WHIPLASH

Don't miss any of Janet Dailey's bestsellers

The New Americana Series
Paradise Peak
Sunrise Canyon
Refuge Cove
Letters from Peaceful Lane
Hart's Hollow Farm

The Tylers of Texas
Texas Forever
Texas Free
Texas Fierce
Texas Tall
Texas Tough
Texas True

Bannon Brothers: Triumph
Bannon Brothers: Honor
Bannon Brothers: Trust
American Destiny
American Dreams
Masquerade
Tangled Vines
Heiress
Rivals

JANET DAILEY

WHIPLASH

KENSINGTON
PUBLISHING CORP.

www.kensingtonbooks.com

KENSINGTON BOOKS are published by

Kensington Publishing Corp.
119 West 40th Street
New York, NY 10018

All Kensington titles, imprints, and distributed lines are available at special quantity discounts for bulk purchases for sales promotion, premiums, fundraising, educational, or institutional use.

Special book excerpts or customized printings can also be created to fit specific needs. For details, write or phone the office of the Kensington Special Sales Manager: Attn. Special Sales Department. Kensington Publishing Corp, 119 West 40th Street, New York, NY 10018. Phone: 1-800-221-2647.

The K logo is a trademark of Kensington Publishing Corp.

Library of Congress Card Catalogue Number: 2021935324

ISBN-13: 978-1-4967-2736-7
ISBN-10: 1-4967-2736-3
First Kensington Hardcover Edition: September 2021

ISBN-13: 978-1-4967-2739-8
ISBN-10: 1-4967-2739-8
First Kensington Trade Edition: September 2021

ISBN-13: 978-1-4967-2742-8 (ebook)
ISBN-10: 1-4967-2742-8 (ebook)

10 9 8 7 6 5 4 3 2 1

Printed in the United States of America

WHIPLASH

CHAPTER ONE

Las Vegas, Nevada
Early November

CASEY BOZEMAN PLANTED HIS FEET IN THE THICK DIRT THAT COV-ered the floor of the vast T-Mobile Arena. As he waited for the first chute to swing open, he willed himself to ignore the lights, the noise, the TV camera crews, and the crowd of nearly 20,000 people who'd come to watch the World Finals of the Professional Bull Riders. His mind was laser focused on one job—protecting the rider who would explode out of the gate astride 1,900 pounds of bucking bull.

A glance to either side confirmed that his teammates, Joel Hatcher and Marcus Jefferson, were in place. Like Casey, they were dressed in loose-fitting athletic gear. Underneath baggy shirts they wore padded vests covered with a rigid shell of high-impact plastic. Another layer of padding was worn under their shorts. The team of bullfighters, as they were called, had worked to-gether for the past five PBR seasons. They trusted each other with their lives. But it was a given that, whatever the cost, the rider's safety always came first.

Farther out in the arena, a mounted roper waited with his lasso ready. If a riderless bull got out of control, it would be his job to rope the animal and herd it back to the exit gate.

The announcer's voice blared over the public address system, introducing the first rider and bull, in sync with the images that flashed onto the huge display screens. In the gated chute, wearing a safety helmet, twenty-year-old Cody Woodbine, ranked fifth in the world standings, was lowering his body onto Cactus Jack, a surly, white-faced behemoth with blunted horns as wide as the front end of a '69 Cadillac.

Casey had faced Cactus Jack before. Some bulls, the good ones, just wanted to dump the cowboy and head back to the pen. Others had murder on their minds. Cactus Jack was one of the second kind.

Inside the chute, the bull was body-slamming the thick steel bars, a move that could break a rider's leg. One of the men, perched on the chute's side rail, shoved a wooden wedge down next to the huge animal to hold him in place. Others pulled the bull rope tight around the animal's body, just behind the shoulders. Cody Woodbine thrust his gloved left hand, fingers up, into the rope handle and wrapped the rope around the handle's base. Casey shifted and danced to keep his muscles loose. His teammates did the same. They had to be ready for anything.

The rules were always the same. At the rider's nod, the gate man would pull a rope to open the chute. When the bull's shoulders cleared the gate, the clock would start. With one hand gripping the rope handle and the other hand in the air, the rider had to stay on the bull for a full eight seconds. For a successful ride, both the bull and the rider would be scored on the basis of fifty points each. For a buck-off, only the bull would be scored.

It was a simple system, but fraught with dangerous surprises.

All eyes were on Cody Woodbine as he hitched forward on the bull until he was sitting almost over his hand. At his nod, the gate swung open, freeing a ton of raw fury.

Streaming snot and manure, Cactus Jack leaped and twisted, then went into a bucking spin to the right—bad for a left-handed rider—but the young cowboy hung on as the digital clock ran up the time, displaying each second by hundredths.

From the back of a bull, eight seconds could seem like forever.

The three bullfighters circled the kicking, spinning bull, ready for a dismount or a buck-off. Casey could see that Woodbine was losing his seat, leaning too far right as he struggled to outlast the clock. But the determined cowboy hung on.

The eight-second whistle blasted. Woodbine had done it. But the young rider was in trouble. As he tumbled off to the right, his left hand twisted under the rope handle and caught fast. Trapped, he flopped like a helpless rag doll against the side of the kicking, spinning bull.

Casey flung himself at the bull, his left arm supporting Woodbine, his right hand clawing at the twisted rope. Joel and Marcus darted in to slow the beast, getting in the bull's face, even grabbing a horn.

Seconds of spinning, jolting terror crawled past before Casey felt the glove loosen. He pulled Woodbine's hand free. The cowboy tumbled aside and rolled clear of the pounding hooves. Dragged away by Marcus and Joel, he was safe. But Casey had gone down with him, and Cactus Jack was looking for somebody to hurt.

As Casey struggled to rise, the massive head filled his vision. He tried to roll to one side, but the horns caught his padded vest with enough force to toss him high over the broad back. As the roper closed in, Casey's body glanced off the bull's side and crashed to earth.

Watching the event alone, on closed circuit TV, Val Champion swallowed a scream. She pressed her hands to her face to block her view of the screen, but she could still hear the announcer's voice over the cheers of the crowd.

"It's 87.5 points for Cody Woodbine on Cactus Jack. But he's going to need that shoulder checked. From here, it looks like it might be dislocated." There was a pause. "And Casey Bozeman is back on his feet, shaken but ready to go. Those bullfighters are tough hombres. They've saved a lot of lives. And now, let's take a look at our next ride."

Lowering her hands, Val sank onto one of the two beds in her room at the Park MGM Hotel. Casey was all right. He would live to face the next bull. And the next. But she wouldn't be watching. She couldn't stand it.

She and Casey were ancient history. She wasn't supposed to care about him anymore. But heaven help her, she did. And caring hurt. It hurt so much that she never wanted to care again.

She needed a drink. She needed more than a drink. But she'd been clean and sober for the five months she'd been out of rehab. She had vowed to stay that way. Besides, her sister Tess would kill her if she smelled the faintest whiff of alcohol on her breath.

The Champion family had come to Vegas bringing two bulls from their Arizona ranch—Whirlwind, a rising star in the rankings, and his younger brother, Whiplash, here as a last-minute reride alternate.

Val's family—big sister, Tess, and adorably pregnant little sister, Lexie, with her wheelchair-bound husband, Shane, were down in the arena watching the event live. Val had tickets, too. But she'd gotten cold feet. Pleading a headache, she'd locked herself in the room she shared with Tess and opted to watch round one on the big-screen TV.

She'd told herself she could handle this. But eight seconds of watching Casey almost die had been enough to convince her she'd misjudged. She'd be smart to sell her tickets for the remaining four nights and spend the money on a flight back to Tucson, with a long Uber ride to the family's remote mountain ranch.

Standing, she switched off the TV, turned off the lights, and walked to the window. The darkened room offered a view of the nearby T-Mobile Arena, lit up like the Fourth of July. Northward, as far as Val's eyes could see, Las Vegas glittered like an endless dumping ground for used Christmas lights and gaudy costume jewelry.

Tacky but strangely beautiful, it called to her with a siren's seductive voice. The hotels and casinos, which she knew by sight, whispered names that resonated like islands in a tale from Sinbad the Sailor. *Bellagio . . . Mirage . . . Aria . . . Paris . . . Venetian . . . Mandalay Bay . . .*

Val turned away from the window. Out there, beyond the glass, was everything she'd left behind, everything she'd run away from to save her body and soul. Four months ago, she'd come home to her family and the ranch, hoping they could make her whole again. She was doing better now. But something was missing. She'd realized it the moment she saw Casey on TV.

Casey. Her first love.

The man she could never be with again.

She'd meant to stay in the room, but her innate restlessness was eating her alive. It wouldn't hurt to take the elevator down to the street and go for a little walk. She didn't have enough money to get into trouble. She'd locked her credit card in the room safe, and she barely had enough cash on her to buy a candy bar or drop a few coins in a cheap slot machine.

She slipped on a flannel-lined denim jacket, twisted up her long red hair with a clip, and covered it with a battered Stetson. For a moment she debated wearing her sunglasses. But it was night outside. Besides, she wanted to blend in with the cowboys and rodeo fans who had swarmed into Vegas for the PBR finals. The movie-star glasses would be out of place.

Deciding to leave her purse, she slipped the key card into the hip pocket of her jeans, put her cell phone in her jacket pocket, and left the room. Tess wouldn't be back here for at least an hour. If she needed to get in touch, she could always call.

Stepping out of the jammed elevator was like plunging into an ocean of noise. People shouted to each other across the crowded lobby and at the registration desk, their voices raised to be heard above the din. From the nearby casino the relentless ding of the slots mingled with the calls of the dealers and occasional whoops from lucky winners. In the bar off the lobby, a country western singer was belting out old Merle Haggard songs.

In the old days, Val could've wandered into the bar and bought herself a free drink with a smile and an empty promise. But those times were behind her. Tonight, she would settle for fresh air.

Zigzagging through the crowd, she made her way out the main entrance to the busy sidewalk. There were signs everywhere welcoming PBR fans and inviting them to come on in and spend their money. People in western gear wandered past, taking in the sights. Ticket hawkers, most of them scammers, waved their wares in front of unwary customers. Girls in skin-tight denim skirts and low-cut blouses prowled the edges of the sidewalk, smiling when a man made eye contact. Val couldn't help feeling sorry for them. She'd known desperate times herself—but never that desperate, thank God.

As she left the shelter of the hotel entrance and launched herself up the Strip, she took a moment to check her surroundings and scan the crowd for anyone who might seem a bit too interested. Old habits died hard. But Val knew there was no need for caution. Nobody was going to recognize her and ask for her autograph. Not that many ever had.

She'd tried the Hollywood thing and had gotten a few small movie parts. But she'd never made it past the bottom third of the credit list. At the time, she'd rationalized that it was because she wouldn't go the casting couch route. But Val knew better. She knew what real talent was. She'd seen it in women like Meryl Streep, Laura Dern, and Cate Blanchett—and she knew she didn't have it. She was merely pretty. And in Hollywood, pretty girls were a dime a dozen.

She'd made a few TV commercials and done some modeling. Between gigs, she'd waited tables to make rent on a one-room studio with roaches in the walls and the bathroom down the hall.

Then she'd met Lenny Fortunato.

The blinking signal at the corner crosswalk ended Val's musings. The light was changing, and she'd already stepped off the curb.

For an instant she hesitated, torn between stepping back and making a dash ahead of the heavy Las Vegas traffic. It was just enough time for a black limo with darkened windows to come barreling around the corner, heading straight toward her.

Val jumped out of the way as it hurtled past, swerving just enough to miss her by an inch.

Pulse slamming, she watched the vehicle merge with the traffic and vanish from sight. A few people glanced at her as they passed, as if curious to see what kind of idiot would step off the curb in front of a moving vehicle. She could just imagine the limo driver cursing the fool woman who'd almost gotten herself killed, which would have caused a major inconvenience for his passengers and probably cut into his tip.

No damage done, except that she'd drawn attention to herself, something she never liked to do. But the walk she'd set out to enjoy was spoiled. It was time to head back to her hotel and wait for Tess to return.

But as she turned around and wove her way back through the crowds, a feeling crept over her—sickening in its familiarity. It was the vague, prickling sense that something was wrong.

The close brush with the limo couldn't have been anything but a coincidence. No one could have known she'd be at that corner, and if anyone inside the vehicle had meant her any harm, the driver wouldn't have swerved.

Maybe she was imagining things. But the chill that crawled along her nerves was too real to be ignored. She should never have left the hotel alone.

Correction—she should've known better than to come to Las Vegas in the first place.

Resisting the urge to rush, she entered the hotel and crossed the lobby to the elevator. A tired-looking couple with two whiny children rode up to her floor and got off with her. Val followed them down the corridor, continuing on after they stopped at their room. Would that have been her life if she'd followed a different path and married Casey? Would it have been enough?

But there was no point in thinking about that now.

Her hand shook as she used the key card to open the door. When she went inside and double locked it behind her, she could feel a headache coming on—maybe karma for lying to Tess earlier. In her purse, she found a bottle of ibuprofen, shook a couple of tablets into her hand, and swallowed them with tap water. There was an ice dispenser and a soda vending machine at the end of the hall, but she didn't want to go out again.

Kicking off her boots, she picked up the TV remote. She wasn't up to watching the PBR finals, but maybe she could find a good movie to pass the time.

As she flipped through channels, she found just the thing— *Voyage to the Black Hole,* a low-budget sci-fi film she'd made years ago with a crew of barely known actors. She'd played a member of a spaceship crew, her single spoken line: *"No damage to report, sir."*

Watching it now might at least be good for a few laughs.

She propped a couple of pillows against the headboard and settled back to watch. She'd known the movie was bad, but until now she hadn't realized what a stinker it really was.

She was chuckling over a dramatic battle scene when the room telephone on the nightstand rang. Val reached for it, then hesitated as the phone rang again, then again. Tess or Lexie would call her cell, not the room number. But what if there was some emergency? Or some question at the front desk? With the phone still ringing, Val picked up the receiver.

"Hello?"

There was no reply.

"Hello?" Her pulse quickened slightly.

Again, there was silence, followed by a faint click and the hum of the dial tone. Nothing more.

CHAPTER TWO

*I*NSIDE THE ARENA, THE LAST RIDE OF THE NIGHT HAD ENDED IN A buck-off. As the fans began filing along the rows and pouring toward the exits, Tess slipped out of her seat and made her way down to the press box. Lexie's husband, Shane Tully, had been a great rider before a fall under a bucking bull had crushed his spine and cost him the use of his legs. Now he was doing color commentary for the PBR finals. Lexie, as always, was at his side.

"So, how did it go?" Tess asked, although their beaming faces had already answered her question.

"Shane did great," Lexie said. "He's already a pro. I was so proud of him."

"And this lady even got in some comments from a wife's point of view," Shane said. "I'd say we were a hit."

Lexie rose from her seat, the curve of her rounded belly just showing beneath her shirt. "I have something else to be happy about, Tess. Before the event, some of the riders' wives came up and introduced themselves. They were so nice; they have a group that gets together at events and stays in touch online. They told me I was already included. It's like I've made all these new friends. They invited me to lunch, and they're even talking about giving me a baby shower."

"That's great." Tess had never needed much of a social life, but she knew how much the support of these women would mean to Lexie. "I'm on my way to check on our bulls," she said. "Are you two going back to the hotel now?"

Shane, darkly handsome, grinned. "We'd planned to go out and kick up our heels. But we're both beat. So, yes, we're going back to our room. Is there something you need, Tess?"

"If you don't mind, could you stop by and see how Val's doing? She seemed a little off when I left her tonight. She said she had a headache. But you know Val. She tends to make excuses when something's bothering her."

"I think what's bothering her is Casey," Lexie said. "Remember last summer when she made us promise not to tell him she was at the ranch? When I asked her why, she said it was water under the bridge. I think she's worried about running into him."

"Maybe it wouldn't be a bad thing if she did," Shane said. "It's been—what? Ten years since they broke up?"

"Nine. But they didn't break up," Lexie said. "She just left without telling him anything. That had to hurt. He got married a few years ago, but it didn't last long."

"Has she ever said why she left?"

"Not to any of us. Casey's such a great guy. I can't help thinking how much happier both their lives would've been if she'd stayed and married him."

"Maybe it's not too late," Shane said. "Maybe they could at least be friends."

"No, leave it alone, both of you," Tess said. "Whatever Val did, she had her reasons, and she doesn't owe any of us an explanation. Pushing her to see Casey again would only open old wounds."

"But you still want us to check on her, don't you?" Lexie asked.

"Yes, but only to make sure she's okay. If there's a problem, call my cell, and I'll come right back."

"Got it, big sister." Shane backed his lightweight power chair away from the press table. Tess stepped aside to clear a path to the exit ramp. Lexie walked at his side, her hand brushing his shoulder. He managed his disability well and rarely complained. But Tess suspected that the cheerful face he put on was mostly for his wife's sake. Before his tragic accident, Shane had lived for the thrill and challenge of riding bulls. He'd been a sure contender for the PBR World Finals. By right, he should be out in that arena competing for the big money. But he would never ride a bull again.

Tess stood for a moment, watching as they disappeared in the milling crowd. She would do anything to protect what was left of her little family, a family that had already known too many losses—her mother decades ago, her brother, Jack, at last year's National Rodeo Finals, her father shortly after that, and her beloved stepmother, murdered by a neighbor this past summer. Only her father's death, from cancer, had been a natural one.

Add to that toll the death of her fiancé, Mitch, who'd died in Afghanistan weeks before the wedding they'd planned. Tess had been even younger than Lexie. Now, at thirty, she still hadn't found anyone else to love. And Val doubtless had her own secret sorrows. The Champions drew tragedy the way some families seemed to draw wealth or scandal.

Turning away, she headed toward the doors at the rear exit of the arena, where the steel-barred complex of pens, chutes, and gates had been set up for the bulls.

She was about to go outside when a voice called her name.

"Tess! Wait up!" Casey, still in protective gear, was striding to catch up with her. Turning back, she greeted him with a smile. Casey, who'd been her brother's best friend, as well as Val's first love, was almost family. Tess was happy to see him, but cautious. If he were to ask her about Val, she would have to choose between lying and breaking the promise she'd made to her sister.

He grinned. A handsome man with George Clooney looks, sandy hair and warm brown eyes, he was huskier than most bullfighters. But it was his strength that had supported Cody Woodbine and kept the young rider's arm from being jerked out of its socket while he was hanging on the side of the bull.

Tess stepped closer, anticipating a brotherly hug, but he put up a warning hand.

"You might want to keep your distance," he said. "I smell like a bull's rear end. I won't be fit for human company till I've had a shower."

"You're fine." Tess gave him a brief hug, remembering how

he'd come to the ranch last year to help bury Jack's casket on a lonely bluff overlooking the pastures. He'd been working the arena when Jack had died under the crushing hooves of a 2,000-pound bull named Train Wreck. Casey would never forgive himself for not being able to save his best friend.

Val had sent a lavish bouquet for Jack's funeral. But even her brother's death hadn't been enough to bring her home. For their father's service, two months later, she'd sent nothing. And she hadn't known about the death of their stepmother, Callie, until she arrived home.

"So how've you been, Tess?" Casey asked.

"The same. Just running the ranch. You know how that goes."

"I ran into Lexie a couple of times over the summer. She told me you were doing a fine job."

"I have good help. Shane's taken over most of the business end, which gives me more time for the animals. Ruben's still there as foreman, of course, watching over us all. And we've brought his son-in-law, Pedro, on full time. He's a good worker, and his wife, Ruben's daughter, is a fine cook. We still miss Callie, but things could be worse."

You should come for a visit, Tess had almost said. But that wouldn't do. Not with Val wanting to avoid him. "But you grew up on a ranch," she said. "You know how it is. Never enough water. Never enough money. Never enough rest."

Casey nodded. "I know. When my dad lost our ranch because he couldn't pay off the loan, it broke his heart. He didn't live long after that. If things had been different, I'd probably be ranching today instead of living out of a suitcase and getting knocked around by bulls."

"Speaking of bulls," Tess said, "I need to go. I was just on my way out back to check on the pair we brought."

"Is it okay if I tag along?" Casey asked. "I've seen Whirlwind buck, but I'm curious about his brother."

She hesitated. The more time she spent with Casey, the more likely he was to bring up Val. But how could she say no? She gave him a nod. "Sure. Come on."

"Don't worry, I'll stay downwind of you." Casey fell into step behind her.

They passed through the huge rear doors and into the covered complex of pens and chutes that housed the bulls for the event. Having Casey with her wouldn't be a problem, Tess told herself. If he hadn't asked about Val by now, he probably didn't plan to.

The softly lit space was equipped with armed guards and security cameras. The animals here were worth big money. The least of them would likely bring more than $50,000 at auction. A world champion bull, like Sweet Pro's Bruiser or Smooth Operator, could be worth as much as half a million—some in prize money, more in future breeding fees.

The smells of manure and warm animal bodies filled the air, along with the peaceful sounds of bulls snoring, snorting, chewing, passing gas, and stirring in their sleep. Some were penned alone, others with their companions.

Tess led Casey through the maze of pens and walkways, toward the far corner of the complex. Ninety-seven bulls had been selected for the finals. Not all of them were here. Some animals, the ones saved for the later rounds, would be arriving in the coming days.

There was nothing ordinary about these bulls. They were the top tier, the bovine version of NFL and NBA athletes. A recognized breed—the American Bucking Bull—they'd been selectively bred for power, agility, and most important of all, for the genetic tendency to buck and buck hard. They'd been raised, tested, and trained for the sport. Their records of ride scores and buck-offs had qualified them to be in the Super Bowl of bull riding.

Every bull here was magnificent. The fact that two of her Alamo Canyon bulls had earned a place among them was enough to make Tess's head spin. What a shame her father hadn't lived to see this. Having his bulls in the PBR World Finals had been Bert Champion's dream since he'd bought and bred his first bucker a dozen years ago.

"Here they are." Tess had stopped beside one of the smaller pens. The two bulls inside were drowsing and chewing their cuds in the low light. "Take a look, Casey. Would you ever believe those two were full brothers?"

"Not if you hadn't told me." Casey studied the pair. He'd always been a good judge of bulls. These two were splendid, but very different from each other.

Casey had faced Whirlwind in the arena more than once. Mottled silver in color, he was on the small side at 1,700 pounds, but quick, alert, and as agile as a cat. His bucking pattern was an unpredictable mix of high leaps and kicks, blinding spins, and sudden direction changes. He was smart and getting smarter, constantly coming up with new ways to throw his rider. With a record of twenty-two outs, all with excellent scores, he'd been ridden the full eight seconds only one time—by Shane Tully.

Casey shifted his attention to Whiplash. Younger than Whirlwind by a year, Whiplash was a good 200 pounds heavier. A brindled black and brown hulk with massive shoulders and haunches, he was all power, and the look he gave Casey was anything but friendly. With a record of thirteen outs in his short career, he had yet to be successfully ridden.

Whirlwind was scheduled to buck tomorrow. Whiplash was a spare, to be used only if another bull was unable to compete or a rider was given a reride. But something told Casey that this year or next, the young bull would get his own chance at greatness.

"So what do you think?" Tess asked him.

"They're like yin and yang," Casey said. "But you've got two great bulls here. I can't wait to see them perform."

"Neither can I," Tess said. "I'm going to be on pins and needles for Whirlwind tomorrow."

"I'm imagining a future bull dynasty here. Are there any more brothers where these two came from?"

The look that flashed in Tess's eyes combined sorrow and anger. "The parents are both gone. There was one more calf, a great yearling, but I lost him, thanks to my own blasted principles.

We were short on money and desperate for an unrelated bull to breed our cows. A rancher in Phoenix had a retired bucker. He agreed to lend me his old bull in exchange for first pick of our yearlings."

"Oh, no." Casey could imagine what was coming.

"Lexie begged me to hide that calf so it wouldn't be chosen. But no, I had to keep my promise and do the right thing. That rancher knew a choice animal when he saw it. He took our yearling, turned right around, and sold it to Brock Tolman."

"Now that is one sad story." Casey knew how much the Champions hated Tolman, a rich Tucson rancher who'd tried to buy Whirlwind. He hadn't succeeded. But now he had the next best thing.

"Lexie's never forgiven me," Tess said. "Lord knows, I'll never forgive myself. But I've kept you here long enough, Casey. I know you're anxious to get out of your gear and take that shower."

"You just can't stand the way I smell," Casey joked. "Do what you need to here. Then I'll walk you back inside."

Tess took a moment to make sure the bulls had food and water for the night. Then Casey walked back with her, as far as the entrance to the locker rooms. "If you've got time while you're here, I'd enjoy taking you, Lexie, and Shane to lunch," he said. "We could catch up over a good meal."

He could sense her hesitation. "We'll see," she hedged. "I know Shane's got a busy schedule. I'll talk to them and let you know."

"Fine. See you around." Casey watched her stride away, tall and lean in her faded blue jeans and dusty cowboy boots, her dark hair caught back in a loose braid. Fiercely independent, Tess shouldered the burdens of her ranch and her family as if it were the whole of her destiny. Casey had known her for a long time. Today he could tell that something was off. She'd seemed edgy and evasive. And her response to his lunch invitation hadn't been like her at all. He could almost believe she was holding something back.

Casey walked down the hall to the locker room and began peeling off the protective layers he'd worn in the arena. Underneath, his body was soaked in sweat. As he stripped down and showered himself clean, he replayed his conversation with Tess. What was going on? Had she said something that he'd missed?

But Casey already knew the answer to that question. It wasn't what she'd said that had him wondering. It was what she *hadn't* said.

This past summer, he'd forced himself to stop asking the Champion sisters about Val. She was gone, and she wasn't coming back. That reality was old news by now, and after what she'd put him through, he was damned fine with it.

When, at seventeen and just out of high school, she'd lit out for the bright lights of Hollywood, Casey, who'd been nineteen at the time, had picked up the pieces of his life, joined the U.S. Army Reserve, and served a deployment in Afghanistan. He'd come home to learn that his parents had lost the family ranch. He'd planned on going to college, but to help out his parents, he found his way to bull riding. He'd competed in high school and had done all right. However, he'd soon discovered that he was better suited to protecting riders than staying on the bulls.

After all that time, the pain of losing Val had never gone away. Even his impulsive marriage to a rodeo queen had failed to mend his shattered heart. But the years had passed, and he'd moved on—into a state of blessed numbness. Even the occasional women in his life had come and gone like roadside attractions along a lonesome highway, seen in the rearview mirror without regret.

So why had his conversation with Tess left him churning with emotions he'd long since buried?

If Tess was keeping something from him, it had to be about Val. But why would she hide it? Why would she hesitate to let him take her family to lunch?

There could only be one reason.

Val was here. And she didn't want to see him.

Val huddled on the bed, staring at the silent room phone. Forty-five minutes had passed without another ring. Maybe the mysterious call had been nothing more than a misdial. Maybe every-thing was fine.

But what if it wasn't? What if someone outside had recognized her, seen her go into the hotel, and called the room to confirm that she was there?

Hotel employees weren't supposed to give out names or room numbers of their guests. But a few bills, slipped into a willing hand, could buy anything, including information.

Why hadn't she been smarter? If she'd had her wits about her, she could have gone into a different hotel, taken the elevator up a couple of floors, and exited by way of the back stairs. Or she could have gone into the nearby arena. But the close call with the limo had left her rattled. She'd panicked and made a foolish mistake.

Maybe she was imagining things—Dr. Rush, her therapist, had suggested as much. But Val had learned to trust her instincts. And now, because of her bad judgment, if anyone meant her harm, they would know right where to find her.

She glanced at the door. There were three locks, including a deadbolt and a chain. Val had secured all of them, but she still felt vulnerable.

The TV was still showing her movie. Settling back on the bed, she willed herself to relax and watch the well-remembered scenes, catching glimpses of herself in the background. Tess should be here before long. By then, Val needed to be calm. It wouldn't do to let her sister know how scared she'd been. Tess had never been afraid of anything. She would either laugh or worry about Val's mental state.

Val's pulse was easing back into its natural rhythm when she heard a sharp knock at the door. Her heart lurched. The knock wouldn't be Tess. Tess had a key card, which she would try to use before discovering that the door was locked from inside.

The knock came again, louder this time. Should she answer or just keep still?

"Val? Are you in there?" The voice was Lexie's. "I'm here with Shane. Are you okay?"

Val began to breathe again. "Hang on. I'm coming." She sprang off the bed, hurried to the door, and released the locks. Lexie stood in the open doorway with Shane in his chair just behind her.

"Tess asked us to check on you," Lexie said.

Val sighed. Tess would do that. "She probably just wanted you to make sure I was sober."

"Don't be like that, Val. Tess cares about you."

"I know she means well. But somebody needs to remind her that I'm not sixteen anymore." Val opened the door wide. "Hey, come on in. I was just watching one of my old movies. It's almost over."

"I've never seen any of your movies, Val." As the door closed behind him, Shane steered his chair into the room and positioned it where he could view the screen. "I'll be damned. There you are, little short skirt, high-heeled boots, and all."

"Male-approved space costume for women." Val sat on the bed and made room for Lexie beside her.

"And the look that captain is giving you as you walk past. Oh, my, what could he be thinking?" Lexie teased.

"Actually, he was a jerk," Val said. "Once he trapped me in his trailer, and I had to fight my way out. He wasn't much of an actor, but then, neither was I. Shane, if you've never seen this movie, believe me, there are reasons for it. Oh, wait for it—my single spoken line. It's coming . . . three, two, one!"

On the screen a younger Val walked up to the captain, hips swaying with each step of her stiletto heels. She gazed up at him from beneath impossibly long false eyelashes. *"No damage to report, sir."*

"Thank you, Corporal Riley." The camera narrowed its focus to the captain's chiseled face. When it panned out again to show the flight deck set, Val's character was gone.

"And that's the last you'll see of me." Val clicked the remote, turning off the TV. "So much for my brilliant movie career."

"Can I ask you a personal question, Val?"

"You can ask. No promise I'll answer."

"I know how hard you must've worked to make it in Hollywood. Did you ever do porn?"

"Good Lord, Lexie!" Shane looked horrified.

Val laughed. Only her adored younger sister could get away with a question like that. "No, sweetheart, I never did. I had offers, and the money was good. But I wanted to be a real actress. I knew that if I were to make a porn film, I'd be branded. I'd never be asked to do anything good. Besides, the men were creepy. Just the thought of what I'd have to do . . ." Val swept her hair back from her face and changed the subject.

"So how did the commentary go, Shane? Do you feel like you did a good job?"

"He did great," Lexie said. "And they even let me say a few words." She frowned. "We were on TV, Val. Didn't you watch us?"

Val shook her head. "Sorry. I turned off the TV after that first ride and went for a walk. I'd seen enough." No need to tell anyone about what she'd experienced on that walk.

"So you did see Casey get tossed?" Shane asked.

"Yes, and I saw that he was fine. After that I left."

The beat of awkward silence was broken by the sound of the door unlocking. Tess stepped into the room.

She smiled at Lexie and Shane. "Hey, thanks for stopping by, you two."

"I was fine, Tess," Val said in a flat voice. "I went for a walk. I didn't go downstairs and drink in the bar or gamble away all our money. And I don't need to be babysat."

"I know that, Val. I just wanted to make sure everything was okay."

"Everything's fine."

"How were the bulls doing, Tess?" Shane asked.

"All right. I just hope Whirlwind puts on a good show tomorrow night. It could make all the difference for our ranch."

"Do you know who'll be riding him?"

"Not yet. We should know sometime tomorrow morning."

"Well," Shane said, stifling a yawn, "if they let me on camera at the right time, I'll put in a good word for him."

Lexie nudged her husband. "I think we're all ready for a good night's sleep. Let's go, honey, and leave these ladies in peace."

Peace? Val bit back a caustic remark as Lexie and Shane left for their own room down the hall. Spending the night in the same room as Tess was bound to be anything but peaceful.

As the door closed, Val secured the locks and turned back to face her sister. "You really didn't need to check on me, Tess," she said. "It's insulting when you do that. I haven't slipped up even once since I came home this summer. No booze, no drugs, and no men."

Tess had taken a seat on the foot of her bed and was pulling off her boots. The thin wool socks beneath were stuck to her feet. One had a hole in the toe. "I know you haven't slipped up," she said. "That wasn't what I was worried about."

"Then what?" Val challenged her. "I could be a blasted nun, and you still wouldn't trust me."

"This isn't about trust, Val. It's about concern. You haven't been yourself since we got here. It's nothing I can put my finger on, just that you seem troubled. Is everything all right?"

Val's first impulse was to tell her to mind her own business. But she was too exhausted for more defiance. Tess had been her big sister her whole life. The two had played together, fought together, shared a hundred adventures on the ranch, gathered eggs in the barn, danced in the rain, and cried together when their mother died. Tess could be bossy and annoying, but in the end, she was family.

"No, everything isn't all right," Val said. "I don't belong here. I want to go home. I can sell my tickets to pay for a flight and a ride. Please don't try to stop me."

"Is it Casey?"

Val didn't answer. Yes, it was Casey. But there were other things as well, things from an ugly past that she wasn't ready to share— things that were coming back to haunt her.

"I talked with Casey tonight," Tess said. "He was interested in seeing the bulls. Your name didn't even come up. He's moved on, Val. If you were to run into each other, I'm sure he'd be fine."

"I suppose he would."

Until he wanted to talk.

Until he started asking questions and demanding answers.

"I understand why you might not be comfortable, Val."

You don't. But at least you're trying.

"I know I can't tell you what to do," Tess continued. "But I'd like to ask a favor. Whirlwind will be bucking tomorrow. Come and support the family—support our bull and all the hope we've invested in him. After that, if you still want to leave, I won't have a problem with it. Does that sound reasonable?"

It did sound reasonable. Given the chance, Val would have made a mad dash for the door and taken a cab to the airport tonight. But even if she were to turn Tess down, selling her remaining tickets and finding a flight to Tucson could take her much of tomorrow. Staying to support the family shouldn't be a big imposition, especially if she could make it onto a red-eye after Whirlwind's turn in the arena.

Meanwhile, as long as she stayed with her family and didn't go out alone, she should be safe from the unseen threat that had set her nerves on edge.

"You know I didn't want to come to Vegas in the first place," Val said. "If Lexie hadn't begged me, I'd be home on the ranch right now."

"I know." Tess pulled her shirt over her head and unhooked her faded cotton bra. Her small-breasted body was lean and sinewy, toned by a lifetime of hard work on the ranch. "So what's it to be? Do you want to tell me now, or think it over while I shower?"

"I'll stay tomorrow for the family. But after that, I'm out of here."

"Fine." Tess shimmied out of her jeans, grabbed her pajamas out of her duffel, and strode naked into the bathroom.

Val waited until she heard the running water. Only then did she slip out of her clothes and pull on her knee-length black nightshirt, which was made like an oversize knit tee. Her sister might not have second thoughts about showing her body, but Tess had no secrets to hide. Val did.

As she pulled the hem of her nightshirt down over hips, her fingers brushed the pale, horizontal scar that crossed below her navel. That scar was her secret. Her pain. The one thing she could never share with anyone—especially not with Casey.

CHAPTER THREE

*T*HE NEXT MORNING, TESS WAS UP EARLY, HER THOUGHTS ON THE busy day ahead. Checking on the bulls would come first. Then, at 8:00, Shane would be filling in for a local host at a TV interview with Clay Rafferty, a founding member of the PBR who was now livestock director—the man responsible for choosing the bulls. Tess had asked and received permission to be part of the small off-camera audience. She'd spoken with Rafferty on the phone and knew him by sight, but she'd never met him in person.

Tess was not easily starstruck, but that morning, as she took extra pains with her hair and clothes, even dabbing on a touch of lipstick and mascara, Val teased her. "Look at you. You've even polished your boots. You wouldn't go to that much trouble for an audience with the Pope."

"Clay Rafferty isn't the Pope," Tess replied. "As far as the future of our ranch is concerned, he's God Almighty."

"In that case, say a few Hail Marys for my sinful soul when you meet him." Still in her nightshirt, Val sat cross-legged on her bed, muttering as she used her smartphone to check on flights to Tucson. Finding a seat at the last minute wasn't going to be easy, but she was set on leaving as soon as possible after Whirlwind's turn in the arena.

Lexie would be skipping the interview. There were times when it didn't suit Shane to appear dependent on his wife, and this was one of them. Val had stepped in and offered to treat Lexie to a shared session of head-to-toe pampering in the hotel spa, followed by a late lunch. Tess was pleased. Not only was Lexie delighted with the plan, but it would keep Val occupied and out of trouble for a good part of the day.

"Have a good time with Lexie." Tess slipped on her leather jacket, grabbed her purse, and headed for the door. "It's really nice of you, Val, to do this for her."

"I do have my rare moments of niceness, don't I?" Val brushed a hand through her flame-colored hair. "Of course, most of the time I'm a total bitch. Give my best to Shane. I know he'll do us proud."

After picking up a coffee to go at the hotel snack bar, Tess set out on foot to cross the short distance to the arena. It was early yet, but she wanted to take her time with the bulls. The November morning was cold for balmy Las Vegas. The stiff breeze ruffled her hair and made her shiver beneath her jacket. She sipped hot coffee as she walked, feeling her body warm as she thought about the day ahead.

She'd spoken with Shane earlier that morning. The interview, to be recorded for later broadcast, would be held in one of the upper rooms that rimmed the arena. Shane, who could access the room by elevator, had already left to make sure everything was set to go. He had a list of questions, but he planned to take the advice an experienced colleague had given him—just let the man talk.

By the time she passed through the arena doors, Tess had finished her coffee. Tossing the paper cup in a handy trash receptacle, she headed for the bull pens in the rear.

The place was teeming with activity this morning. Owners and their workers were busy caring for the bulls—feeding and watering them, grooming them, inspecting them for any sign of injury or malaise, and seeing that their pens had clean bedding underfoot. To the stock contractors who bred, raised, and trained them, these bulls were like family. Every bull that burst out of that bucking chute for a few seconds of glory carried somebody's hopes and dreams.

But that didn't mean they weren't dangerous. Some bulls would attack without provocation or warning. And any bull, when angered, challenged, or threatened, was capable of killing. They were so powerful that even when a bull was only doing his job, a stomp or shove could crush a man's bones.

That was how Jack had died at last year's National Rodeo Finals. It was the reason Shane was in a wheelchair. And it was the reason the sport needed men like Casey Bozeman.

Tess found her bulls and refilled their food and water. Whiplash ignored her and went for the food. Whirlwind sidled up to the rails, expecting his usual morning ear scratch.

Whirlwind had been spoiled by Lexie. As a calf, he'd followed her around the ranch like a puppy. Even as a full-grown bull, he was attached to her. Tess had disapproved of her sister's making a pet of the bull; but this morning she reached over the rail, found the special spot behind his ear, and gave it a good scratch. Whirlwind sighed and closed his eyes.

"Do your best out there tonight, big boy," she murmured. "We'll be rooting for you."

"Do you always talk to your bulls, Miss Champion?"

Tess went rigid. There was no mistaking that deep voice with its mocking tone. She turned around to find herself face-to-face with Brock Tolman.

Tess was a tall woman, but at six feet four, he loomed over her. Dark, with roughhewn features, he was dressed in spotless jeans, a denim shirt, and a flawlessly tailored black leather blazer. The bolo clip that lay below his collar was a chunk of veined turquoise mounted in Navajo silver that wouldn't have been out of place in a museum.

From his python skin boots to his custom-made Stetson, every inch of the man exuded money, power, and sheer ruthlessness. For a moment, the rage that welled in Tess robbed her of speech. From the time he'd stolen a piece of choice pastureland from her father to his current scheming to buy her bulls and take over her family ranch, Brock Tolman had proved that he'd do anything to get what he wanted.

Struggling for composure, she found her voice. "I'd watch my step if I were you, Mr. Tolman. You don't want to get bull manure on those fancy boots of yours."

He chuckled, a rumble rising from deep in his chest. "Take it easy," he said. "I just stopped by to congratulate you on having two bulls in the world finals." His gaze shifted to the pen. "So that's Whiplash. He's a big boy. And young as he is, I'll bet he's still putting on weight. He could be a full ton by the time he's finished growing. I hope he gets a chance to buck this week. I'd enjoy watching him."

"In case you're about to ask, the answer is no, he's not for sale. Not for any price, especially to you. Besides, you've already got the bloodline in that yearling I traded to Alma Jensen. How did you manage to get your greedy hands on him?"

Tolman ignored the jab. "Just a stroke of luck. Jensen actually contacted me. He almost turned cartwheels when he found out what I was willing to pay for that yearling. Still, it was a gamble. I won't even know if he's a bucker till we test him next spring."

"You'll forgive me if I hope he turns out to be a dink."

"He won't. Not if he's anything like his brothers. It's too bad you didn't register him for the ABBI futurity events. It had to be done before he was a year old. Now it's too late."

Tess knew what he was talking about. The organization that kept records of bull lineage also had a program of training and futurity events for promising young bulls, giving them a chance to compete for big money with lightweight bucking dummies on their backs as they matured. Many of the top bulls in the sport had been through the program, and it showed.

Tess shook her head. "That would've been like registering a kid for the right preschool so he could get into Harvard. A small outfit like ours can't spare the time or the money. You're on your own with the yearling."

"Understood. But getting him to where his brothers are is going to take years. I'm still in the market for either of your bulls—or both—if you decide to sell."

"Don't hold your breath. I wouldn't sell you one of these bulls for a million dollars. For that matter, I wouldn't sell you a three-legged mule."

"We'll see." Tolman studied the two bulls in the pen. Tess was aware that he had several bulls of his own in the finals. Clearly, he'd brought along a hired hand to take care of them while he strutted around the arena like a glorified barnyard rooster.

"Have you heard who'll be riding Whirlwind tonight?" he asked her.

"No, I was just going to—" Tess broke off as she caught the knowing glint in his eye. "You already know, don't you?"

"I do." He smiled, clearly enjoying himself.

"Well, are you going to tell me?"

"Maybe. But I'd rather see you beg."

Tess bit back a curse. "You're the last person I'd beg for anything, Mr. Tolman. I can always go and find out for myself. But since you're dying to tell me, why don't you just save me the trouble?"

Again he chuckled, the sound deep and disturbingly warm. "All right. You win. Are you sure you don't want to venture a guess?"

"Just tell me."

"Would you believe R.J. McClintock?"

"You're kidding." R.J. McClintock, last year's world champion, was currently in second place. A successful ride with a big score could put him in first. "And he chose a rookie bull that's been successfully ridden only once? Why, for heaven's sake?"

"He didn't choose Whirlwind. He drew him. But R.J. is a great believer in luck. This early in the competition, he was willing to gamble. So tonight, all eyes will be on your bull."

Shaken, Tess clasped the top rail of the pen. "I almost wish you hadn't told me. Now I'll be on pins and needles all day."

"I just wanted to see your face when you heard the news." He glanced at his watch, a high-end platinum Rolex. "I take it you're going to the interview with Clay."

"I am." His use of Rafferty's first name was not lost on her. The bastard was showing off.

"I'm going, too. I'll walk with you," he said.

It wasn't a question. It was more like an order. Brock Tolman was trying to control her, the way he controlled everyone and everything around him. For now, Tess hid her annoyance. She would allow him to escort her to the interview. But once that was over, she was going to get as far away from him as she could manage. She didn't trust the man—never had and never would. Right now, he was pretending to be a gentleman. But she knew better. He was as treacherous as a rattlesnake, biding his time, waiting to strike when she least expected it.

"I watched Shane's commentary last night," he said as they walked back inside the arena. "He did a good job. I was proud of him."

"Yes, he did." Tess had almost forgotten that Shane had shown up on the Tolman Ranch as a homeless teen, been taken in, and had lived there for years. It was where he'd learned to ride bulls. He and Tolman had parted ways this past summer, shortly before Shane's accident. Despite some hard feelings, Tolman had stepped forward to get Shane the medical help he needed. The man wasn't a complete monster. But that only made anticipating his moves more of a challenge.

"I suppose you know that Shane's going to be a father," she said.

"Yes, I'm happy for him. In a different world, I could look forward to being an adoptive grandfather."

Startled, Tess glanced up at him. This was something new.

"He didn't tell you?" Tolman raised a dark smudge of an eyebrow. "But knowing Shane, of course he wouldn't. After his accident, I offered to make him my legal heir if he'd agree to stay and run my ranch. He turned me down flat. He wanted to strike out on his own."

"As you see, he's done all right for himself."

"Yes, he has. But now that he's about to become a father, I can't help hoping he'll change his mind."

Tess's pulse slammed. "Are you saying the offer's still on the table?"

"It was never off the table. My one try at marriage convinced me that I'm not parent material. Shane's the closest thing to a son I ever had—the closest I'll ever have. If he were to come back to me, his family would want for nothing—education, travel, the best of whatever they need. And his descendants would be heirs to the Tolman Ranch. How could a man with his family's best interests at heart turn down an offer like that?"

Tess fell silent as they entered the elevator for the ride to the top floor of the arena. At home, Shane and Lexie had the master bedroom to themselves, with a private bath. Everything else was shared. They didn't even have space for a nursery. Shane was a partner in the Alamo Canyon Ranch and was entitled to a share of the profits, but the ranch barely made enough to pay its bills, and money was a constant worry. When Lexie wasn't working cattle, she was helping Shane with the many small tasks that challenged his disability. In a few months she'd have a baby to care for. How could they not take Brock Tolman up on his offer? It would be a dream come true for them.

And what would the Alamo Canyon Ranch do without their help? Tess had come to depend on Shane's management skills in the office and on Lexie for her knowledge of modern animal care. The ranch didn't have money for more hired help, and Val was as flighty as a sparrow. Odds were Tess would have to sell out—and a ready buyer was standing right next to her.

As the elevator stopped, her simmering anger rose to a high boil. Brock Tolman had tried to buy her bulls. He had tried to get his hands on her ranch. And now he was trying to take her family.

If his plan worked, he would end up with everything he wanted.

Val and Lexie sat side by side in the pink mani-pedi chairs, chatting while their feet were being smoothed and softened, the toenails trimmed, filed, and polished. Val had chosen traditional red, to match her fingernails. Lexie was going with bright blue.

They'd had a relaxing time in the hotel spa, enjoying a sauna, a massage, a facial, and the mani-pedi treatment that would soon be finished. Next they would have their damp hair styled and makeup applied before getting dressed and going to lunch.

The spa routine was nothing new to Val. She'd had it done on a regular basis when she was still trying to be a movie star. Today she realized she hadn't missed it. But Lexie was having a good time, and Val enjoyed spoiling her little sister.

Earlier that morning, she'd booked the last seat on a flight that left Las Vegas at 11:15 tomorrow morning. She'd hoped to get away sooner, but at least it would buy time for the agency she'd contacted to sell her three remaining PBR tickets. Meanwhile, she would keep to safe surroundings, just in case the threat that had thrown her into a panic last night was real.

"Val?" Lexie's voice brought her back to the present. "Could I ask you a question?"

Val glanced down at the two young Asian pedicurists, who appeared to be sisters. They spoke minimal English and weren't likely to be interested in a personal conversation.

"You can ask, honey. But I won't promise to answer," she said.

"What really happened between you and Casey?" Lexie asked. "What made you leave without telling him? Did you have a fight?"

Val suppressed a sigh. She should've known this was coming.

"I mean, Casey's such a great man," Lexie chatted on. "Any woman would be lucky to have him. And I've talked to him. I can tell he still loves you."

Val took a moment to weigh her answer. She didn't want to lie, but neither did she want to reveal too much of the truth.

"Casey might have feelings for the girl I was back in high school. But the person I am now—he doesn't even know me. And if he did, I can't imagine he'd like me."

"But why did you leave, Val? You were so young, just out of high school and not even eighteen yet."

Maybe a half-lie wouldn't hurt, Val thought. "Casey and I had been dating for a couple of years. I knew he wanted to marry me as soon as I finished school. His folks still had their ranch, and he was going to take it over when they passed on. But I had my dreams, and I didn't want to give them up. I couldn't see myself herding cows, scrubbing floors, and changing diapers for the rest of my life. It wasn't what I wanted. So I left before he could change my mind. End of story. Does that make sense?"

"Yes, but . . ." Lexie paused. Val waited, sensing another question.

"What about Dad?" Lexie asked. "You never came home while he was alive, not even when Jack died. And you didn't come to his funeral. You didn't even send flowers."

"Our father disowned me when I left," Val said—the truth but not all of it. "He forbade me to go to Hollywood—said that I'd fall into bad ways. He swore that if I ever came back, I wouldn't be welcomed. He was a hard man, Lexie. You know that."

"Yes, I know. I saw how he drove Jack and Tess to make something of the ranch—his legacy, he always called it. But he was always kind to me. I loved him."

Of course, she did, Val thought. Lexie loved everybody, and everybody loved her. She had all the good qualities that had passed down through the family and, unlike Val, none of the bad ones.

"That's enough questions for now," Val said, pretending to admire her fresh crimson toenails. "Where in the hotel would you like to go for lunch when we're finished here?"

"I saw this cute-looking French place on the mezzanine," Lexie said. "We passed it on the way here. French food might be a nice change from the ranch. And after that, maybe we can go outside and do some window-shopping. Even if we can't afford the clothes and jewelry, it's always fun to look."

Warning bells went off in Val's head. She'd felt safe enough in the spa, and the restaurant would probably be all right. But if the unseen presence she'd sensed was more than just her jumpy nerves, leaving the hotel to shop would be too risky. Taking a chance with her own safety would be foolish enough. But exposing Lexie and the baby to danger would be unthinkable.

"Sorry, honey," she said. "By the time we finish with lunch, I'm going to be ready for a nap. And with the baby, you should rest, too. There's always tomorrow. Maybe some of those cowboy wives you met would like to go with you."

Lexie didn't argue, but disappointment was written all over her pretty face. Val felt like a spoilsport. But she couldn't take a chance, not with Lexie.

Not even if she was only jumping at shadows.

What if the fear she felt was all in her head? With all the booze and cocaine that had gone through her system before rehab, a little craziness would come as no surprise. She had no solid evidence that she was being watched. Even the phone call could've been a simple misdial. Hearing an unfamiliar voice, the caller could have simply hung up. But her instincts were warning her of danger. And Val trusted her gut more than she trusted the flawed logic in her brain.

Forty minutes later, pampered, painted, and fluffed to perfection, they strolled back along the mezzanine toward the French restaurant. Seeing their reflection in a shop window, Lexie giggled. "We look like we're trolling for men, don't we?"

Val gave her a smile. "I haven't seen any men to compare with the one you've already got."

"But what about you?" Lexie teased. "Hey, that old guy over there with the walker's giving you the eye. He looks rich. Do you know how I can tell? Expensive boots."

"I'm not in the market for a man, not even if he's rich. Come on, you troublemaker." Val nudged her sister into the restaurant, which was decorated with posters of the Eiffel Tower, the Arc de Triomphe, and other well-known French scenes. Wrought iron bistro tables and chairs were arranged under artificial trees. Édith Piaf's voice crooned "La Vie en Rose" over a hidden speaker.

A young waiter who spoke with a comical fake French accent ushered them to a table and gave them menus. The few customers in the place, all women, looked like out-of-towners. Val hadn't expected much from the food, but the quiche Lorraine they ordered with tall glasses of iced tea was surprisingly good.

Lexie finished her plate and put down her napkin. "Thank you for today, Val. With Shane and the ranch taking so much energy these past few months, I'd almost forgotten how to be good to my-self. I feel like a real live girl again."

"My pleasure. And wait till Shane sees how gorgeous you look. You'll knock his socks off." Val found her credit card in her purse and held it up to summon the waiter. The spa sessions would go on the hotel bill, but she wanted lunch to be her treat.

"You can put your card away, *madame,*" the waiter said. "A gentle-man already paid for your lunch."

"But who—?" Val glanced around restaurant, seeing only women at the tables and the bar.

Lexie hooted with laughter. "See, Val? I told you that old rich dude had his eye on you. He's probably outside waiting for you to thank him."

Val struggled to ignore the tension crawling along her nerves. Lexie could be right. But what if she was wrong?

"The gentleman, was he old?" she asked the waiter. "White hair, using a walker?"

"Nope." The waiter shook his head, dropping the fake accent. "It was a guy in a suit, maybe about forty, black hair. He gave me fifty bucks, said that should cover any order, plus the tip."

Val's throat had gone rigid. She forced the words. "But I didn't see anybody."

"Oh, yeah—he came by before you got here. He said two ladies would be showing up, and he described you both, even your clothes."

Val fought back waves of panic. Only the manicurists had known where she and Lexie were going for lunch. The two girls had looked completely innocent. But they'd passed on what they'd heard.

Passed on to whom? That was the question.

She forced herself to speak calmly. "I'm sure there's an expla-nation for all this," she said, rising and reaching for Lexie's hand. "Come on, let's go."

The elevator was only a few doors away. It was empty when they stepped inside. Val willed her hand not to shake as she pushed the button for their floor.

"That was creepy," Lexie said. "Who do you think paid for our lunch?"

"I don't know," Val said. "I used to hang out with some people here. Maybe one of them is playing games, having a little fun. But be careful, Lexie. Until we learn what's going on, don't go anywhere alone."

Lexie stared at her. "This is serious, isn't it? You're scared, Val. I can tell."

"Not scared. Just puzzled." One more half-lie. "But let's not tell Tess or Shane. They'll only worry, and there's nothing they can do. Okay?"

"Okay for now. But if there's something going on—"

"Yes, I'll let you know. Meanwhile, keep your door locked until Shane gets back. If you need anything, call me. I'll be right down the hall."

The elevator door opened. Val stayed in the hall until Lexie had gone into her room. Then, ready for anything, she used her key card to open the room she shared with Tess.

No one was inside. Only the made-up beds and general tidying told her that room service had been there.

She double-locked the door. Then, trembling, she sank onto the bed and buried her face in her hands. When she'd come out of rehab and gone home to her family, she'd told herself the past was buried. But here, in the city she'd never wanted to see again, it appeared that her past had come back to haunt her.

She'd dismissed the limo and the phone call as coincidence. But what had happened in the restaurant had been no accident. Someone was sending her a message that no one could misunderstand. Whoever it was, they wanted her scared. They wanted her to know that they had eyes and ears everywhere, and when they tired of their game, they would reel her in like a hooked fish.

She could only try to guess the reason. When she was Lenny Fortunato's girl, she'd seen things. Bad things. Maybe somebody out there thought she'd seen too much.

Right now, all she wanted to do was get on that plane, go home to the ranch, and never come back here. But something had changed. Whoever was stalking her, they knew about Lexie. To get what they wanted from Val, they could use her sister, even hurt her.

How could she go home and leave her precious, pregnant sister exposed? And what about Shane and Tess? Her shadowed past had put them all in danger.

There was only one right thing to do—cancel her flight, cancel the sale of her arena tickets, and stay in Las Vegas until she knew that her family was safe—even if it meant confronting the demons of her past.

CHAPTER FOUR

VAL SAT ALONE, ONE FACE IN THE CROWD OF ALMOST 20,000 WHO'D come to watch the second night of the PBR World Finals. Lexie had promised to sit with her, but at the last minute she'd been called to be with Shane at the press table. Not that Val minded. There were worse things than being alone, and she was undoubtedly safer here than in her hotel room.

She'd never been in the T-Mobile Arena before, but growing up, she'd seen smaller places like it—the seemingly endless rings of seats, rising to the vast dome of the ceiling, where rows of lights and two giant display screens hung suspended from steel beams; and the central floor, normally a basketball court, that had been replaced by a thick layer of dirt hauled in for the five-day PBR event. Toward one end of the floor was a box-like structure known as the shark cage, which sheltered TV and video cameras, members of the press, and a few privileged guests. The platform on top served both as a stage and an emergency escape from charging bulls.

Every available surface was plastered with ads promoting the event's sponsors. There were ads for outdoor gear and cowboy clothes, for beer and whiskey, for farm and construction equipment, for tires, motor oil, and all kinds of vehicles. Even the riders and bullfighters wore logos on their clothing. Every ad meant money that went to the PBR for event costs, prizes, salaries, and other expenses.

Adjusting the bill of the baseball cap that covered her hair, she settled back to watch the ceremony that opened every major PBR event—the presentation of the flag, the singing of the national anthem, and a prayer, followed by the lighting of the giant PBR letters on the ground and the introduction of each rider as they walked forward between the flames to stand in a line.

Val's seat was in an upper section, but the screens at either end of the arena gave her a close-up view of the action. Despite her resolve, she found herself scanning the nearest screen and the arena below for one face, one familiar set of broad shoulders, one man with an easy, confident way of moving. The first rider was mounting his bull in the chute before her eyes found him, poised for action near the gate, his face shadowed by the straw hat he wore.

Her breath caught at the sight of him. She hadn't seen Casey in more than nine years. But she'd thought of him far more often than she'd wanted to. A woman never forgot her first love, especially when that first love was Casey Bozeman.

In the bad times—and there'd been plenty of those—the memory of his strong arms had been there, supporting and tormenting her, and she'd shed tears because she knew that no matter what happened, she could never go back to him again.

Especially not now.

The gate swung open and a hulking, tan monster of a bull with a wide rack of horns exploded into the arena. The rider lasted barely three seconds before a twisting leap sent him flying off into the dirt. He landed clear of the pounding hooves. But he was hurt, and the bull wasn't finished with him. Turning, the beast lowered its head to do more damage.

The bullfighting team was already in action. Casey flung himself between the bull and the downed rider, grabbing the horns and taking the hit while one teammate dragged the rider out of the way. The second man diverted the bull in time to keep Casey from being shoved backward and crushed.

While the crowd cheered, Val closed her eyes and forced herself to take deep breaths. Acts of courage like this one were what fans had come to see. But watching Casey flirt with death only served as a bittersweet reminder of what the years had cost her.

Why had she let her sisters talk her into coming here? She could have stayed home in Arizona and spared herself the pain of memories that should have stayed buried.

It was all she could do to keep from bolting out of her seat, plunging down the aisle, and fleeing into the cool night. But she'd promised her family she would stay and see Whirlwind buck. And given the unseen threat, rushing outside would be the most foolhardy thing she could do. She had little choice except to stay and watch.

Of the thirty-five riders who'd qualified for the finals, there were seventeen left to ride in this round. At the end of the night, those with lower scores would be eliminated from competition. Tomorrow another round would begin with the riders who remained. The stakes, in terms of prize money and prestige, couldn't be higher—for the bulls as well as for the riders.

With the rides happening in rapid succession, the time passed swiftly. Typically, the higher-ranked riders were saved for later in the event. Val already knew that Whirlwind would be bucking last, but she'd lost track of the count.

Her seat in the upper stands gave her an eagle's-eye view into the bucking chutes. Now she could make out Tess, in the Kelly-green shirt she wore for luck moving behind the complex of gates and passageways that connected the chutes to the pens. Val's interest quickened. If Tess was there, it had to mean that Whirlwind was about to buck.

Tess leaned over the top rail of the narrow holding pen to attach the flank strap in front of Whirlwind's hindquarters. Made of soft cotton, it provided enough pressure to make the bull want to kick higher. Some critics of bull riding claimed that the strap constricted the bull's testicles, causing pain. There was no truth to that. But the thin strap was slightly uncomfortable. It wasn't attached until the bull was ready to go into the chute. And it was taken off as soon as the bull left the arena.

It was common custom for the stock contractor to attach and

remove the strap. But getting it around the bull, which involved dropping it down one side of the narrow pen, catching it with a hook, and pulling it up the other side, was a challenge to manage alone. Tess was struggling when she heard a familiar voice.

"How about I give you a hand?"

Tess's heart skipped. The speaker was Clay Rafferty, the PBR livestock director Shane had interviewed that morning. Close to sixty, and heavier than he'd been in his bull riding days, he was an easygoing man with friendly blue eyes. Tess had been introduced to him by Shane after the interview. She was still starstruck.

With expert skill he hooked the end of the strap Tess had dropped, pulled it up, and passed it across Whirlwind's back for her to tie. "Nice bull you've got there," he said. "He's smart. I like smart. And that's an impressive buck-off streak he's got."

"I know he's got talent and heart," Tess said. "But I've seen the other bulls here, and I'm familiar with their pedigrees. Some of them are sons and grandsons of legendary bulls like Bushwacker and Asteroid. Compared to them, my bulls are just mutts."

"Don't sell your bulls short. When that gate swings open and a bull comes rocketing out of the chute, it doesn't matter what his pedigree is. All that matters is how hard he can buck."

"Thanks for that," Tess said. "I'm really hoping he'll buck off R.J. McClintock tonight."

"That would be fine," Rafferty said. "But let me offer you a word of wisdom. At the end of the night, nobody remembers one more buck-off. What you want is for this bull to give R.J. a ninety-point ride. That's what'll get Whirlwind noticed and give him the points to move up in the rankings."

"Thank you. I just wish you could make Whirlwind understand that."

Rafferty grinned. "I know. Like any bull, he'll do whatever the hell he wants. And your other bull will do the same. I'm anxious to see him buck with a world-class rider." He tipped his weathered Stetson. "Good luck out there."

Tess gazed after him as he walked away. Had he meant that Whiplash would get his chance in the arena?

But Tess had little time to think about that. Whirlwind was

lunging against the gate of the holding pen as the chute boss ordered him moved forward to chute number three.

Tess mounted the metal stairs to the platform above the chutes. Standing there, looking down into the chute, was R.J. McClintock. Dark, lean, and as tough as barbed wire, he chose to wear a broad-brimmed black hat instead of a helmet. His thin, bony face was a study in concentration. But when he sensed Tess behind him, he turned and gave her a nod and an easy smile. He was a living legend, his body a mass of scars and metal. Each new injury threatened to end his career. But he continued to ride as if there were no tomorrow.

There were two rides ahead of him—both buck-offs, over fast, with no score for the riders. Tess's heart crept into her throat as McClintock shoved his mouthpiece between his teeth, checked his glove, and moved between the bars above the chute. As the announcer blared out his name and the name of the bull, he lowered himself onto Whirlwind's back.

Casey planted himself a few yards clear of the gate and waited while McClintock rubbed the rosined surface of his bull rope, thrust his glove into the handle, and wrapped the rope tight. This was the moment the Champion family had lived for—the most famous rider in the world on their bull. Casey could only wish them—and Whirlwind—the best.

As McClintock made the final adjustments and moved forward over his hand, Casey forced himself to focus. Whirlwind was an easygoing bull who usually went right out the exit gate, but anything could happen, and he needed to be ready.

For the danger-charged seconds ahead, he needed to ignore the feeling that somewhere, in that vast sea of faces, was the one he'd told himself he never wanted to see again.

No one had told him that Val was in Las Vegas. But it made sense that she would be here for her family. And Tess's reticence yesterday had confirmed it. Val was here. He could almost feel her watching him. But right now he couldn't allow that to matter. He had a job to do.

At a nod from McClintock, the gate swung open. Whirlwind exploded out with a giant, twisting leap that raised a dust cloud when he landed. The leap was followed by a storm of spinning kicks, so high that his silver body was almost vertical. Whirlwind had already learned that if he could make the rider lean back, a twist of his rump would be enough to fling him to the dirt. But McClintock stayed in place, arm raised, legs forward, in perfect position as the digital clock spun off the seconds. Four . . . five . . .

Casey could almost sense the young bull's frustration as he bucked harder, trying tricks that had thrown off lesser riders in the past. When his spin suddenly changed directions, away from the rider's hand, McClintock leaned dangerously, almost sliding off to the side. But he was still hanging on when the eight-second whistle blasted the air. The crowd erupted with wild cheers as he freed his hand from the rope, slid to the ground, and rolled clear, unhurt.

As Whirlwind trotted out the open gate, the score for the ride was posted—46.5 points for the rider, 46 points for the bull, for a spectacular 92.5 total, enough to put McClintock solidly in the lead and assure Whirlwind's place as a rising star.

Job done for the night, Casey took off his straw Resistol hat and wiped a sleeve across his damp forehead before heading back through the chute area to the locker room. Tess and her sisters would be over the moon. As a friend, there was no way he could leave without taking time to congratulate them.

Would he see Val? Did he want to?

For now, that decision was out of his hands.

He found Tess by the holding pen, where she'd just unfastened Whirlwind's flank strap. She was watching the bull disappear down the passageway. For the moment, she was alone.

"So, how does it feel, Tess?" he asked her.

She turned, and he saw the tears flowing down her cheeks. "Oh, Casey! It's too much!" She stumbled into his open arms. He hugged her like a brother, patting her back as she sobbed. Tess was one of the least emotional women he'd ever known, but tonight had opened the floodgates.

"Excuse me, am I intruding?" The deep voice broke them apart. Brock Tolman had just stepped around the chutes.

Tess wiped her eyes and squared her jaw. "Not at all," she said.

"I just came back to congratulate you on your bull," he said. "That was quite a show he put on."

"Now you know why we wouldn't sell him," she said. "But thank you, anyway."

He nodded, his expression darkening. "I won't keep you," he said, "especially since I've clearly interrupted something. Enjoy the glory while it lasts, Tess." He turned away and vanished in the direction of the exit. Looking past him, Casey saw R.J. McClintock striding toward them, with Lexie behind him. She was bouncing like an excited puppy.

There was no sign of Val. Maybe his hunch had been wrong, and she was still off in La-La Land trying to be a star. Or maybe, by now, she'd married some rich used car dealer and put the Alamo Canyon Ranch behind her for good. Whatever—he couldn't let it matter anymore. And things were getting crowded back here. It was time to leave the Champions to their celebration.

He gave Lexie a high five, then headed back toward the locker room to shower and change. He had just stepped inside when he realized his straw hat was missing.

He recalled having it in the arena. He'd taken it off to wipe his forehead after the last ride. Distracted, he must've dropped it. He'd had the fool hat for so long that it had become a sort of lucky talisman. If he didn't get it now, it would be swept up and thrown in the trash. With a mutter of impatience, he left the locker room to retrace his steps.

By now, most of the fans had left the arena. The cleaning crew was already at work. Casey spotted his hat where he remembered taking it off. It was lying undamaged on the dirt. With a wave to the cleaners, he jogged out into the arena, picked up the hat, and walked back toward the gate.

At the last moment, something—a sound, perhaps, or just a feeling—made him turn around and look back across the arena. Coming down the steps from the upper tier of seats was the lone figure of a woman in jeans, a denim jacket, and a baseball cap. He couldn't see her face or even her hair, but as he watched her he knew, with a certainty that crushed his heart in his chest, that it was Val.

Val had stayed in her seat, waiting for the crowds to clear before making her way down to find her sisters and Shane. She'd had her reasons for not leaving earlier. Being packed tight in a mob of strangers had always made her nervous. She also knew that the area around the chutes would be busy until the press and other people involved in the event had packed up and gone. There was no reason to rush down there, she'd told herself. Lexie and Tess knew where she was. They wouldn't go anywhere without her.

But Val had delayed for another reason—a reason that vanished like smoke in the wind when she looked across the arena and saw Casey standing by the gate, looking up at her.

She had hoped to avoid him, knowing that whatever they had to say to each other was bound to hurt. Now it was too late. He had seen her, and she had no place to run.

He stayed where he was, waiting for her to come to him. Val forced herself to keep moving. What would he say to her? Did he hate her for what she'd done? Or would Casey's big, forgiving heart still hold some love?

Love would be the worst. Hate would make things so much simpler.

Please hate me, Casey, she thought.

She could see him clearly now, as she crossed the walkway at the foot of the arena and descended the steps to the floor. He stood with his head up, his hat in his hand. His body, made bulkier by the padded armor beneath his loose-fitting shirt, appeared as strong and fit as ever. But his face had a careworn look, the eyes creased at the corners, the hair touched with gray at the temples.

His impassive expression masked his emotions. But that was no surprise. Casey was a proud man, and even though it had been years ago, she'd hurt him deeply.

She stopped an arm's length from him. He made no move to reach out to her.

"Hello, Casey," she said.

He cleared his throat. "Hello, Val. I had a feeling you might be here."

"I almost didn't come. But Whirlwind . . ." The words trailed off. She remembered how they used to talk for hours, lying on an old sleeping bag in the bed of the pickup, gazing up at the stars. She could tell him anything back then. Now they'd become uncomfortable strangers.

"I understand why you're here," he said. "You want to support your family. I guess you and your sisters will be celebrating tonight."

"I doubt there'll be much of a celebration, with Lexie pregnant and me on the wagon. And you know Tess—she's always been a stick in the mud. We'll probably just go to bed."

Val gave herself a mental slap. She hadn't wanted to mention anything about her personal life, especially any hint that she'd been in rehab.

He reached out as if about to lift the cap off her head; then he appeared to change his mind. "You look good, Val," he said. "The Hollywood lifestyle must agree with you."

"Believe me, the so-called Hollywood lifestyle isn't all it's cracked up to be. For now, it feels good to be away from there." She'd said enough, Val cautioned herself. It was time to cut and run before he started asking questions, forcing her to lie.

"Sorry, I didn't mean to keep you this long," she said. "You must be anxious to change your clothes and get out of here. Good to see you, Casey. Maybe we'll bump into each other again."

Before he could respond, she spun away from him and fled up the lower flight of stairs to the nearest exit. The double doors at the top were closed, but she was able to push one open. It clicked shut behind her as she plunged out onto the concourse.

Only then did she realize her mistake.

She'd meant to head back behind the chute area to find her sisters. But the encounter with Casey had thrown her off balance.

Gazing into his earnest brown eyes, she'd realized that she couldn't deceive him with casual talk. He knew her too well. Stay, and he would strip away her disguise. He would see her for what she was. Just wanting to get away, she'd fled up the stairs and out through the exit doors.

She could hardly go back the way she'd come. That would only mean more questions and more lies. For now, all she could do was walk around the concourse and give him time to leave before she went in to find her family.

The concourse was almost empty. The overhead lights had been dimmed, the concession booths and ticket windows closed for the night. Here and there, custodians were sweeping up fallen debris and emptying the trash receptacles into a wheeled cart. None of them paid her any attention as she passed. From somewhere out of sight, she could hear the whirr of an industrial floor polisher.

After ten or fifteen minutes, Val paused to get her bearings. By now, Casey would've had plenty of time to leave. It would be all right for her to go back inside. But all the doors looked the same, and all of them were closed. The stenciled section numbers were of no help because she hadn't taken notice of where she'd started. But never mind. All she needed to do was open any door and step back into the arena. She would see at once where she was and know where she needed to go.

She walked to the nearest set of double doors and pushed the handle.

Nothing moved. The doors were solidly locked.

Fear trickled upward from the pit of her stomach. Turning back the way she'd come, she walked to the next set of doors and pushed the bar. Locked again.

As the next set of doors also failed to open, Val realized her mistake. To exit the arena, she'd pushed a door open from the inside, but once she'd gone out, the door had closed and locked behind her. It could only be opened from the inside or with some kind of key. She was locked out of the arena.

Taking a deep breath, Val told herself not to worry. She'd seen people cleaning up. Surely one of them would be able to open a door for her. If all else failed, she had her phone in her jacket. She could call Tess to come and let her in.

But she could no longer hear the floor polisher. And when she walked partway around the concourse, she couldn't see any of the custodial staff.

As the lights darkened overhead, Val pulled her phone out. Dead. When was the last time she'd charged it?

Feeling like a fool, she thrust the phone back into her pocket. There had to be something she could do. The outside doors were made of reinforced glass. Beyond them, she could see streetlights and hotels, glittering in the night. She could probably get out that way. But she wouldn't be able to get in again. She'd be stuck outside, with nowhere to go except back to the hotel.

Val was weighing her options when she heard it—faintly at first, then growing closer and more distinct, the sound echoing along the concourse—the sharp cadence of footsteps.

"Hello," she called in the direction of the sound.

There was no reply. But the footsteps kept coming closer, their rhythm steady and unchanging.

Val felt the gooseflesh rise on her arms. Fear crawled along her nerves. "Hello!" she called again. "Who are you? Answer me."

Again, there was no reply, only the sound of footsteps, ringing through the silent concourse.

Was she losing her mind? Maybe. But after what had happened at lunch today, she couldn't dismiss any possibility.

Fear exploded in her. She pounded on the nearest door. Surely there had to be someone inside the arena who could hear her. "I'm locked out!" she shouted, pounding harder. "Let me in!"

Seconds crawled past. She could still hear the footsteps, coming closer. She could feel her heart hammering her ribs. Should she run, try to hide, or just scream and pray that she'd be heard?

At that moment there was a sound from the other side of the entrance, metal parts moving, the creak of a hinge as the door opened. Casey stood there in the glow of the exit light. "Val, are you okay?" He'd changed into jeans and a leather jacket. "Your sisters were worried when you didn't show up."

"Close the door!" she gasped, stumbling over the threshold. "Somebody's out there!"

"Wait." Casey opened the door wider. Now Val could see the glow of a flashlight. It came closer as a security guard walked up to them. "Is everything all right?" The guard, young, with an acne-scarred face, was wearing earbuds. The rap music coming through them was so loud that Val could hear it from where she stood. That would explain why he hadn't heard her shouting.

"Everything's fine," Casey said. "The lady just locked her-self out."

The guard walked away, the sound of his footfalls a match to the ones that had terrified Val earlier. Relief buckled her knees. Shaking, she stumbled toward the steps that led back down to the chute level.

"Val, what is it?" Casey had paused to close the door. He crossed the distance between them in a single stride, caught her shoulder, and pulled her around to face him. His eyes examined her face in the glow of the exit light. "What's the matter? You look like you've seen a ghost. Are you sick?"

"No, nothing like that. Just a little scare out there when I dis-covered I was locked out."

"A little scare? You looked terrified when I opened that door."

"It was nothing. Just a silly mistake. I heard that guard coming and I thought he might be somebody else." As soon as the words were out, Val realized she'd said too much.

"What do you mean, somebody else?" Casey demanded. "Val, are you in some kind of danger?"

"It's nothing. I'll be fine. Just let me go, Casey. Forget you even saw me tonight."

Before he could reply, Casey's cell phone jingled. Releasing her, he pulled it out of his pocket and glanced at the caller ID be-fore answering.

"Hey, Tess . . . Yes, I found her. Everything's fine. She just took the wrong door and got locked out . . . No need to wait. Go on back to the hotel. I'll see that she gets there."

Val knew she could walk away now; and maybe she should. But

she also knew Casey. He wouldn't be satisfied with the crumbs of information she'd tossed him. Protection was his livelihood and to him, it wasn't just a job. It was ingrained in his nature.

Whatever she might have done to him in the past, he wasn't likely to back off until he felt sure that she was safe.

"You don't have to escort me back to the hotel, Casey," she said. "If I hurry, I can catch up with my family."

"No, you don't," he said. "After what just happened, I can't just turn you loose. I'm taking you for coffee, and you're going to tell me what spooked you so badly."

"Blast it, stop trying to big-brother me. This is none of your concern, and I'm not going to let you get involved."

The narrow-eyed look he gave her was a sign she remembered from the old days. It meant that he'd dug in his heels and wouldn't be moved. "I'd say it's a little late for that," he said. "Come on, let's go."

With a sigh, Val gave in. After all, this was a man who routinely faced charging bulls.

But she had to shut the door on Casey Bozeman and lock it for keeps. There were too many secrets she couldn't let him know. And Casey, as she remembered, had a way of wearing her down until nothing was left but raw, bleeding truth.

Only one plan came to Val's mind. Lie through her teeth, then run for her life.

CHAPTER FIVE

CASEY STUDIED VAL WHERE SHE SAT ACROSS FROM HIM IN THE shadowed corner booth. The radiant, laughing girl he remembered was still beautiful, but she had a frayed look. She was too thin, her features too sharply chiseled. Her stunning green eyes were restless, their gaze darting here and there as if hesitant to meet his.

She'd never made it big in Hollywood. Casey would have known if she had. He'd seen every one of her movies, even the ones in which she was little more than a walk-on. For a time, he'd hoped she'd come back to him. After a while he'd forced himself to give up and move on.

Even now, looking at her across the booth, he knew better than to think tonight would make any difference. He and Val were history. But she would always be a part of who he was. And he still cared enough to worry about her.

Was that all, the caring? Or was the memory of loving her still heating his blood?

He'd invited her for coffee. But in his truck, on the way to the café he had in mind, they'd both confessed they were hungry, so they'd ordered nachos to share and two Cokes—a favorite from the old days. Casey would've preferred a cold beer, but he remembered Val saying she was on the wagon. Did that mean she'd had an alcohol problem? Once he'd known her so well. Now he hardly knew her at all.

"So you're back at the ranch," he said, making small talk while they waited for their order. "Do you plan to stay?"

"Maybe." She shrugged and sipped her Coke. "But only if I can find a way to earn my keep. I never was much of a cowgirl, as you know."

"Yes, I know." Casey had to lean close to hear her. Some noisy cowboys at a nearby table were whooping and laughing, their raised voices drowning out even the country music that blasted from the speakers.

"We can't talk in here." Val had to raise her voice. "Maybe you should just forget it and take me back to the hotel."

"I've got a better idea." Casey motioned to the waitress. "We'll take those nachos to go," he said, handing her some bills. "Keep the change."

Minutes later, they carried the boxed nachos, their drinks, and some napkins out to the truck. Casey opened the door for her. When she was settled in the seat, he passed her the food and drinks. "Remember how we used to do this at that old drive-in before they tore it down?" he teased as he climbed into the driver's side.

"At least you've got a fancier truck now," she said, opening the box on the console. "But I'm not about to join you on a trip down memory lane. Eat up. Then you can take me back to the hotel."

"All in good time." Casey sampled a nacho chip, dripping with cheese and garnished with jalapeños. If she didn't want to talk about the past, that was fine. It would only open old wounds. But he wasn't about to let her go until he understood what lay behind the terror in her eyes.

The nachos weren't as tasty as the ones Val remembered from the old days, shared in the front seat of Casey's dad's old pickup, while they watched the movie between cheese-flavored kisses. The old drive-in theater had been a relic of an earlier time. But it had fed Val's desire for a glittering life beyond small-town Arizona. Even on the nights when he'd driven her home to the ranch and they'd parked at the top of the pass to lie under the stars in the open truck bed, she'd known that she wanted to leave—and that she would. She just hadn't known how it would happen, or how soon.

"So, tell me," he said. "Why were you so afraid, back there on the concourse? Who did you think was after you?"

"It doesn't matter. I was just imagining. It turned out to be nothing—just a security guard. You saw that for yourself."

"I know you better than that, Val. You were terrified. Who did you think was following you? An old boyfriend, maybe? One who never got over you? Tell me. I want to help if I can."

"Leave it alone, Casey. This isn't your concern."

"I'll be the judge of that. Just tell me."

She pushed the nachos away, her appetite gone. "Is that what you think, an old boyfriend? Fine. We'll let it go at that. I've dated some creeps in my time, mostly to get ahead in the business. See where it got me. Now, take me back to the hotel."

"You never could look at me when you were lying."

"Stop it. You think you can just walk into my life again and start fixing things. Well, you can't. It's too late for that, Casey. Now start the truck and take me back to the hotel."

"All right." He gathered up the napkins and closed the nacho box. "Five more minutes, and I promise to take you back. You can sit there like a stubborn bump on a log, or you can tell me the truth. Your choice."

He settled back in his seat, one hand resting on the wheel as the minutes scrolled past on the dashboard clock. Casey knew her all too well, Val thought. If one thing could break her, it was silence.

"I'm not just being stubborn," she said. "There's a reason I don't want to tell you."

"Go on."

"Only if you promise not to get involved. Not in any way. All right?"

He hesitated. "All right. But if you're in danger—"

"No, you have to promise."

Lights from a nearby vehicle pulling out of the parking lot cast his features into stark light and shadow. His strong chin had a slight dimple. Val remembered how much all the girls had loved that dimple.

"Fine, I promise—for now," he said. "Tell me."

Val took a deep breath. She'd wanted to tell him, she realized. Heaven help her, she was so scared. She needed to tell somebody— even if she couldn't tell him everything.

"A few years ago, I spent some time here in Vegas. I got mixed up with the wrong people, and I saw some bad things."

"What kind of bad things?"

"Bad. Telling you isn't part of our deal. You're better off not knowing. I can swear that I wasn't involved. But I was a witness."

"And now all this is coming back to haunt you?"

"I'm pretty sure somebody recognized me. And they're trying to get to me." She told him about the limo, the phone call, and finally the lunch incident. "That's when I knew I wasn't just imagining things. Somebody's watching me. Maybe even here, tonight. But I don't know what they want. Is it a threat, maybe a warning, or even a game? Anyway, you can understand why I panicked out there on the concourse."

His face, in the faint glow of the parking lot's overhead light, revealed nothing but worry and concern. "Do you have to stay in town, Val? Can't you just go home?"

"I almost did. I even had a flight booked. But then I realized that if I left, they could still hurt my family. They saw me with Lexie, and they would know about the others, too. I can't let anything happen to them."

"You could go to the police."

"What could I tell the police? That somebody paid for my lunch? It would be a waste of time." Val stirred in the seat. "That's all you're going to get. So it had better be enough for a ride back to the hotel."

"I still wish you'd let me help," he said.

"Even if I did, there's nothing you could do."

"I could protect you."

"Stay out of this, Casey. These people play rough. So far they're only letting me know they're watching me. But I know what they can do. I've seen it. Now let's go."

"Damn it, Val—" He bit back whatever else he'd meant to say. After turning on the headlights, he scooped up the nacho box and the plastic cups. "Just give me a minute to dump these in the trash. Then we'll be on our way."

He climbed out of the truck, which was parked facing the side of the restaurant. The headlights illuminated the trash bin and a newspaper rack with the front page of the *Las Vegas Review Journal* on display.

Val gave the headline, and its accompanying photo, a quick glance at first. Then, as what she was seeing sank in, her pulse lurched.

With a shaking hand, she lowered the window. "Casey," she called, trying to sound calm. "Would you get me one of those newspapers? I want to check for write-ups about the finals. I've got change if you need it."

"No, that's fine. I've got it." Casey dropped some coins into the slot, retrieved the last paper in the box, and without looking at the front page, passed it through the window. Val thanked him, took the paper, and doubled it, hiding the headline in the fold. She would read it later, alone in the hotel.

She should have known better than to confide in Casey. Some things about the man would never change—like the protective instincts that were almost a compulsion and his way of rushing into danger with no thought for his own safety. That was what made him so well suited for his job.

If Casey were to see that newspaper story and piece it together with what she'd told him, there'd be no way she could keep him from wanting to learn more. There was just one thing she could do to keep him safe—and to protect her own secrets.

She had to end this now.

* * *

Casey had offered to walk Val to the elevator in her hotel. But she'd insisted on being let off in the parking lot. Her last words to him, spoken as if she were auditioning for a TV commercial, had been something like, "Thanks for everything, Casey. I hope you'll understand that I can't see you again. You're a good man, just bad timing all around. Have a happy life. Good night and goodbye."

She'd bailed out of the door and fled without giving him a chance to respond, or even to help her out of the truck. Casey could only watch her as she rushed away, clutching her purse and the folded newspaper, dodging foot traffic, and pausing to glance around before she disappeared into the hotel's main entrance.

Now, as he pulled out of the parking lot and drove back to the small hotel he'd found on a quiet side street, Casey put his mind to sorting out what had just happened.

It was like Val to run away from things she didn't want to face. But this wasn't just avoidance on her part. He'd seen the look in her eyes as she'd told him goodbye. It was stark fear.

Walk away, his sensible side argued. *She doesn't want your help, let alone deserve it. The woman wrecked your life once. She'd do it again in a heartbeat.*

But common sense had already lost the battle. As he drove and pondered his options, one thing became more and more certain.

Whatever was going on, this wasn't over.

He remembered the newspaper Val had asked him to buy. She'd claimed that she wanted to read about the PBR finals. But any coverage in that issue would have been about yesterday's event. Whirlwind's performance with R.J. McClintock would be covered in tomorrow morning's paper. The edition she'd asked for was old news.

So why had she wanted to read it? And why would she lie about the reason?

From the truck, Val would have seen only the front page. Something in the headline must have caught her eye. But Casey had paid no attention when he took the paper out of the stand. If he wanted to know what had set her off, he would have to find another copy.

At this late hour, most newspapers would be gone, either sold or cleared out to make room for the next morning's edition. Casey stopped at two convenience stores on the way to his hotel. Their papers were gone. Only then did he remember that his hotel had a paper delivered to the lobby every day.

He made it back in time to save the scattered pages from the janitor's trash barrel. Gathering them, he carried the paper into the elevator and up to his room, where he arranged it on one of the two beds.

It was the front page he needed—that and any pages that might have related or continued articles. At first he saw nothing but minor news items, editorials, and ads. Then he turned the pages over and saw the headline that Val had spotted.

LANZONI CHARGED, DENIED BAIL

Las Vegas businessman and alleged crime boss, Carlo Lanzoni, appeared in First District Court on Tuesday to face charges of racketeering, extortion, and murder. He was charged on all counts and denied bail. The trial date will be set pending investigation by a grand jury.

There were more details in the article, accompanied by a photo of a middle-aged man with thinning gray-streaked hair, dark eyes overhung by beetling brows, and a jaw framed by sagging jowls. He looked like a bus driver or maybe a construction boss. But looks could be deceiving.

As Casey reread the article, his nerves crawled. Val had mentioned that she'd gotten mixed up with some unsavory people and implied that she'd witnessed some criminal acts. Given her reaction to the headline, it was no challenge to put two and two together.

If she'd been recognized, and Lanzoni's thugs thought she might be planning to talk, Val's life was in danger.

Val was one of those women who left a trail of wreckage everywhere she went, he reminded himself. He had every reason to turn his back on her. But right now, it didn't matter what she'd done or who she'd been with. He needed to keep her safe.

Val crossed the lobby, dodged a cluster of partying cowboys, and headed for the bank of elevators. Stepping inside the first one to open, she punched the button for the floor above her room, then stayed on past the stop and got out the next time the door opened. She needed to read the newspaper, but she didn't want Tess to know about it. She also needed to make sure she wasn't being followed.

Along one side of the alcove that housed the elevators was a low, upholstered bench. Taking a seat, Val unfolded the paper. The sight of Carlo Lanzoni's face in the photo triggered a stomach spasm so sharp that she had to gasp. Even without reading the article, she could guess what was going on. Lanzoni was in jail. But that didn't mean she was safe. The man was like an evil spider with a network of webs as broad as the state of Nevada. He had eyes and ears everywhere, and an army of paid informants that included public officials and police officers. For him, running his organization from a prison cell and keeping watch on anyone he needed to control would be no problem.

She forced herself to read the news article, once, then again, memorizing the content before crumpling the newspaper and stuffing it into a nearby waste can. Stepping into the elevator, she pushed the button for the floor above her room. She would take the stairs the rest of the way down—a needless precaution, maybe, but she couldn't be too careful—not only for her own safety but for her sister's.

As the elevator hummed downward, she thought about what she'd read. *Racketeering, extortion, and murder.* Those were the charges. But whose murder? How many murders had Lanzoni committed, not with his own hands but on his orders? Dozens, almost certainly.

Solid evidence of just one killing would be enough to convict him. If Val came forward, her testimony could put Carlo Lanzoni behind bars for life.

But at what cost to her and her loved ones?

At least she could understand why she was being watched, and most likely warned. But why would it matter when there'd been so many other hits—most of them carried out by Lanzoni's bodyguard, a coldly handsome brute named Dimitri who killed as efficiently as a machine. She couldn't be the only witness left alive. There had to be others who had more to gain and less to lose.

Still tormenting herself with questions, she left the stairwell and walked down the hall to the room she shared with Tess. Before using her card, she took a deep breath and arranged her expression in a smile. She'd told her sister nothing about her past or about her present danger. Knowing would only set Tess off and distract her when she needed to focus on the bulls.

Val walked into the room to find Tess sitting up in bed, checking her phone. "I've got some good news," she said. "Clay Rafferty wants to buck Whirlwind a second time in round four. And Whiplash will be on standby for the next reride. Rafferty really seems to like our bulls. Let's hope they don't disappoint him."

"That's great." Val tossed her purse on the bed and headed for the bathroom.

"Hey, wait," Tess said. "You were gone for quite a while. How did it go with Casey?"

"It didn't go anywhere," Val said. "We just talked—and agreed to stay distant friends. We won't be spending any more time together."

"Okay. So why did he just call and ask me if you'd made it back to the room? And why did he sound worried when I told him I hadn't seen you?"

Val sighed. "You know Casey. Overprotective is his middle name. After he let me off, I took a little walk to clear my head. That was all."

"Maybe you should call him and let him know you're here now," Tess said.

"My phone needs charging. Anyway, you're the one who's got his cell number. Why don't you call him?"

Tess raised an eyebrow. "Goodness, it sounds like things really didn't go well between the two of you."

"What did you expect? We're not teenagers anymore. We've grown up. We're different people now."

"Fine. I'll call him." Tess scrolled her phone, then paused. "I just remembered something weird. About fifteen minutes ago, the room phone rang. I thought it might be the desk calling about something, so I picked up and answered. Nobody replied, but I could hear a sound, like rustling, and then the line went dead."

Val's shrug masked a shudder of apprehension. "Probably just a mistake. Or some scumbag looking for an empty room to rob. Just to be safe, we need to make sure our door's securely locked, even when we leave. Remember to call Casey, will you?"

Val ducked into the bathroom and closed the door behind her. She felt vaguely ill. The nachos and Coke had congealed in her stomach, but even when she tried to throw up, nothing happened. Maybe she should tell Tess what was going on. But her family would be safer not knowing. Any efforts on their part to protect her would only put them all at risk.

One question still bothered her. She mulled it over while she brushed her teeth and washed her face. If Lanzoni feared she might testify against him, why hadn't his people killed her? It would be easy enough, especially if Dimitri was still doing his job.

Only one answer came to mind. Her death or disappearance could result in more charges, more investigations, perhaps even more arrests. And so far, their subtle scare tactics were working. Val had no desire to put herself or her family at risk. Surely the DA would have enough on Lanzoni to convict him without her help.

But what if she were wrong? Of all the terrors plaguing her, the most frightening was fear of the unknown.

By the time Val walked out of the bathroom, Tess had turned off her bedside lamp. She lay on her side, with the pillow doubled under her head. "I called Casey. When I asked him why he'd seemed so worried, he shut right down. What's going on, Val?"

"Nothing." Val sat on the foot of her bed in the dim light, her back toward her sister as she undressed and pulled the black sleepshirt over her head.

"It didn't strike me as nothing," Tess said.

"All right. We had an argument. Things got a little heated. I got out of the truck and walked back to the hotel by myself." Val was lying through her teeth, but it was for a good cause, she told herself. Blast Casey—she could punch him for alerting Tess to her possible danger.

"I've been thinking," Val said, although the idea had just struck her. "I won't have much to do tomorrow. Lexie will be with the wives' group she met, and you'll be looking after the bulls. What do you say I tag along with you and give you a hand? I can shovel manure and scoop bull chow as well as the next flunky."

"Uh—sure, Val. I'd like that. But weren't you planning to fly out tomorrow?"

Val shrugged. "I changed my mind. I was thinking maybe it's time I got more involved in the family business."

"Oh. Okay then." Tess sounded surprised. Not that Val could blame her. On the ranch, she'd filled in for the cook and given the old house a badly needed refurbishing for Lexie's wedding. But she'd never offered her help with the stock.

Val still wasn't keen on working with the bulls. But helping Tess would give her something to do and a safe place to be. Right now that was important.

"I'll be leaving here by seven o'clock and grabbing coffee on the way," Tess said. "We can have breakfast after the bulls have been taken care of. Do you think you can drag yourself out of bed in time to go with me?"

"We'll see." Val was tired, and she'd never been an early-morning person. "If you have to leave without me, I can always join you later."

Tess sighed. "Whatever. But you know what Dad would have

said. Hungry bulls need to be fed. You can sleep on your own time." She turned over and pulled the covers up to her chin. Within a few minutes her breathing became deep and even.

Exhausted but too wired to sleep, Val lay in the dark, listening to voices passing in the hall and to the whir and bump of the elevators. Faintly, through the window, she could hear the sound of traffic. Vegas was known as Sin City. Once, two years that seemed like a lifetime ago, she'd fed off the energy and excitement that pulsed through the place. Now it only grated on her nerves. All she wanted was to be somewhere else.

Why had she agreed to come here? She could have stayed home, safe from the dangers of her past. Safe from Casey and the way he made her feel.

She'd promised herself that she wouldn't think about him. But she couldn't help recalling the physical jolt she'd felt when she'd first seen him, standing at the foot of the stairs in the arena. And afterward, in the truck—how her pulse had quickened when she'd sensed him looking at her. Even after so many years, the man could turn her on with a look or a touch.

But that was just one reason why she had to stay away from him.

Would she see him tomorrow morning? Not likely. He'd probably be working out at a gym somewhere. Lives depended on the bullfighters being in top condition. Casey wasn't getting any younger, but she could imagine how his body must look without clothes—the sculpted shoulders and taut, narrow hips and flat belly; the crisp V of hair that traced a shadowy path down his muscular torso to . . .

Stop it!

Casey was the last man she should be fantasizing about. Being with him tonight had stirred feelings that she'd done her best to bury. But she would never act on those feelings. If he were to find out what she'd done and what she'd become, he would turn his face away and never look at her again.

Drifting now, she could feel the dream rising out of her memory like a poisonous tide. Helpless to resist, she was swept back eighteen months in time, to a one-room apartment on a seedy Vegas backstreet, in a neighborhood so rough that even the police tended to avoid it.

She kept to the shadows, the hood of her sweatshirt drawn tight around her face, hiding everything but her eyes. A mile distant, the hotels along the strip glittered like fantasy towers from another world—a world apart from this potholed street where homeless people camped on the sidewalks and whores came to crash after a night of working the tourist spots—a street where anything could be bought if you had the cash and knew where to look.

It was sometime after midnight, not a safe time for a woman to be alone on the street. But Lenny, who was in trouble with the boss, didn't want to be seen. So when he'd needed a hit, he'd given her a wad of cash and sent her out to score some cocaine.

She already knew where to go, who to find, and how much to pay. The deal was done in a matter of minutes. With the packet of white powder tucked into the kangaroo pouch of her sweatshirt, she turned around and headed back down the block, to the entrance of the three-story apartment house.

The stairwell reeked of stale cigarette smoke and urine. But they wouldn't be here long, Val reminded herself. Soon Lenny's luck at the gaming tables was bound to change. He'd get the cash to repay Lanzoni for the protection money he'd held back, and everything would be all right again.

The door to their room was on the second floor, next to a recess in the wall where a rusted, broken vending machine stood. Val was fumbling for the key she'd thrust into the pocket of her jeans when she heard voices from the room inside.

"No . . . Please, I'm sorry, so sorry . . ." The pleading voice was Lenny's. "For God's sake, Dimitri, tell Lanzoni I'll make it up. He won't get anything if I'm dead."

"It's a little late for that. Lanzoni won't work with a man

he doesn't trust. You've crossed him one time too many." Val recognized the chilling voice with its Slavic accent. "Here's a present from the boss. Nice knowing you, Lenny."

Val heard the muffled sound of a shot from Dimitri's .38, equipped with a silencer. She ducked on the far side of the vending machine and squeezed against the wall, expecting him to come bursting into the hall. Instead, what she heard was the bathroom and closet doors slamming open, drawers being pulled out and thrown, and even the bed being moved. He would have seen her clothes in the room and her purse hanging on the bedpost. That meant, in order to finish the job, Dimitri would have to kill her, too.

Seconds later, having failed to find his quarry, he stepped out of the room, closed the door behind him, and stood looking up and down the stairwell. He was so close that Val could have reached out and touched his pantleg. She held her breath. Any second now, he would turn and see her, squeezed between the wall and the old vending machine.

Just then a gang of teenage boys came pouring inside from the street. Laughing and jostling each other, they pounded up the stairs and spilled into the hallway. With a muttered curse, Dimitri turned aside, headed down the stairs and out the door. As the boys disappeared into one of the rooms, Val heard the sound of a powerful car roaring away.

Minutes passed before she dared to squeeze out of her hiding place. What if Dimitri was tricking her? What if he planned to come back?

Val thrashed and twisted in the bed, struggling to wake from what she knew was coming—the part that would haunt her to the end of her days. But sleep held her captive, forcing her to go on.

Her first impulse was to flee to the roof, where she could hide and watch for Dimitri's return. But what if Lenny was still alive? She couldn't go without checking.

The door had locked when Dimitri closed it, but she still had her key. Hand shaking, she thrust it into the lock and turned the latch.

The room, lit by a guttering candle she'd left on the counter, was a wreck. Dimitri had destroyed the place looking for her— and probably for any hidden cash or drugs. Val had closed the door behind her when she saw the body sprawled facedown on the filthy carpet. No breath. No movement. Not much blood. Dimitri liked to kill with a single clean shot to the side of the head. Still, she needed to turn Lenny over and make sure she wouldn't be leaving him alive.

Tugging and lifting, she managed to roll him onto his back. Only then did she force herself to look down at his lifeless face.

Val awoke with a violent jerk. Stifling a scream, she lay quivering in the dark as the dream dissolved around her. She could hear the faint rumble of cartwheels passing the door and the soft rush of her sister's breathing in the next bed.

It had only been a bad dream—one she'd had so many times before that it had taken on the aspect of a stage play.

But this time, something about the dream had been different.

When she'd turned the dead man over, it hadn't been Lenny Fortunato she'd seen.

It had been Casey.

CHAPTER SIX

WHEN VAL OPENED HER EYES AGAIN IT WAS ALMOST 8:00. MORN-ing light was streaming through the blinds, and Tess was gone.

With a groan, she sat up, flung back the covers, and swung her legs off the bed. Last night, after the awful dream, she'd tried for more than an hour to go back to sleep. Finally, she'd gone into the bathroom, found a bottle of over-the-counter sleeping tablets in Tess's travel kit, and taken just one—or had it been two? What-ever she'd taken had knocked her out. She hadn't even heard her sister get up and leave.

Tess was probably disgusted with her. Flighty, irresponsible Val, with her pickled brain. Val, who couldn't be counted on to show up for anything on time.

Well, she was trying, blast it. She wanted to be someone her family could depend on. But it wasn't always easy—hell, it was *never* easy. Especially when her inner demons reared their heads, as they had last night. But she couldn't just give up and walk away. Her sisters and the Alamo Canyon Ranch were her last refuge—her one chance to heal.

She was still worried about Casey—maybe the dream had been a manifestation of that anxiety. He was a family friend, and she couldn't avoid seeing him. But she'd been wise to end any notion of a relationship last night. Trying to protect her would only put him in danger. And learning the truth about her past would de-stroy him in ways he could never imagine.

In the bathroom, she brushed her teeth, raked back her hair, and applied a few dabs of foundation to her tired face. In her younger years, she hadn't needed anything more than a touch of lipstick. But this morning, she looked . . . old, damn it, even though she was only twenty-seven.

She dressed hurriedly in the jeans and shirt she'd worn the day before. Mucking out the bull pen, if Tess would still let her help, would be a waste of clean clothes. She could shower and change later.

After disconnecting her cell phone from the charger, she dropped it into her purse and headed out of the room. In the doorway, she hesitated, then hung the DO NOT DISTURB tag on the outside doorknob. The room wouldn't get made up, but at least the cleaner wouldn't be coming in. After her experience with the manicurists, she was afraid to trust anyone.

As an afterthought, she broke off a loose thread from the lining of her jacket and placed it to lie between the door and the frame. If she came back to find the thread in place, she would know the door hadn't been opened.

What if she was being overly cautious? What if the sense of being watched, the phone calls, even the incident in the restaurant, were just harmless events playing on her fears?

What if she was becoming irrational?

Deciding to skip coffee, she left the hotel and crossed the short distance to the arena at a jog. The main entrance was open, but aside from a few maintenance people passing in and out of the arena, the concourse was almost empty.

Val had gone partway around when she realized she didn't know how to get from here to the bull pens. Maybe there was another entrance in the back. That could explain why she hadn't yet seen anybody involved with the PBR.

She was about to go outside and look for another way in when she saw a strange man coming around the concourse toward her.

Dimitri! That was her first thought. But no, this man was a stranger—tall and lanky, dressed in new jeans and a plaid western shirt topped by a quilted Carhartt vest. His long-jawed face was untanned, his felt Stetson oddly set on his head, as if it were the wrong size. All in all, he struck her as someone trying to pass as a cowboy. The impression was confirmed when she noticed the wingtip oxfords showing below his jeans.

As they came even, she pretended to ignore him. But as she passed within hearing, he spoke her name.

"Miss Champion."

Her pulse lurched. Her first impulse was to run, but the stranger looked fit enough to catch her easily. And there was no one close by to hear a scream for help. Drawing on her acting skills, she gave him a puzzled look. "I'm sorry, sir," she said. "I believe you've mistaken me for somebody else."

"I don't think so, Miss Valerie Champion." He thrust an official-looking photo ID toward her. "Paul Brandt, Assistant District Attorney for Clark County."

Val willed her emotions to freeze. A new scene in her nightmare had opened. What happened next would be out of her hands. All she could do was try to appear calm and reasonable.

"Am I in trouble?" she asked, masking her anxiety with a smile.

"Not necessarily." He appeared to be about forty, with a flat voice that played on her nerves like a bow on a cheap violin. "Is there someplace where we can talk?"

"That depends. What's this about, Mr. Brandt?" she asked.

"I think you know." He ushered her through a door that opened into the darkened arena. "We should be all right in here for a few minutes. Have a seat."

Val chose a shadowed row, slipped into a seat, and prepared herself for a grilling. She knew better than to lie. But she'd be smart to reveal as little as possible.

Brandt took a seat next to her. "I need to be someplace," she said. "Please make this quick."

"Very well." He cleared his throat. "How much do you know about the case against Carlo Lanzoni?"

"Only what I read in the paper last night."

"According to police files, you were Lenny Fortunato's girl-friend. Is that correct?"

"Yes." If he was waiting for her to explain, he would have to wait a long time.

"And you know that Fortunato was murdered."

"Yes."

"A woman's clothes were found in the room with his body. Were they yours?"

"They were."

"Where were you when Lenny Fortunato was killed?"

Val felt a chill. "Am I a suspect?"

"Not at this time. We want to know what you witnessed. Were you in the room?"

"No, I'd just returned from an errand. I was outside in the hall."

His look told her he'd guessed the nature of her errand. But to her relief, he simply nodded. "Tell me everything you saw and heard."

Val made her story as brief as possible. But she knew that anything that strayed from the truth could get her in trouble later. "I hid until I heard Dimitri's car leave," she finished. "Then I went back into the room to make sure Lenny didn't need my help. But he didn't. He was dead."

"You could've called the police."

"I know. But I was too scared. I grabbed my purse, left everything else, and ran—caught a bus all the way to California." She didn't mention that she'd sold the cocaine to a dealer for enough money to get her out of town. "I'm clean and sober now, living with my sisters on our ranch. I only wish I'd never come back here."

"But you're sure the shooter was Dimitri, and you heard him say he was acting on Lanzoni's orders?"

"Yes." Val's heart had begun to pound. She knew what was coming next.

"Would you be willing to testify to that before the grand jury hearing?" Brandt asked.

Val's mouth had gone dry. She shook her head. "Lanzoni's

people are watching me. They've got eyes and ears everywhere. And I know what they're capable of doing."

"We could protect you."

"That's a joke." Val felt her anger rising. "Could you protect my family? Could you protect my sister's unborn baby? I can't risk their safety. For all I know, I've even put them at risk by talking to you. Find some other way to get Lanzoni convicted for murder."

"We've tried. We're aware that Dimitri killed people. But we have no solid proof that he was acting on Lanzoni's orders—only you can give us that."

Val's stomach clenched. She took a breath, willing herself not to show the strain. "I take it you haven't got Dimitri," she said. "If you had him, you wouldn't need me."

"Don't bet on it. We'd have to make him talk, and Dimitri's a hard nut to crack. He'd lawyer up. Without a reliable witness— like yourself—he'd likely get off. And no, we haven't got him. We've been after the slippery bastard for years. But he's an expert at wiping out his own trail. That includes not leaving behind any witnesses. Last we heard, he'd left town—maybe to freelance while his boss is in lockup."

Val rose from her seat. "Well, if you catch him, give me a call. Otherwise, my answer is a definite no. I won't risk my family. And I can't risk talking to you again. So I suggest you leave here the way you came in—without me."

Brandt stood with her and pressed a business card into her hand. "Call me if you change your mind—or if you learn any-thing new."

"You know where I stand. Don't count on it. And don't come near me again."

Brandt's expression hardened. "You're not entirely in the clear. For all we know, you could've set Lenny Fortunato up—let Lan-zoni know where to find him and made yourself scarce while Dim-itri carried out the hit. That would make you an accessory to murder. You could be charged."

"Don't threaten me, Mr. Brandt." Val's simmering temper

boiled over. "Just remember that if anything happens to me, or to my family, it's on you!"

Turning abruptly, she made her way down the stairs. Now that she could see the chutes, she knew how to get to the bulls and find her sister.

Behind her, the door opened and closed as Brandt left. Val didn't look back. But she was shaking with every step. Brandt wouldn't give up on her. And neither would Lanzoni's goons—especially if Dimitri was involved. She was under pressure from both sides.

A uniformed security guard stood at the entrance to the chute area. Seeing Val approach, he waved her through. Only when she glanced up did she recognize the acne-scarred face beneath his cap. He was the guard who'd been on the concourse last night—the one who'd scared her so needlessly.

She gave him a nod. But one thing struck her. She'd seen him on the night shift. Now here he was, still working in the morning. Never mind, there had to be a reasonable explanation. Maybe his shift was just ending, or maybe he was putting in overtime.

But how long had he been standing there? Long enough to see her with Brandt? Long enough to overhear their conversation?

A nervous shudder passed through her body. What was wrong with her? She was jumping at shadows now, suspecting everyone. And she hated it.

As she passed the empty chutes and press area, she could hear the bulls and smell the warm, earthy aromas of hay and manure. A young cowboy with the look of a rider gave her a "howdy, ma'am" and a tip of the hat as she passed him. Two more did the same. Strange, amid the danger, how safe she felt here. She'd spent the past years of her life amid the hollow glitz and glamour of Hollywood and the dark underbelly of Las Vegas. But this world of polite cowboys and magnificent animals, a world where people worked with their hands and honored their values and traditions, had become a refuge for her.

But how could she earn a place here, where her sisters already belonged? With her new life under threat, how could she find a way to hold on to what she'd found?

Gazing across the sea of bulls and pens, she could make out Tess's dark head at the far corner of the complex. Val sighed. By now, her sister would have finished taking care of the bulls. Tess might not say a lot, but she'd be angry and disgusted. Once again, scatterbrained Val had been too lazy to drag herself out of bed and show up for work.

But it was too late to change what had happened this morning. Right now it was time to face her sister and apologize. Too bad she wasn't ready to tell Tess the truth as well.

Val negotiated the pathways between the blocks of pens, stepping around bags of feed, piles of wood shavings, hoses, and wheelbarrows. This morning the bulls were awake and active, eating, lowing, rubbing against the rails, and dropping piles of manure that steamed in the morning chill.

As she walked toward the rear of the complex, Val struggled with what she would say to Tess. She couldn't talk about the nature of her dream or her encounter with Paul Brandt. All she could do was keep her excuse simple—she'd just failed to wake up in time. Nothing else would be needed except a plea for forgiveness.

She hated lying. It went against her nature. And she'd been telling far too many lies lately. It couldn't be helped. But it didn't make her like herself any better.

She was piecing together the right words when she happened to glance in Tess's direction. Her sister wasn't alone. Standing next to her, with a folded newspaper tucked under his arm, was Casey.

Val could only see part of the newspaper, but she could tell that it was the same edition she'd asked him to buy last night. How much had he told Tess? Probably everything he knew. Why else would he have brought the newspaper? And why else would Tess be standing ramrod stiff, arms crossed over her chest, as she waited.

Val braced herself for a storm as she came within speaking distance. Forget sleeping late. Forget the apology. This was real trouble. And it was her own fault for trusting Casey with her secrets.

"I can't believe you kept this from our family, Val." Tess's voice shook, whether from anger or fear, Val couldn't be sure. "Why didn't you tell *me*, at least?"

"I didn't want to get you involved," Val said. "It's my problem and no one else's. Not even Casey's." She turned toward him, eyes blazing fury. "How could you break your promise? I thought I could trust you!"

Casey stood firm, his expression resolute. "I meant to keep my promise, Val. But that was before I saw this newspaper headline and read the article. That was when I decided your safety was more important than my word. I meant to meet you here this morning and let you be the one to tell Tess your story. But when you didn't show up, I told her myself."

Val took a moment to regroup her thoughts. Tess and Casey didn't know everything. They didn't know about Lenny or how he'd died. And they didn't know about Brandt's threat to charge her if she refused to testify. For now she would keep those things to herself. She might be on a collision course with disaster, but she'd be damned if she was going to take anybody else down with her.

She faced the two of them, hands on hips. "Well, I have one thing to say to you both. Stop treating me like a child. This is my problem. It has nothing to do with either of you. I can deal with it myself."

"You're wrong, Val," Tess said. "I know you've been on your own for a long time. But you're back with your family now. We have each other's backs, no matter what."

Val shook her head. "You don't understand. You weren't around when I made the stupid mistakes that got me into this mess. And there's no way you can help me out of it now. These are bad people. My worst fear is that they might go after you or Lexie as a way of getting to me. That's why I canceled my flight home."

"We have to warn Lexie," Tess said. "Or at least we should let Shane know. Then he can decide whether to tell her. I don't want her upset—with the pregnancy, she's already so emotional."

"Do you want me to tell him?" Casey had stepped back from the conversation. He stood next to the rails, reaching over to scratch the special spot behind Whirlwind's ear. The silver bull's eyes were closed. On the far side of the pen, Whiplash raked the wood shavings with one horn and snorted at the white bull in the next enclosure.

"That's a good idea, your talking to Shane," Tess said. "If Val and I were to take him aside, Lexie would be suspicious. But with you, it would just be man talk."

"I'll catch him later this morning," Casey said. "Don't worry, I won't raise any alarms with Lexie."

"And, Val, you're not to go out alone, hear?" Tess added. "Tonight I'll be behind the chutes in case Whiplash is needed for a reride. You can come with me."

Val sighed. As usual, Tess had taken charge. But for now, that would have to be all right. And being close to the action would at least be more interesting, and safer, than sitting in the stands. The finals had three more nights to go. Then she and her family could load the bulls in the trailer and put Las Vegas in the rear-view mirror. If neither bull was needed for Saturday night, and if Shane wasn't needed for the TV commentary, they could go even earlier.

"I'm fine with that, Tess," she said. "Now, if there's anything left to do, you can put me to work."

"It's all done." Tess's frown spoke volumes. "There's nothing going on till eleven o'clock, when Shane will be showing up with a cameraman to do a spot on our bulls. Whirlwind's stirred some interest with that ninety-point ride. And the little bit of pub-licity will be good for the ranch—providing they actually use it on the air."

"That's great." Val resolved to stay out of camera range. The last thing she needed was for her face to show up on television.

"So it sounds like you've got some time before then," Casey said. "My truck's out back. What do you say I treat you ladies to brunch at the Bellagio?"

Val was about to make an excuse, but Tess jumped at the idea. "Thanks. I've been so busy I haven't had a decent meal since we rolled into town."

"Great. Follow me." He led the way past the loading chutes that opened onto the parking lot. With little choice except to go along,

Val tagged after her sister. As they approached the rear gate, she happened to glance back, over her shoulder.

The guard was still in place, watching them leave.

Casey kept an eye on Val as they filled their plates from the lavish buffet. She'd barely looked at him or spoken a word since they'd left the arena. He understood that she was angry, but that wasn't all he was seeing.

Except for the past few years, he'd known Val for most of their lives. In that time—and because he'd loved her—he'd learned to read every nuance of her emotions. Some things didn't change. What he was seeing now was more than anger. Val was scared—beyond scared. She was terrified.

There had to be more to her story than what she'd told him.

In order to keep her safe, he needed to understand the danger. But that wasn't going to be easy. He'd committed a breach of trust when he'd seen fit to warn Tess. Val had never been quick to forgive wrongs. But he had to try.

His chance came when they'd almost finished the meal and Tess left the table to visit the restroom. Val stared down at her plate. She'd picked at her food, eating only a few bites.

"Are you all right?" Casey asked her.

"What do you think?" She looked up at him, her jade eyes blazing. "Why can't you just leave things alone, Casey? None of this is any of your business."

"It's my business if it threatens people I care about," he said. "What am I supposed to tell Shane? And what am I supposed to do if somebody tries to hurt you or your sisters? What if some tragedy happens, and I could've stopped it if I'd known what to expect?"

"You know right where to twist the knife in, don't you? Guilt through the heart."

"I think we both know how." Casey crumpled his napkin and left it by the plate. "Right now, I don't give a damn why you left me, Val. I don't care what you've done or who you've been with in the years between. Since my parents died, you and your sisters are the closest thing to family I've got left. Watching Jack die in the arena was the worst thing I've ever been through. I don't want to see any more of your family get hurt."

"Not even if it's me—and it's all my own fault?" Val had lowered her voice.

"Whose fault it is doesn't matter to me. And it shouldn't matter to you." Casey could see Tess coming from the direction of the restroom. He leaned closer to Val. "We need to talk. I'll be busy until after the competition. Maybe then?"

"Ask me later." She rose as Tess came back to the table.

"Ready to go?" Tess didn't sit down again. "I should be getting back for the TV interview."

"Let's go then." Casey laid a tip on the table and fished for his keys. "Don't worry, I'll make sure Shane knows what's going on."

Val sat wedged between Tess and Casey in the front seat of the truck. Casey drove in silence, and Val made a show of checking her phone. The ride from the Bellagio back to the arena was a short one. But to Val, it seemed to take forever. She felt like a child who'd been caught misbehaving and was being hauled home by her parents to be sent to her room.

She'd wanted to keep her family clear of her troubles. But then Casey had gotten involved and brought Tess into the picture. Soon Shane would be made aware, too, as would Lexie if he chose to tell her.

But Casey had been right about one thing. She couldn't keep her family safe by herself. If they were in danger, they needed to know about it so they could protect each other.

But only she knew the whole story—the heartbreak, the failures, the addiction, and the gut-wrenching terror she couldn't seem to leave behind. How would they feel toward her if they were to learn the truth?

She'd assumed that Lenny's murder would be old news by now—that coming here with her family would be safe. How wrong she'd been. Heaven help her, what a godawful mess she'd made of things!

Touching her shirt pocket, she felt the card Paul Brandt had given her. She'd been tempted to throw it away. But that would've been foolish. Calling Brandt and agreeing to testify for the DA, which would hopefully put Lanzoni behind bars for life, would be the right thing to do.

But also the most dangerous.

Maybe she could get her family back to the ranch, then call Brandt from Ajo and agree to come back to Vegas for the grand jury hearing.

And then what? Witness protection? A new identity? No contact with her family? She'd rather go to prison.

Casey let the two women off at the rear gate to the bull pens. As he helped Val to the ground, his eyes met hers with a questioning look as if to ask, *Can we talk later?*

Val's silence left the question unanswered.

Tess was already hurrying toward the rear gate. Val followed her. They found Shane outside the pen, setting up with the camera crew. Lexie was with him, making sure he had what he needed.

Tess had described the interview over lunch—the main idea being that not all stock contractors were men. Lexie would tell how she'd been present at Whirlwind's birth and pretty much hand-raised the silver bull. Tess would talk about Whiplash, the differences between the two brother bulls, and her hopes for the future of the ranch.

As for Val, she wanted no part in it. Finding a nearby empty pen, out of camera range, she perched on the top rail to watch.

The interview would be edited down to five minutes. But this was Shane's first such project. He wanted it to be perfect. Val watched as he had the cameraman try different shots and angles. She had liked her brother-in-law from their first meeting. It was a pleasure to see him working at something he so clearly enjoyed— something he could do as capably as any man with two good legs.

On the edge of her vision, Val saw that Casey had returned. He stood near the loading chutes, keeping out of the way. Val waited, wondering if he meant to join her. Was that what she wanted?

But he'd probably just come by to talk with Shane, as he'd

promised to do. Disappointed in spite of herself, Val resolved to ignore him and watch the shoot.

Earlier today, the bulls had been moved to adjoining, smaller pens so Tess could work on Whirlwind, checking his limbs, grooming his coat, and massaging his muscles with an electronic stimulator. The new arrangement also made it possible for the camera crew to get in close without having to worry about Whiplash, who had an irascible streak and couldn't be trusted.

Tess was doing her part of the interview in Whirlwind's enclosure, standing next to the bull, scratching his ear to keep him calm while she talked. The cameraman had climbed the rails that separated the two pens and was shooting down at her. Val was watching her sister when another visitor showed up.

"So you're the prodigal Champion sister."

Startled by the deep voice at her side, Val had to grab the rail to keep her balance. Turning, she saw a tall man with rough-hewn features, dark hair, and dark eyes, standing an arm's length away from her. Everything from his expensive Stetson to his custom-designed boots reeked of money. Attractive . . . but not really her type, Val concluded. Too confident, probably more than a little controlling.

"Brock Tolman," he introduced himself with a nod. "You may have heard of me—nothing good if it came from your sisters."

"Oh, of course! Brock Tolman—the devil incarnate!"

His laugh was deep, warm, and real, which made Val like him somewhat better, although she still saw him as an enemy. "Since that's not likely to change, I'll take it as a compliment," he said.

"Tess says you'd do anything to get your hands on our bulls and our land. Is that right?"

Tolman didn't answer. His attention had pivoted toward the interview that was being shot. Val remembered Lexie saying that Shane had lived on the Tolman Ranch outside Tucson since his teens. He'd left there after a falling out. But Tolman had stepped in to help after Shane's accident, and the two still maintained a friendly but distant relationship.

It made sense that Brock Tolman might want to watch his former protégé at work. But as Val followed the line of his gaze, she realized it wasn't Shane the man was watching. His eyes were lingering on—

Lexie's scream cut off the thought. The cameraman, shooting down at Tess, had lost his balance and toppled backward six feet into the pen behind him—Whiplash's pen.

As the camera crashed outside the rails, the fallen man struggled to get up and climb to safety. But he'd landed hard. His left leg appeared to be injured, maybe broken. It collapsed beneath him as he tried to pull himself up on the rails.

Whiplash had been standing on the far side of the pen. Agitated by the stranger in his territory, he snorted and pawed the shavings. As the terrified man tried once more to pull himself up, the huge bull lowered his head and raked the ground with a horn.

"Don't move!" The shout came from Casey as he shot forward. Covering the distance in a flash, he vaulted over the rails, into the pen. Arms waving, he sprang between the bull and the injured man. "Somebody get him out!" he shouted.

Casey! No!

Helpless, Val could only watch as Casey pitted himself against the 1,900-pound bull. She'd seen Casey struck and tossed in the arena, but then he'd been wearing padded body armor. This time he was in street clothes, with nothing to protect him.

Whiplash had never met a man he didn't hate. His horns, though blunted at the tips, were long enough to gore an enemy through the middle, and he knew how to use them. Val had seen what was left of a coyote that had wandered into Whiplash's pasture at the ranch. Casey was facing death.

CHAPTER SEVEN

BROCK TOLMAN AND THE SOUND MAN SPRANG INTO ACTION.
Unlatching the gate, they opened it far enough for Tolman to slip
through into the pen. Casey moved like a shadow between the
bull and the injured man, waving his hat, swatting Whiplash on
the nose to distract him as Tolman worked his arms beneath the
cameraman, hoisted him to his feet, and supported him to safety.

The man holding the gate hesitated, waiting for Casey to follow. "Close it!" Casey yelled as the bull swung toward the opening.
"Close it now!" The gate clanged shut. The bull pivoted back toward Casey.

Alone in the pen with Whiplash, Casey gave the snorting bull a
hard slap with the hat. "Come on, big boy," he muttered. As the
bull charged, he flung down the hat and raced for the rails. By
the time Whiplash had finished stomping the hat into a shapeless
lump, Casey had scrambled over the side of the pen.

Within minutes, a crowd had gathered. Tess had left Whirlwind's pen to keep from being crushed by the silver bull, who was
body-slamming the rails. Brock Tolman was comforting the injured cameraman. Lexie was with Shane. Somebody had called
for an ambulance. The wail of a siren could already be heard in
the distance.

Val had begun to breathe again. She'd lost sight of Casey, but at
least she knew he was safe. Slipping down from her perch, she put
a hand to her face. It came away wet with tears.

Furiously, she wiped them away with her sleeve. Big girls didn't cry, and she was a big girl, wasn't she? She'd just seen an act of amazing bravery from the man she'd lost forever. But that was no reason for tears, was it?

Maybe not. But the tears still flowed, releasing emotions she'd buried for years. Loath to humiliate herself, she fled out the back gate to the parking lot. There, hidden between two empty stock trailers, she buried her face in her hands and broke down. Her shoulders shook with sobs as the relief, the fear, the regret, and the raw, aching love overflowed and spilled out of her.

"Val?" The voice was Casey's. He touched her shoulder.

"Leave me alone." She jerked away from him, turning her back to hide her tears.

"Look at me." Taking her shoulders, he turned her gently back toward him. His eyes took in her tear-stained face. "What's the matter?"

"Nothing. I was scared, that's all. Now go away."

"I'm not going anywhere until I find out what's happening with you."

She glared up at him. "Just go. I mean it, Casey. I hurt you once. But the first time was nothing compared to how I could hurt you now. I'm a mess. I'm nothing but—"

His mouth stopped her words. He kissed her long and hard and deep, melting her resistance and burning away the lost years between them. She could feel his beating heart as he held her close. Their kiss recalled old times when everything was new and there was nothing more important in the world than being crazy in love. But this time their coming together was more poignant, more bittersweet. They were two wounded souls, reaching out of pain to find each other.

But it wasn't enough. And it wasn't right. When his hand wandered to her breast, Val forced herself to push away from him. Her lips were moist and swollen from his kiss, and there was nothing she wanted more than to go back to the way things had been the moment before—and to go on from there. But she couldn't let it happen.

"We can't do this, Casey," she said.

"Why the hell not?" His husky tone bordered on a growl. "Right now it strikes me as a damned good idea."

When Val didn't answer, he dropped his arms and took a breath. "You win, Val. But I need to know why. I need answers, and it's time you gave them to me."

Val gave in. She couldn't tell him everything. But at least she could give him enough to make sense of the way she was behaving. "It might take time," she said.

"Fine. My truck's not far. How about going for a ride?"

"Now?"

"Now. I just need to call your sister."

Tess took the call next to the bull pens. By now both Whirlwind and Whiplash were calmer. But with the cameraman on his way to the hospital, the shoot was over.

"Hi." She recognized the name on the caller ID. "Are you all right, Casey?"

"Fine. I've got Val with me. I'll have her back in plenty of time for tonight. But I need a favor."

"Name it. After what you did here, I owe you."

"I was doing my job and you don't owe me a blasted thing. But I promised you I'd talk to Shane and warn him about the threat to Val. I was waiting for him when things went crazy, and now—"

"I understand. Now you're with Val, and that's important, too. Shane's off checking the rescued camera to see what's salvageable. But don't worry. I'll talk to him."

"Is everything else okay? How's the cameraman?"

"Bad break. He's on his way to the hospital. But at least, thanks to you, he didn't get stomped. The bulls are fine. So's everybody else. So take a break. Tell Val I'll see her later."

Tess ended the call with a sigh. If ever any two people were meant to be together, it was Casey and Val. But how could they find their way past the wreckage that Val had brought home with her?

Maybe they could at least become friends and move forward from there. It was the best she could hope for.

Tess checked the bulls one last time and went to look for Shane. She found him at a table in the press room, viewing the video footage from the interview. Seated next to him was Brock Tolman.

Tess was about to turn and leave when Shane saw her. "Hey, Tess, come look at this," he said. "We've got some good shots. I just hope I can get the interview edited in time for the nightly news."

Ignoring Tolman, Tess leaned over her brother-in-law's shoulder to see the viewing screen. "Not bad," she said. "You're lucky the camera didn't get smashed to pieces."

"It's too bad there's no footage of the real action," Tolman said, glancing up at Tess. "Your boyfriend was a hero, holding off that bull the way he did. You must be proud of him."

"My boyfriend?" Tess stared at him, startled. "Casey isn't my boyfriend."

"That's not the impression I got the last time I saw you with him. As I recall, you were in his arms."

A beat of silence passed before Tess remembered—she'd been weeping with joy over Whirlwind's performance, with Casey comforting her. Tolman had come from behind the chutes, then hurriedly left.

"Casey was my brother Jack's best friend," she said. "We've known each other since I was in pigtails. What you saw was a brotherly hug."

Tess didn't wait for his reaction. Why should it matter what Brock Tolman thought about her nonexistent love life? She should be asking herself what he was doing here with Shane. Had Tolman presented his offer for Shane and Lexie to live on his ranch? Was she about to lose part of her family?

"Where's Lexie?" she asked Shane, changing the subject.

"She's napping on the couch next door. I think the excitement wore her out."

"Then I need to have a word with you, Shane. In private." She gave Tolman a sharp look.

"I can take a hint," he said, rising. "I'll see you around, Shane. Let me know when your interview airs. I'd be interested in watching." He turned to Tess. "Two of my bulls will be bucking tonight. Wish me luck."

"I should be wishing the bulls luck," Tess said. "Oh, and thank you for rescuing the cameraman. You deserve some credit, too."

"Credit had nothing to do with it." Tolman paused in the doorway, one dark eyebrow raised. "Have a nice afternoon, Miss Champion."

"*Miss* Champion?" Shane shook his head as Tolman vanished down the hallway. "What was that about?"

"We're not exactly friends, you know," Tess said. "The man would do anything to get his greedy hands on our ranch. But I'm wise to him, and he knows it."

"So what was it you wanted to say?" Shane asked.

Tess told him everything she'd heard about Val. When she'd finished, he gave a low whistle.

"I had a feeling that something was up with Val," he said. "But this? Good Lord, Tess, it's like something out of *The Godfather*."

"Val's scared, Shane. And she's afraid her family might be threatened. That's why I'm telling you now. Whether you think Lexie can handle it is up to you. But either way, you'll need to protect her. Don't let her wander off alone."

"I brought a legal gun," Shane said. "For now, it's locked in the room safe. Maybe I ought to keep it on me."

"That's not a bad idea. But it's up to you. I know you'll do whatever it takes to protect Lexie and the baby."

"What about you?" he asked.

"I'll watch my back. I'll be fine. You don't have to stay, you know. None of us do. We could load the bulls and check out tonight if we had to."

"You know better than to suggest that, Tess. Having our bulls in the world finals is too important to us—to the family and the ranch—to walk away because of a threat. We'll just have to stay alert. That's all."

"We'll all do our best to protect Val," Tess said. "I only hope she'll let Casey help, too."

Casey had driven the short distance out of town to Lake Las Vegas, a peaceful expanse of water created by a dam and framed by parks, golf courses, and resorts. Pulling onto a rise with a view of water, palm trees, and distant mountains, he parked and turned toward Val. "If you're ready to tell me your story, I'm ready to listen," he said.

With a ragged sigh, Val unfastened her seat belt. "I wish I could ask for your promise not to judge me. But after what you're about to hear . . ."

"Just tell me, Val. I wouldn't ask if I didn't care about you."

After a long silence, she spoke again. "You know I never made it big as an actress."

"I know. I saw every one of your movies."

"I tried to make it happen. I tried for years, went to every audition." She paused. "I know what you're wondering. I promised myself I wouldn't sleep with men to get parts, and I didn't. Maybe it would've made a difference. I'll never know."

"I wouldn't blame you if you had. But it's not my place to judge." Casey checked the impulse to reach for her hand and hold it.

"I was waiting tables at a Howard Johnson when a good-looking man introduced himself. His name was Lenny Fortunato, and he told me he was a talent agent. If I signed on with him, he said he could get me into private parties and introduce me to people who could help my career. I was desperate enough to believe him. By the time I realized that Lenny was a small-time hood, and the parties we went to were for people connected to the mob, I was hooked on the lifestyle—the booze, the blow, and Lenny. I never made another movie."

Oh, Val . . . Casey ached to take her in his arms and just hold her. But he sensed that she wouldn't want that. And he needed to hear her story.

"I lost track of time. But at some point, Lenny had a chance to move to Las Vegas and work as an enforcer, collecting protection money for Carlo Lanzoni. For a while, the money was good. We lived high—the clothes and jewelry, the car, the fancy apartment— but Lenny's gambling debts got him into trouble. To pay, he started holding out on his boss. When Lanzoni found out, every- thing changed. The apartment, the car, the clothes and jewelry, we lost it all. We had to go into hiding."

"Why didn't you just leave him?"

"There were times when I almost did. But in my own mixed-up way, I thought I could save Lenny. I thought he needed me. The reality was, I was being used. But I was in too deep to understand that.

"We were living in this one-room dump, in the worst part of town. Late one night, Lenny sent me out to score some cocaine. While I was gone, Dimitri, Lanzoni's hit man, showed up. I got back in time to listen through the door. I heard Dimitri say that Lanzoni had ordered the hit. I heard Lenny begging for his life and then the shot. Dimitri would've killed me, too. He'd seen my clothes and knew I was living there. But I'd found a place to hide. When he finally left and I saw that Lenny was dead, I ran. I ran all the way back to LA."

Val was shaking by the time she paused in her story. Casey reached out to comfort her, but she pushed his hand away. "So now you know the worst of it. Do I make you angry, Casey? Do I make you sick? Do you want to throw me out of the car like a piece of trash and drive away?"

His gaze took her in—the proud defiance in the way she hid her awful wounds. He felt no disgust, no anger, no pity. Only com- passion. But he resisted the urge to take her in his arms. She was too raw for that.

"I can imagine the strength it must've taken to save yourself," he said. "So tell me the rest. What did you do?"

"I managed to get a waitress job in a cheap dive. I was barely surviving, and I was still an addict, but I hadn't given up on my dream. I made up my mind that I was going to get into rehab, go back to Hollywood, and take some honest-to-goodness acting lessons before I tried again.

"I finally got into a charity program and spent the time it took to get clean. But when I told my counselor my plan, she said, 'Val, return to that life and you'll fall right back into the pit. If you want to heal, go home. Go back to your ranch and your family.' I took her advice and went home. I thought I was going to be all right. And for a few months I was. Then I came back here."

She stared down at her hands for a moment, then looked back at Casey. Her beautiful green eyes were laced with red from her tears. "I'm scared, Casey. Not just for me, but for my family. I never would've come here if I'd known that Lanzoni had been arrested and I was the only witness who could tie him to a murder—"

"Wait," Casey said. "How do you know you're the only witness? Think how many hits Lanzoni must've ordered over the years. There've got to be others."

She shook her head. "Dimitri always covered his tracks. No witnesses. I got lucky."

"Again, how do you know that?"

"A man from the DA's office got in touch with me about testifying to the grand jury. Paul Brandt was his name—he showed me his ID. He was the one who told me. He said that—" Her voice broke. She shook her head.

"What is it?" Casey laid a hand on her arm. "What aren't you telling me?"

"When I told him I was scared to testify, he said they could make me. If I didn't cooperate, they could accuse me of setting Lenny up and charge me as an accessory."

"Damn it, Val, you always did find ways of getting yourself into hot water." Acting on impulse, he gathered her close. This time she didn't resist. Trembling, she burrowed against his chest like a frightened child. Casey buried his lips in her hair, breathing its familiar fragrance and feeling its silky texture. She fit naturally in his arms, just as she had so many years ago. But this was a different Val he was holding—so strong and yet so vulnerable. He would do anything to keep her safe. That included finding Paul Brandt, whoever the hell he was, and letting him know that Val had friends who'd stand up against his bullying.

"I've got your back, girl," he murmured. "All the people who care about you have got your back. We won't let anything happen to you."

"No!" She stirred and pushed away from him. "Don't you see? My worst fear is that Lanzoni's people will go after Tess or Lexie and Shane, or even you. I have to handle this on my own."

With a sigh, he settled back in the seat. "What if you *can't* handle it on your own? They could kill you, Val. In fact, I can't help wondering why they haven't tried."

"I've wondered the same thing. There's no date for the grand jury yet. Maybe they're playing me, waiting to see what I'll do. Dimitri usually does the dirty work. Brandt told me he was out of town, but when he gets back, things could get ugly."

She shuddered. "He's the coldest person I've ever known, Casey, like someone out of a gangster movie. Killing is a business to him. Some people fix cars or sell real estate. Dimitri kills whomever he's paid to kill. Flat rate for a gunshot. Extra for custom work."

"We should get you someplace safe. Given what you've told me, he could have an old score to settle."

"I know. I'd be like an unfinished job to him. He'd track me down just for that. But I can't go off and leave my family here. I'm not even sure I'd be safe on the ranch. Its location is public record." She yanked her seat belt into place and clicked the buckle. "We need to be getting back. Tess should be at the hotel. You can take me there."

"You'll call ahead to make sure, won't you? Did she happen to bring a gun?"

"Of course I'll call her. And yes, she has a gun, and she knows how to use it, which is a good thing, since I hate guns myself. Stop mothering me, Casey. I'm a big girl, and this isn't your fight."

"That's where you're wrong." Casey started the truck, backed up, and swung onto the road. "I'm here for you, Val. And I won't be going anywhere until I know you're out of danger."

"I can't ask you to do that," she said. "What I told you earlier still stands. We can't be together. There are too many things that I can't change."

They drove back to town, Casey keeping his eyes on the road, Val playing with her phone. Maybe he ought to listen to her warning and move on. But he knew better than to lie to himself. Val might be a walking minefield of painful secrets. But he was hooked on her—probably for life. He'd never gotten over her leaving him. Even after he'd wed Candy, after a hot couple of weeks, Val's memory had come between them. It had probably played a part in driving his wife to the affair that had ended their marriage.

Candy had since married a wealthy Phoenix restaurant owner. She probably had a couple of kids by now. She and Casey hadn't kept in touch. There was no reason to.

And now Val was back in his life—broken, troubled, and still heartbreakingly beautiful. If he let her, she was capable of wrecking his life all over again. But as long as she needed him, there could be no walking away. Whether he liked it or not, Val was in his blood, and in his heart.

The T-Mobile Arena was full to the rafters for the third night of the PBR World Finals. By now the original field of thirty-five riders had been whittled by more than half. Only the best and luckiest remained. The stakes were higher, the competition keener than ever.

From behind the chutes with Tess, Val watched the opening ceremony. It was always much the same but never ceased to be moving—the flags, streaming behind riders on galloping horses; the pledge; then the national anthem, sung tonight by a young Navajo girl, followed by a prayer. Life had made Val a cynic. But she felt the sincerity of belief in God and country here, and she respected it.

Cheers rocked the arena as the giant PBR letters blazed, and the competing riders walked forward to stand before the crowd. R.J. McClintock, who'd scored on Whirlwind, was among them, as were cowboys from Texas, Montana, Oklahoma, and Utah, and several high-ranking Brazilian riders.

Behind the chutes, Whiplash waited in his pen. If something were to go wrong with a ride—for example, if the bull were to stumble and fall, strike the chute coming out, or fail to perform, the rider would be offered a reride later in the program. Only then would Whiplash get his chance to buck.

If that were to happen, it could be a great moment for the Alamo Canyon Ranch. Val could feel Tess's excitement as they waited for the first ride. If only she could relax and enjoy the event with her sister. But her mind was on other things—all of them troubling—as she waited for her first sight of Casey in the arena, where anything could happen. Her heart would be in her throat until the event was over.

Dressed in his gear, Casey waited for the first bucking chute to open. Earlier, he'd glimpsed Val with Tess, headed back to the holding area. She'd be safe there, which was fortunate because Casey couldn't protect her, or even consciously worry about her, while he was doing his job.

In front of the stands, Sam Callahan, the official clown of the PBR, was just finishing his act. A beloved fixture of all the big events, Sam was a skilled bullfighter, as well as a gifted entertainer. He wore clown makeup with his regular gear but could be counted on to help in an emergency.

As Sam doffed his hat and took refuge atop the shark cage, the PA system blared the name of the first rider. The face of a young Brazilian named Alonzo Santos, currently in fourth place, flashed onto the screen. He would be riding a bull named Blackjack.

Casey was familiar with Blackjack. The bull had never been a problem, but there was always a first time. He moved into position as Santos shifted forward and gave a nod.

The gate swung open. Kicking and leaping, Blackjack flew out backward. His hindquarters slammed the gate. Stunned, the black bull kept bucking, but not with his usual energy. Santos lasted eight seconds and made a safe dismount, but the score would be low.

The red flag thrown out by the judges signaled a reride option. As expected, Santos accepted the offer.

As the exit gate closed behind Blackjack, Casey couldn't hold back a grin. Spotting Tess and Val behind the chutes, he gave them a thumbs-up. Whiplash would get his chance.

The reride would take place later in the program, which gave Tess time to prepare her bull. After the morning's drama in his pen, the big brindle was still testy. Tess had put him back into the larger pen with his brother before the move to the reride pen. Being with Whirlwind tended to calm him. But this time it wasn't helping. Whiplash snorted and pawed the shavings as she came with Val and one of the men to move him to the narrow chute, where he'd be fitted with a flank strap.

Bulls were herded safely through the complex of pens and chutes by means of gates that could be opened and closed to form pathways. If a bull balked, a touch from a low-voltage prod called a Hot Shot—more annoying than painful—would be enough to get him moving.

Most experienced bulls knew where to go and needed no urging. But Whiplash was in no mood to cooperate. It took three mild jolts from the Hot Shot to get him in place for the flank strap. By then he was plain mad.

"This is going to be a disaster!" Tess raked her hair back from her perspiring face after finally placing the strap with the help of a chute man. Memories of unruly bulls trying to climb out of the bucking chute flashed through her mind. If Whiplash proved to be unmanageable, his career in the PBR would be over before it began.

Val had come to stand beside her. "Poor guy, he's having a rough time of it," she said. "I can imagine how he feels. But he deserves his chance at the big time."

"Should I tell the boss to call up another bull?" the chute man asked.

Tess studied Whiplash through the rails, so powerful and yet so young, maybe even a little scared. She laid a hand on his massive shoulder and felt a quiver pass through his body.

"No," she said. "I'd never forgive myself if I didn't let him do this. Tell your boss he's ready."

During the break before the second half of competition, Casey saw Whiplash being herded into chute number three. Even at a distance he could tell the big brindle was wired. He was banging against the rails and tossing his head, his blunted horns clattering against the gate. An unruly bull could make for an exciting ride. But something told Casey that Alonzo Santos was going to have his hands full, and so was the protection team.

Glancing above the chutes, he saw Val and Tess on the walkway, in plain sight of the crowd. Lexie was with Shane at the press table. It crossed Casey's mind to worry about having Val so exposed, but he dismissed the thought. She and Tess would want a clear view of their bull when he bucked. And surely she'd be safe enough there, where no unauthorized person could get near her.

After Sam's brief entertainment, the action picked up again. Bucking out of the first chute was a young Cherokee, Tom Blackhorse. He lasted eight seconds on his bull, with a score of 87.5 to move up in the rankings. The second ride was a quick buck-off with no score for the rider. Then it was Whiplash's turn.

The brindle bull was banging against the inside of the chute. Santos lowered himself partway, then backed off to save his legs. A chute man shoved a tall, wooden wedge down one side of the rails, pinning Whiplash's body in place while Santos settled onto his back. Whiplash snorted and tossed his head, trying to buck while the rider tightened his rope. After several tension-fraught seconds, Santos gave the nod and the gate swung open.

Whiplash came barreling out of the chute like a runaway locomotive. Casey closed in with his teammates, studying every move. The 1,900-pound brindle had a low forward leap, flowing into a wrecking ball of a back kick with a twist at the top that was powerful enough to throw any rider. From close up, Casey could see the fire in his eye. This bull wasn't just bucking. He was enraged—

and that made him all the more dangerous.

Santos had hung on, but he was losing control. At seven seconds, propelled by a giant kick, he flew forward like a marble out of a slingshot, tumbling over the bull's head before he crunched into the dirt.

As his teammates rushed to aid the injured Santos, and Sam Callahan sprinted across the arena to help, Casey sprang forward to divert the bull.

"Remember me, big boy?" he muttered, swatting Whiplash's nose with his hat. "C'mon, let's play!"

Whiplash charged. Dodging, Casey felt a horn strike his body armor. He stumbled to one side, catching himself with a hand in the dirt as the bull swung back toward him with murder in his eyes.

CHAPTER EIGHT

*C*ASEY RARELY HAD TIME TO BE AFRAID IN THE ARENA. BUT HE COULD feel the cold sweat as Whiplash came at him again. He managed to jump aside, but the blow from the horn had thrown his timing off. His knees felt like jelly. As the bull swung back toward him, he knew he was in trouble.

Only the roper's lasso, flying around Whiplash's neck, saved Casey from a pounding. Light-headed, he hunched over his knees as the well-trained horse herded the bull out through the gate.

Santos was on his feet, being supported out by the medical team. His helmet had protected his head, but he was limping and clasping his shoulder. Too bad. The young Brazilian would likely be out of the competition. But his injuries could've been far worse.

Still catching his breath, Casey glanced up at the scoreboard— zero points for the rider; forty-five points for the bull. A great score for Whiplash.

"Are you okay?" Casey felt a hand on his shoulder. Sam had come out from the sidelines to check on him.

"Just a little shook up, Sam." Casey straightened and gave a wave to show the crowd he was unhurt. "I'll be fine."

They stood a moment longer, waiting for the arena to clear. "That's one rank bull," Sam said. "Reminds me of Bodacious. Did you ever see him in the arena? This one bucks like him and throws 'em over his head the same way."

"I don't know if that's good or bad," Casey said, recalling the huge yellow bull, one of the greatest buckers ever, who was retired early for injuring so many riders. Whiplash could have a great career or, if tonight's behavior continued, he might prove too dangerous for the arena.

Sam glanced toward the chutes. "Looks like they're ready to go again. You be careful, hear?"

As Sam trotted back to his perch on the shark cage, Casey looked up at the platform above the chutes. Tess had gone back to take care of her bull, but Val was still there, watching him with an anxious expression. He gave her a thumbs-up to let her know he was all right. By then the next rider was mounting his bull.

Val could feel the hammering of her heart. She waited a moment for her pulse to slow before moving toward the metal steps at the end of the platform. Twice today she'd watched Casey risk his life against Whiplash, as well as the other bulls in the arena. Every time the horns and hooves came too close, she'd died a little inside.

Did the wrenching terror she felt every time Casey faced danger mean that she still loved him?

But she had no right to ask that question. She'd lost Casey the night she'd loaded her old Pontiac and set off for California. For her, there could be no turning back.

As she reached the end of the platform and started down the steps, she happened to glance up. A face caught her eye—one face amid hundreds in the high-priced seat section above the chutes.

Her throat jerked, shutting off her breath as she recognized the ivory skin, the coal-black hair, the chiseled features and—perhaps filled in by memory—the blue eyes, as glassy and expressionless as the eyes of an old-fashioned china doll.

She was looking at Dimitri.

After Casey changed out of his gear, he found Val with Tess next to the bulls. Whiplash had been moved into the shared pen with his brother, but he had yet to calm down. He was snorting, pawing, and bellowing challenges to his neighbors.

Val greeted Casey with a smile as fragile as a snowflake. Her colorless face told him at once that something was wrong, finding out more might be best done in private.

Tess was busy with the bulls, refilling their feeders and fussing over them as if they were the children she'd never had. "Wasn't Whiplash amazing? Maybe by next season, he'll have a buck-off streak going. A bull who's never been ridden can attract a lot of attention."

"I saw what he did to you, Casey." The stress in Val's voice betrayed her state of mind. "Are you all right?"

"I'm fine. He got me pretty good. I'll have a bruise where the horn hit. But that's what the body armor's for. Will you walk with me, Val?"

She nodded. Still, she seemed closed off. He could only hope she'd open up when they were alone.

"You won't mind if I take her away for a few minutes, will you, Tess?" he asked out of politeness.

"Not a bit. But Lexie and Shane want to go out to a late dinner somewhere. They'll be showing up here in about fifteen minutes. You're welcome to come along, Casey."

He glanced down at Val. She gave a slight shake of her head. His cue. "Thanks," he said, "but it's been a long, rough night. I'll pass."

"Count me out, too," Val said. "I'm dead on my feet, and I don't have much appetite."

"You're sure?"

"Yes." Val managed a faint smile. "Have a good time. Casey can drop me off at the hotel. Don't worry, if you're not there, I'll make sure the door's locked. And if the house phone rings, I won't answer it."

They walked out into the parking lot, where he'd left his truck. Casey guided her with his hand on the small of her back. He could feel the tension in her rigid spine and in her silence. All he wanted was to take her in his arms, kiss her, and tell her everything was going to be all right. But he couldn't promise that. And he knew better than to lie.

"Thanks for getting me off the hook," he said. "I really wasn't up to a late dinner."

"Neither was I."

"But that doesn't mean you have to rush back to the hotel, does it?"

She didn't answer. At the far end of the lot, Casey could see the bulky outline of his truck backlit by a neon sky, reflecting the gaudy lights of the Strip. The night was chilly, her jacket too thin for the cold. She was shivering.

Slipping off his leather jacket, he laid it around her shoulders. She settled into the warmth with a murmur of gratitude.

"What's wrong, Val?" he asked. "You know you can tell me."

She walked a few steps in silence, then took a ragged breath. "It's Dimitri. I saw him tonight, in the stands above the chutes."

Casey's pulse slammed. "You're sure?"

"I'm sure. He wasn't close, but I know it was him. And I'm sure he saw me. He couldn't have missed me, standing there on the platform." Her voice broke. "I'm scared, Casey. Not just for me, but for my family, even for you."

They had reached his truck. Sheltered by the open passenger door, he wrapped her in his arms, cradling her fiercely, as if challenging the whole world to try to do her harm. Holding her and feeling her breathe, Casey felt a strange sense that fate had come around as it was meant to. Crazy, passionate Val was back, turning his life to a chaotic mess.

Damn it, but he'd missed her!

"You'll freeze." She pulled away, slipped out of his coat, and handed it back to him. He helped her into the truck before putting it back on. The lining still held traces of her warmth and her subtle fragrance.

"Does Tess know about Dimitri?" he asked as he started the truck and backed it out of the parking spot.

"I meant to tell her, but I was waiting for the right time. Now that I know he's in town, and that he's seen me, I need to tell her—and tell Shane, too."

He swung the truck into the heavy traffic on the Strip. "You can't fight a professional hit man on your own, Val. Maybe you need to go to the police."

"I can't. I know for a fact that Lanzoni has eyes and ears on the police force. That would put all of you in danger." She huddled close to the heat coming out of the vent in the dashboard. "But I've got the number of Paul Brandt, the assistant DA. He could have Dimitri picked up without involving me."

"Can you trust him?"

"As much as I can trust anybody. Brandt contacted me in the arena, dressed as a cowboy. When I pressed him, he implied that if the DA could get their hands on Dimitri, they might not need me to testify."

"But then Brandt threatened to charge you."

"I'm hoping he was only trying to scare me." She glanced out the side window of the truck. "This isn't the way back to the hotel, Casey. Where are you taking us?"

"Someplace where you'll be safe," he said. "We can call Tess after we get there."

Val watched the lights streak past the window as Casey made a right turn off the Strip and wound through the side streets, past casinos, chain restaurants, strip clubs, and bars. Every few minutes he checked the rearview mirror, as if making sure they weren't being followed.

At last he turned off the street at a small neon sign and continued down a narrow driveway overgrown with shrubbery. "Here we are." He parked in front of a small two-story hotel in the middle of a block. "Las Vegas's best kept secret. This is where I always stay when the PBR is in town."

"You've brought me to your hotel room?" Val realized immediately that she'd asked a needless question.

"That's the idea." Casey came around to help her out of the

truck. "But don't worry. My intentions are strictly honorable. And there are two beds in the room. You'll be safe."

As safe as you want to be.

He didn't add the words, but Val understood as clearly as if he'd spoken them. Spending the night here with Casey was a risky proposition in more ways than one. But she was too tired and too scared to argue.

The lobby had an old-fashioned coziness about it—the over-stuffed furniture and oriental rugs, the weathered brick fireplace with its glowing coals and a plump tabby cat curled on the hearth, paperbacks on a corner bookshelf, and even free coffee and pastries on a table next to the stairs. Val could understand why Casey was partial to the place. It was a tiny island of calm amid the endless assault of bright lights, deafening noise, and hordes of people that typified Las Vegas.

Casey spoke a few words to the elderly woman behind the desk, probably arranging to pay for the extra guest. Whatever he said caused the woman to smile and give Val a friendly nod.

"How did you ever find this place?" Val asked him as they climbed the stairs to the second floor.

"My secret."

"Since it's a secret, I'm guessing it involved a woman."

"No comment. We're not kids anymore, Val. By now, we've both been around the block a time or two."

He unlocked a door and turned on the light. The room was small but charming, with two quilt-covered double beds, a miniature desk, and French doors opening onto a miniature balcony that overlooked the courtyard in back. Val was taking it all in when a disconcerting thought struck her.

"What is it?" Casey studied her expression. "Not classy enough for you?"

"Stop that. It's lovely. But I don't even have a toothbrush. And I don't have anything to wear to bed. It's chilly, and I don't fancy tripping around in my birthday suit."

Val kept the truth to herself. Whatever she had to do, whatever lies she had to tell, she couldn't let Casey see what had happened to her body.

He gave her a teasing look. "You mean you've forgotten the fun we had, skinny-dipping by moonlight in that canyon pool? You weren't so modest back then."

"I remember how cold the water was."

"I remember how beautiful you were—and how I had to warm you."

Val remembered, too—lying in his arms on the blanket, loving him with every part of her—loving him as she'd never wanted to love anyone else again. But she couldn't think about that now. The sweet, innocent passion they'd shared was lost forever.

"Don't, Casey," she said. "I'm not seventeen anymore. I'd feel a lot more comfortable with something on, even if it's just an old T-shirt. Otherwise, I'll sleep in my clothes."

"Relax." He rummaged in his duffel bag, which lay on a luggage rack at the foot of his bed, and came up with a faded, light blue T-shirt. "Here you go." He tossed it to her. "I brought it to sleep in, but it's all yours. It should be long enough to cover what you want covered."

Val held the shirt up to check its length. "Yes, it'll do. Thanks."

"There's a new spare toothbrush in my shaving kit. You'll see it on the bathroom sink. If you want to go in first, I'll call Tess while I'm waiting."

"Thanks. And maybe you can do something about the heat. It's freezing in here."

"I'll try. But the antiquated heating and plumbing in this place are the price you pay for its charm. Good luck with the hot water."

In the bathroom, with its exposed pipes and claw-footed tub, Val brushed her teeth, washed her face, and stripped down to change into the tee Casey had lent her. As she shook it out, his clean, manly scent rose from the fabric, stirring memories of sun-warmed afternoons, riding in the canyon, stopping in the shade of a sandstone cliff, the subtle aroma filling her senses as he held her close. . . .

As she raised her arms to pull the shirt over her head, she glimpsed her body in the cabinet mirror. Even after all this time, the pale scar, crossing her belly below the navel, was clearly visible, as were the faint, slightly puckered streaks below it. Each one of those marks was a scar on her soul. Not even her sisters knew about them. And the last person she would choose to set eyes on them was Casey.

He had brought her here to protect her. But tonight, alone with him, she'd be facing a new and different kind of danger. It would be up to her to protect herself—and him—from a secret that could shatter them both.

She thrust her arms into the sleeves of the shirt and pulled it down past her hips. It covered her to midthigh. As an afterthought, she reached for her panties and slipped them back on, pulling them as high as the waist band would reach. That would have to do.

He grinned as she came out of the bathroom, carrying her folded clothes. "That old shirt looks better on you than it ever did on me," he said.

Val ignored the teasing compliment. "Did you talk to Tess?" she asked him.

"I did. She was at dinner. I told her you spotted an old enemy in the crowd, and I brought you here to keep you safe. She said she'd be careful, and that she'd let Shane know. I think they've decided to tell Lexie."

"That should be fine. Lexie's tougher than she looks. She's already been through a lot with Shane." Val laid her clothes on the desk. As Casey disappeared into the bathroom, she turned back the covers on her bed and eased between the sheets. She gasped. The bed was icy cold.

Teeth chattering, she curled into a ball beneath the covers. The cold wouldn't last long, she told herself. The heat from her body would soon warm the bed.

Minutes later, Casey emerged from the bathroom. The long-legged thermals he'd put on hung loosely from his narrow hips. His upper body, bare to the navel with a V of dark hair tapering downward from his chest, was solid, sculpted muscle, the skin nicked by scars.

Still chilly, Val was sitting up in bed with the covers pulled to her chin. She fought the urge to devour him with her eyes. Casey would know, and he'd likely see it as an invitation. Was that what she wanted? If the answer was yes, then she was an even bigger fool than she'd feared. She'd have been smarter to go back to the hotel with Tess.

When he turned aside to lay his clothes on his suitcase, Val could see the ugly bruise where Whiplash's horn had clipped him. It was as big as the palm of her hand, its color deepening from red to purple.

"That looks bad." She spoke through chattering teeth. "It must hurt a lot."

"I've had worse. In my line of work, you get used to being knocked around. It's part of the entertainment." He turned back to look at her. "Sounds like you're still cold."

"This bed's freezing. Didn't you have any luck with the heater?"

"I tried. But I think it needs fixing, and nobody's gotten around to it. Vegas doesn't usually get this cold in November. There's an extra blanket on the top shelf of the wardrobe. It's yours. I'll get it."

"No, you take it. This is your room, and I've already taken your shirt."

"You always were a muleheaded little thing. Fine. At least I can say I offered."

She'd expected him to argue and insist on her taking the blanket, but to Val's surprise, he took it out of the wardrobe and spread it on his own bed. With a mischievous glance, he switched off the lights except for one side lamp. Then, turning down the covers, he stretched out on his side, facing her.

"Now, Miss Val Champion, I have a proposal for you. You can stay where you are and freeze your lovely butt off, or"—he patted the empty space next to him—"you can come over here with me. Understand that all I'm offering you is a warm night's sleep. I promise to be a perfect gentleman. And you'll be free to go back to your own chilly bed any time you want. If you insist, I'll even get up and drive you back to your hotel."

"You never change, Casey Bozeman! You're incorrigible!"

He laughed. "Come on. We need to talk. We might as well be warm while we're doing it."

He was the picture of sly innocence. Could she trust him? More to the point, could she trust herself?

She was looking at a very sexy trap, and Casey was the bait. But this wasn't just about sex. Being with him this week had stirred emotions she'd been forced to bury years ago. Bringing them back would be like ripping scars off old wounds—not just for her but for him.

But one truth remained. Of the men she'd known, Casey was the only one who really knew her. He was her childhood friend, her surrogate brother, and her first love.

She'd be taking a fearful chance. But she needed to be in his arms, if only for tonight.

She gave him a smile that he would recognize as forced. "If I decide to go back to my bed, can I take the blanket with me?" she teased, stalling for time to gather her courage.

"Nope. Your choice. We can snuggle and talk and keep each other warm, or we can stay like this." His voice deepened. "Damn it, Val, no more games. Just get over here! I won't bite you, and this room isn't going to get any warmer."

Surrendering at last, Val extinguished the lamp on the bedside table, then swung her bare feet to the cold floor.

Casey raised the covers and pulled them over her as she eased in beside him. The bed was still chilly, but his body was a block of heat. She snuggled against his side, her head pillowed in the curve of his arm. The warmth, the clean aroma of his skin, the sound of his breathing—some things never changed. It was like coming home.

"You said we should talk," she murmured.

"In a bit. Let's get you warm first." He shifted her in the bed, spooning behind her, his lap cradling her hips, his arm resting on her waist.

Oh, Casey . . . Val hid a freshet of tears. She'd known that she would want him if they were to get this close. She just hadn't realized how much. Knowing that they could never go back to the boy and girl they'd been only sharpened the pain.

"Warm yet?" His lips nuzzled the back of her neck.

"Getting there," she whispered, knowing that unless she left now, this could only end one way. It wasn't too late to change her mind. But she needed him. She needed to touch him in all the places she remembered; to feel him filling the lonely hollow inside her. Just for now, she needed to forget everything but this time and place and this man with his arms around her.

Where her hips nested against him, she could feel his arousal jutting beneath the soft fabric of his thermals. She lay still for a moment. Then, heart pounding, she took his hand where it lay across her waist and moved it up beneath the shirt, to cradle her breast.

"Damn it, Val, what took you so long?" His breath quickened and deepened. Shifting above her, he pushed up her shirt to uncover both breasts. In the darkness, Val could barely see his shadowed face as he bent to nip, suckle, and lick them. Every stroke of his tongue drove her to a frenzy of need. She arched upward, fingers raking his hair, clasping his shoulders, holding him to her.

Pausing, he made a move to pull the T-shirt off over her head. Protective of what he mustn't see, she stopped him. "No—leave it. It's cold."

To her relief, he let the shirt go. His hand ranged downward. Her heart stopped for an instant as his fingers found the waistband of her panties. The scars—

But no, it was all right. He moved lower to run a finger beneath the leg band and stroke her moisture-slicked folds, kissing her mouth as his finger did its magic. She gasped as a miniature earthquake shook her. He chuckled. "I'll be damned, it still works. Just like it used to at those drive-in movies."

"Casey—" She was still quivering inside. All she could think of was wanting more.

"I think we need to shed some clothes," he muttered. Hooking the panties with his thumbs, he jerked them downward, off her hips. Leaving her to finish, he swung out of bed. She heard the soft sound of his thermals dropping to the floor and a faint rustling as he took a moment to protect her.

When he slipped back into bed beside her, she welcomed him with her arms and a deep kiss. Her tongue played with his, thrusting and teasing until she felt his breath quicken. Strange how well she knew him, even after so many years. "Now," she whispered, reaching down to guide him. "Yes . . ."

As he glided into her wet, pulsing center, she forgot about the scars, the past, and the threats that lurked outside this safe little room. Nothing mattered but now, with Casey inside her, Casey loving her, lifting her, bringing her home at last.

Casey . . .

Afterward they lay side by side. Val had pulled the shirt back down and was drifting on a sea of contentment when Casey spoke. "Now we talk."

"Why now?" Val muttered, rousing.

"Because we might not have a better chance. And because the next time you walk away from me without a word, Val, I want to know why."

The warm, blissful mood had cooled. "Haven't I already told you enough? I'm not the innocent girl you knew in your teens. I've been an alcoholic. I've been on drugs. I've lived with a mobster and witnessed his murder. Do I need to go on?"

"Val, I don't give a damn where you've been or what you've done. I've wanted you from the second you walked into that arena. I still want you. But not just for a one-night stand."

"Don't make me do this," she said. "If I could go back and change things, I'd do it in a heartbeat. But I can't, not even for you. The girl you loved is gone, Casey—so far gone that she might as well have died. That's all you need to know."

"Yet here you are."

"Yes, a stranger. A one-night stand, as you put it. Maybe this was a bad idea."

"I'm not sorry. Are you?"

"I'll chalk it up to a very good time." Val knew her reply would sting, but maybe that was what he needed. "Now, can we go to sleep?"

"Fine." He exhaled. "Just one more question. The first time you left, without even telling me, I never knew why. I've wondered all these years. I'd like to know now."

She should have known this was coming. But at least she had her answer ready, half-truth that it was. "My reasons were totally selfish," she said. "I wanted my dream. I knew that if I stayed in Arizona, I'd never have a chance to make it come true. And I knew that if I told you my plan, you'd talk me out of going. That's it."

"It strikes me that your dream turned out to be more of a nightmare."

"True. But it was my choice. And if I hadn't gone, I'd still be longing for what I might've missed. Somewhere I have an old Neil Diamond album with a song about a girl who took a chance and paid her dime and went to Hollywood. That was me."

"I know that song. The girl died."

"So did the girl who loved you, Casey."

He lay still, taking his time before he spoke again. "Be careful out there, Val. Don't let those bastards get close to you. I'll protect you when I can, but I can't be with you all the time."

"I understand," Val said, but she sensed that understanding wasn't enough—maybe for him, but not for her.

Suddenly, like a light coming on, she knew what she needed to say. "But I'm through being protected. I'm through burdening people I care about with my problems. I got myself into this mess. Whatever it takes, I'm going to get myself out of it, starting first thing tomorrow."

"Do you have a plan in mind?" He didn't sound convinced.

"It's still coming together. But my best option might be to call Brandt. If he can have Dimitri picked up and held, maybe we can strike a deal."

"That could be dangerous, Val."

"Maybe so. But I need to take responsibility for this mess. It's time I grew up and stopped depending on other people, like you and Tess, to hold my hand and keep me safe."

Casey failed to suppress a groan. "Do me one favor. Sleep on those words tonight and see how they sound to you in the morning. In the cold light of day, you might want to change your mind."

She shook her head. "My mind is made up. I'm done with being everybody's problem child—Val the black sheep; poor Val, who's screwed up her life so badly that she'll never be right again. I've done reckless things, but I'm not a fool, Casey. I'm going to prove it."

Casey pushed himself onto an elbow to brush a kiss on her forehead. He hadn't paid any attention to the pain in his bruised side while they were making love, but now it was hurting. It would be worse in the morning. Maybe he should take something to ease the pain.

"Okay," he conceded. "I'll do my best to get used to the new and improved Val. Just remember that there are people who care about you—including me. And don't be too proud to ask for help. Now, what do you say we get some sleep?"

"Good plan. I'm already ahead of you." She turned away from him, her back curving against his side. Casey closed his eyes and listened, waiting for the even cadence of her breathing to tell him she was asleep. The change never came. He imagined her lying there in the dark, wide awake, her agile mind spinning dangerous new schemes—schemes that could get her killed.

Val was the only woman he'd ever truly loved. He had little doubt that he would love her forever. But he couldn't trust her to make wise decisions, or even to tell him the unvarnished truth.

Her acting skills may not have made her a movie star, but she wasn't above using them on him. Back in the day, they'd worked. But now he was older and wiser. When she'd told him about her past, he'd looked into those beguiling green eyes and sensed that she was holding back even more secrets—maybe dangerous secrets.

She reminded him of a hummingbird—her beauty flashing as she darted one way, then another. Now, suddenly, she seemed determined to face down the Las Vegas mob. Heedless of the deadly risk, she was out to prove that she could take on career criminals and hired killers. He could only hope that she'd come to her senses before somebody got hurt.

As she sighed and nestled closer to him, Casey felt a surge of love that almost tore him apart. If he had any sense, he'd walk away now. But that wasn't going to happen. He would be there to protect her any way he could.

Cradling her with his body, he leaned close and kissed the fragrant nape of her neck.

Val, Val . . . you scare the living hell out of me!

CHAPTER NINE

WHEN CASEY WOKE AT 7:15, THERE WAS NO SIGN OF VAL. HE SAT up in bed, wincing as his bruised side shot daggers through his body. His curses purpled the air. If he hadn't gotten up and taken those pain pills in the night, to help him sleep, he might have heard her getting ready to leave. He might have even been able to talk some sense into the woman before she went charging out to do battle.

The side of the bed where she'd slept was as cold as the room. Rising, he checked for a note or anything else she might have left. Nothing. She'd probably just slipped out of bed, pulled on her clothes, and called a cab from the lobby. He could ask the desk clerk what time she'd left, but it wouldn't make much difference. She was gone.

Making love to her last night had probably been a bad idea. But he wasn't sorry. Having Val in his arms, in his bed, had been like old times and more. The sensual heat was still there, but it was tempered with bittersweetness—an awareness of who they were now and the pain they'd both known—that had deepened the connection, making it all the more precious. And he'd sensed that what he'd felt, she'd felt, too.

But now she was gone again. That was Val. Much as he loved her, it was something that he suspected would never change.

A hot shower eased the stiffness in his side. He'd have the sports doctor take a look at it, maybe tape it before he geared up tonight. But right now that was the least of his worries. This morning, Val could already be rushing into danger. He needed to stop her, or at least protect her.

He could try calling her cell. But in her present frame of mind, she'd only accuse him of being overprotective. Alerting Tess would make sense. But at this hour she'd be at the arena, looking after her bulls. Catching her there later might be easier.

Right now there was one thing he could do—talk to Paul Brandt, find out exactly what the DA's office was demanding of Val, and what they would do to keep her safe. If Val found out he'd been checking up on her, she would no doubt be furious. But Casey would stop at nothing to protect her—and the people who were the closest thing he had to family.

Val had mentioned having Brandt's card, which probably had both his cell and office number. Casey's only way to reach Brandt would be through the District Attorney's office. He checked the time. It was coming up on 8:00, a likely hour for the office to open. He'd just have time to shave and dress before he made the call.

Val had told him how Brandt had dressed as a cowboy and tracked her down in the arena. In order to do that, he must've had her under close watch ahead of time. If the DA could track her movements, so could the mob. Surely she was aware of that. But she hadn't seemed to care.

Taking a seat, he googled the number of the Clark County District Attorney. At two minutes after 8:00, he entered the number on his phone.

A woman he guessed to be the receptionist picked up on the third ring. "District Attorney's office. How may I help you?"

"I need to speak with Assistant District Attorney Mr. Brandt. It's urgent."

There was a beat of silence. "Mr. Brandt did you say?"

"Yes, Mr. Paul Brandt. With a B. Is he available?"

Again, there was a pause. "I'm sorry, sir," the woman said. "You must be mistaken. There's no Mr. Brandt working here."

Casey's pulse lurched. "Do you happen to know anything about a Mr. Brandt—anything that might help me reach him?"

"Again, I'm sorry. I've never heard of—oh, wait! Can you hold while I check on something?"

Casey waited, his nerves crawling with tension. After a few minutes, the woman's voice came back on the phone. "I've got it, sir, but beyond that, I can't be much help. Paul Brandt worked here before my time. But he passed away three years ago, in a car accident."

"Thank you for meeting me, Mr. Brandt." Val slipped into the booth in an obscure diner off the west side of I-15. She'd phoned the cell number on Brandt's card from her hotel room, where she'd taken time to shower and change. Tess had already left for the arena, which saved some awkward explaining.

It was Brandt who'd suggested their meeting place, a short cab ride from the hotel. On the way, she'd checked her cell phone to make sure it was turned off. She didn't want any disruptive calls, especially from Casey. She was determined to handle this business by herself.

"So you're sure it was Dimitri you saw?" Brandt was wearing an expensive-looking jacket and tie, which suited him better than the fake cowboy getup he'd had on the day before.

"I'm positive. How could anybody mistake that face? He always reminded me of a vampire."

"I didn't realize the man was a rodeo buff." Brandt stirred creamer into his coffee. He'd ordered a cup for Val, but she was too nervous to drink it.

"He may have shown up because of me. I know he saw me, and I got the impression he wanted me to see him. He wanted to scare me."

"And did he?" The corner of Brandt's mouth twitched in a half smile.

"Dimitri is a scary man."

"Yes, he is. So what are you proposing we do, Miss Champion?"

"If you can keep Dimitri in custody and guarantee my family's safety, I'd be willing to help put Lanzoni away. I'd also be willing to testify against Dimitri, but only if you could guarantee he'd stay behind bars. I can't have him coming after me or hurting the people I love."

Brandt leaned back in the booth, studying her from beneath his thick eyebrows. "Would you consider witness protection?"

"No, I've been away from my family too long. I'm just getting to know them again."

"I see." Brandt frowned. "Here's something I want you to think about. Dimitri, as you know, is a businessman. Killing is his stock and trade—his job. I've only known him to kill for two reasons—for money or to get rid of witnesses. He doesn't kill out of anger or even for revenge because there's nothing in it for him. Do you agree?"

"From what little I know of the man, yes, I suppose I do."

"Picture this, then. Let's say Dimitri is being paid, by Lanzoni's contacts, to keep you from testifying. If Lanzoni is convicted on your testimony, he'll never be free again. And if Lanzoni is no longer paying, Dimitri will have no more reason to concern himself with you. On the other hand, if you don't testify, and if Lanzoni goes free, the threat of what you know will always be there. You'll never be able to stop looking over your shoulder."

"So you're saying we should leave Dimitri alone?"

"Why wake a sleeping tiger? We don't even know if he's working for Lanzoni right now."

"Well, somebody's trying to scare me. I'm not imagining that."

"True. But Dimitri doesn't operate that way. If he'd been paid to kill you, you'd be dead by now. I don't believe you're in as much danger as you fear you might be." Brandt emptied his coffee cup and set it down with a *click*. "So what's it to be? Are you willing to testify?"

Val took a moment to study him across the table—the high-end Rolex on his wrist, the jacket and tie that were designer brands she recognized. How much did an assistant DA get paid these days?

She had hoped for clarity, but this conversation had led her down a rabbit hole. Maybe Brandt was on the level, but it was too soon to make up her mind.

"I don't know what to say," she hedged. "My offer to testify hinged on your arresting Dimitri. Now you're telling me to leave him alone. I'm going to need more time to think this over."

His expression didn't change. "Take all the time you want. But we can't justify protecting you until you agree to help us."

"And what about your threat to have me charged as an accessory?"

He gave her a thin smile. "Only a threat, of course—providing you cooperate."

"I understand." She slid out of the booth and stood. "I'll call you when I've made a decision."

He stood with her and offered a handshake. His grip was professional, his palm smooth and cold. "And you can trust me to call you if the situation changes. To take Lanzoni to trial and put him away, we'll need to build an ironclad case. Your testimony could make all the difference." He glanced out the window, where his silver-gray Jaguar was parked. "I'd be happy to drive you back to your hotel."

"Thank you, but under the circumstances, we probably shouldn't be seen together. I can wave down a cab."

"Of course. I'll be waiting to hear from you." After opening the door for her, he slid into his car, started the engine, and roared off in the direction of the freeway.

Getting a cab took only a few minutes. Val took a deep breath as she settled into the backseat. She'd hoped that the meeting with Paul Brandt would give her some answers. Instead she'd come away with nothing but more questions. She was disappointed and more than a little worried about the whole arrangement.

Fishing her cell phone out of her purse, she switched it back on. There were three voice messages from Casey, probably reading her the riot act for walking out on him. Why couldn't he understand that she needed to be an adult and clean up her own mess, dangerous as it was?

She played back the messages, each one more urgent than the last.

Val, I need to talk to you. It's important. Please call me as soon as you get this.

Damn it, Val, turn on your phone and call me!

Listen to me, Val. Whatever you do, don't talk to Brandt. I checked him out. He's not who he says he is. The real Brandt is dead. The man who contacted you is probably working for Lanzoni. Where the hell are you? Call me. I need to know you're all right.

Val played the third message again to make sure she'd heard it correctly. Her hands were shaking. She'd sensed that something was off about Paul Brandt—the expensive watch, clothes, and car, and the things he'd told her. But with all that, she'd never suspected the truth. Thank heaven she hadn't made him any promises. But that didn't mean she was safe.

One thing was for sure—she wasn't about to call Casey back and tell him what she'd done. Not yet at least. But he deserved to know she was safe. Instead of making a call, she pecked out a brief text and sent it to him.

Got it. Ok. Talk soon.

When there was no reply to the text, she asked the cab driver to take her to the parking lot behind the arena. On the way, she forced herself to recall every detail of the unsettling conversation with the man who'd called himself Paul Brandt.

If he was working for Lanzoni, why would he urge her to testify against his boss? There had to be a reason. Maybe he was fishing, to see how much of a danger she might be, or to see if she could be used in some way.

Or to calculate whether I'm worth killing.

In the arena parking lot, Val directed the driver to stop next to the ranch's big SUV, specially modified with a side ramp for Shane's wheelchair and a heavy-duty hitch for pulling the trailer with the two bulls. Her eyes scanned the lot for Casey's pickup, but it didn't seem to be here. Maybe he was out looking for her. Or maybe he'd given up on her and decided to go his own way.

After paying the driver and sending the cab off, she found her set of spare SUV keys in her purse. Earlier she'd mentioned to Casey that Tess had a gun. But that had skated the edge of a lie, implying that she kept it with her. Tess did own a gun, but it wasn't in the room. It was locked in the SUV's glove compartment.

The pistol, a compact SIG Sauer P365, was where she remembered, hidden in its holster beneath a stack of maps and registration papers. After checking the loaded magazine, Val tucked it into her purse, locked the glove compartment and the vehicle, and headed across the lot toward the gate to the bull pens.

The gate guard let her pass with a wave and a friendly nod. Val recognized the acne-scarred man who'd scared her that night on the concourse. She gave him a smile, hoping the young fellow had a girlfriend who could look past his unfortunate face. Those deep scars were downright painful to look at.

She found Tess, Lexie, and Shane outside the pen where Whirlwind and Whiplash were kept. Whiplash, calm now, was munching cud on the far side of the pen. Whirlwind was leaning against the rails, eyes blissfully closed as Lexie scratched behind his ears.

Only then did Val remember that Whirlwind would be bucking again tonight in round four. Another high-scoring ride, or even a spectacular buck-off, would raise his earning power, both in the arena and as a stud. It would be something for the whole Alamo Canyon Ranch family to celebrate.

She had been remiss, Val scolded herself. She'd come to Las Vegas to support her family and cheer on their bulls. Instead, she'd been caught up in the peril and intrigue of the coming Lanzoni hearing and the heart-tearing reminder that she was in love with a man she could never have.

Put it aside for now. Paul Brandt is a fake. Lanzoni's people are playing games with you, but nobody's done you harm. Chances are the real DA doesn't even know you exist. Nobody with any authority has asked you to testify. As for Casey, that's a dead-end road. So put it aside, all of it, and be here for your family.

* * *

Tess leaned on the rails, watching the bulls and chatting with her sisters. She wanted to enjoy the moment—to be totally caught up in the excitement of a dream come true. But part of her was worried about Val.

The fact that Val had spent the night with Casey was a promising sign. Seeing the two of them together was Tess's best hope for her wayward sister. Casey would anchor Val, support her, and love her as no other man could. But from the look of Val this morning, things hadn't gone well. She was pensive and nervous, her eyes laced with red.

It might help if Val would talk to her. But growing up, the two of them had never been close. And now that Val was home from her misadventures, Tess had stepped into the role of stern parent. Under the circumstances, Val would be even less inclined to confide in her. Lexie might have better luck. But Lexie had moved on. She was totally wrapped up in her husband and their coming baby.

Now Val was gazing out toward the parking lot, as if waiting for Casey to show up. But there was no sign of him. Tess sighed. If she'd known how stressful this trip would be for Val, she wouldn't have prodded Lexie to talk her sister into coming along. Val had agreed mostly out of guilt. Now she was paying the price.

"I thought I'd find you here." The brusque voice was the last one Tess wanted to hear. Brock Tolman had come around the corner of the pens. Today he was dressed in work clothes—weathered jeans, a faded flannel shirt, and beat-up sneakers. Tess knew that two of his bulls were bucking tonight. But it was hard to believe that he was actually getting his hands dirty.

She checked the sarcastic remark she'd been tempted to make as Shane greeted him.

"What's up, Brock?" he asked, turning his chair to face his former mentor.

"Just some good news to pass on. I was talking with Clay Rafferty. He wants Whiplash on standby in the reride pen again tomorrow night in the final rounds. The fans want a chance to see him buck again. I told Clay I'd let you know." Tolman answered Shane's question, but he was looking at Tess.

I told Clay. Why was the man always dropping names, showing off his friendships with important people? Tess found it annoying, but the news about Whiplash was a gift.

"I mentioned to Clay you might be planning to leave early, since Whirlwind will be finished bucking tonight," he said. "It won't be a problem to stay through Saturday, will it?"

Tess glanced at Val. She knew her sister wanted to get away from the danger she was in. But Val smiled and nodded. "It's fine," she said. "I hope Whiplash gets another chance to show his stuff."

"I'll let Clay know," Tolman said. "We'll be sharing lunch today. Tess, I thought you might like to come along. Clay said he'd be happy to have you join us. It'll be shop talk, but you might learn a few things."

For a moment, Tess was shocked into silence. From somewhere behind her, she heard Val snicker. "Of course," she said, finding her voice. "I'd be happy to come. Thanks for including me. I'm not dressed—" Tess broke off, wanting to bite her tongue. This wasn't a date.

"You're fine," Tolman said. "Just come as you are. That's what we'll be doing. Can I pick you up here?"

"Sure . . . and thanks." She hated being in debt to the wretched man, but she would give her teeth for more time with Clay Rafferty.

As Tolman walked out of hearing, Val's face broke into an impish grin. "I'll be damned, Tess. That man's got a thing for you."

Tess went hot. "That sneaky, underhanded snake? No way! He cheated Dad out of that land he was buying, and he'd cheat us out of our ranch in a heartbeat. He never does anything unless it gets him something he wants. I wouldn't trust him to walk my dog."

"Uh-huh." Still smiling, Val turned away and walked out toward the parking lot.

* * *

The November sky was muddy gray, the sun a faint glow behind the clouds as it climbed toward its daily peak. Val could hear the late-morning traffic as she stood in the parking lot, checking her phone.

No texts. No voice messages. No sign of Casey or his truck.

He had to be all right, Val told herself. Maybe he'd given up on her. Or maybe he was just giving her space. In the short time they'd been together here in Vegas, she'd fallen right back into the old pattern of depending on him. Not a healthy thing. Maybe Casey had been wise enough to realize that. Maybe he'd cut her loose for a good reason.

Stop it, Val! It doesn't matter! You're a big girl now!

Hearing the blast of a horn, she moved out of the way as a big truck, towing a long stock trailer, swung into the parking lot and pulled up to the unloading chutes. By now, Val knew that the bulls inside it were arriving for the final championship rounds tomorrow. These would be the top-ranked animals, the PBR superstars, some of them valued in the hundreds of thousands of dollars.

Val might have enjoyed watching them be unloaded. But she had other things on her mind. Waiting around to hear from Casey had given her time for some deep thought.

She had vowed to solve her issues with the Lanzoni case on her own. Even though her meeting with the man calling himself Paul Brandt had been a disaster, her resolve hadn't changed. But she was up against ruthless, deceptive people. If the morning's encounter with Brandt had taught her anything, it was that they weren't going away. She couldn't beat them alone. And after talking with the fake Paul Brandt, she knew she couldn't keep herself or her family safe by doing nothing.

So she'd made a plan. Now it was up to her to carry it out. Tess had gone to lunch. Lexie was off somewhere with Shane, and Casey was making himself scarce. Alone, she'd paused on her way outside to speak with the guard.

"I have an errand to run. I might be a couple of hours. When my sister comes back, could you let her know that I've gone? Oh, and also tell Mr. Bozeman, one of the bullfighters. You know him, right?"

"Sure." He'd given her a lazy, gap-toothed grin. "No problem."

That done, she'd hurried on outside.

Now, pulling her jacket tighter around her, she watched the parking lot entrance. At last a mustard-colored taxi appeared, the one she'd called for. When she stepped into view and waved an arm, the cab headed in her direction and stopped in front of her.

"Where to, ma'am?" the gray-haired driver asked as she slid into the backseat.

Val took a breath and squared her shoulders. "Take me to the Clark County Regional Justice Center," she said.

Casey swore as he viewed the damage to the passenger side of his truck. The old woman had T-boned him with a vintage red Cadillac the size of a World War II landing barge. His right front fender, wheel, and part of the hood were history. But at least nobody had been hurt.

The tiny, white-haired lady wearing a fox stole with the little heads intact waggled a bejeweled and manicured finger at him. "Everybody knows this is my street, young man. And everybody knows that I don't brake for that blasted stop sign the city put up. I was here first. You should have seen me coming."

Casey held his tongue, feeling as if he'd wandered onto the set of a TV sitcom. He'd gone to the gym and spent a couple of hours working off his frustration, then stopped at a coffee shop he liked and took a shortcut back to the hotel to change before going to find Val. The shortcut had been an unlucky choice.

Any plans he might've had were probably shot for the day. By the time he'd seen to the tow, called his insurance company, and arranged for a replacement vehicle, he'd be due at the arena. He'd tried to call Val, but the blasted woman had turned her phone off again, probably because she was up to some deviltry and didn't want him interfering. Fuming, he'd left her a message.

Now the police were arriving. A husky, tired-looking cop climbed out of his patrol car, looked at the scene, and shook his head.

"Not again, Madge," he said. "You know I'm going to have to write you a ticket."

She shrugged. "Write me a dozen tickets if you want. You know the mayor is my nephew. He'll let me off, like he always does."

The officer interviewed Casey separately. "Sorry," he said, "Madge does this every few months. Luckily, it's a slow neighborhood. She hasn't hurt anybody yet, but she's banged up a few cars with that old Caddy. Her kids have tried to take her keys away, but she's threatened to disinherit them if they do."

"How does she get insurance?" Casey asked. "She's got it, I hope?"

The cop chuckled. "You bet your life she's got it. Her brother owns a controlling interest in the insurance company. They'll treat you like royalty as long as you promise not to sue." He surveyed the smashed truck. "You'll want to take your belongings out before the tow truck gets here."

Casey thought about what he'd need to take. "I've got a pistol in the glove box. It's legal."

"Fine. I'll need to see the gun and the permit. Then you can sign these papers. I'll give you a copy of Madge's insurance card, and you'll be free to go."

Madge's Cadillac had survived the crash with a mangled grill. The cop released her to leave the scene. Casey finished stuffing his papers and a few other belongings into his gym bag and settled back in the driver's seat to wait for the tow truck.

Given the threat to Val, it would be a good idea to keep the pistol, a compact Smith & Wesson 40C, with him. If he needed to protect her, it could make all the difference. The challenge would be convincing the woman that she needed protection. Her new plan, whatever it was, was bound to put her in more danger than ever. She was probably in danger now, and he couldn't even reach her by phone.

He tried again. Her phone was still turned off. Swearing, he jammed his phone back into his pocket.

Where are you, Val? And what the hell are you up to?

*   *   *

Assistant District Attorney Mac Halvorsen, assigned to the Lanzoni case, was midfortyish and balding, with the photo of a pretty
wife and two youngsters displayed on his desk. When Val told
him, briefly, why she'd come, he buzzed the receptionist and
asked her to reschedule his next two appointments.

"Now tell me everything," he said.

"I will," Val replied. "But only if you'll promise to answer my
questions. Before I agree to cooperate, I need to know what's
going on with the case. And I need to know how I can protect myself and my family."

"You realize this is an ongoing investigation. There are things I
can't—"

"I know. I also know that if I don't like my options, I can get up
and walk out of here."

"Understood. Tell me your story, and I'll tell you your options."

"You can't force me to testify in court, is that right?"

"That's right."

"And I'm not being recorded?"

"We can't do that without your consent."

"And can I be granted immunity from any charges?"

"If you agree to testify."

"All right." Val began her story by describing briefly how she'd
met Lenny Fortunato and how they'd come to be in Las Vegas,
working for Carlo Lanzoni.

"Were you part of his organization?" Halvorsen asked.

"No, I was just Lenny's girlfriend. But I saw and heard things."
Even the memory made Val cringe. How could she have been so
foolish?

"I'm aware that Fortunato was found murdered, presumably by
Lanzoni's hit man," Halvorsen said. "The CSI team found a woman's
clothes and toiletries in his apartment. Were those yours?"

"Yes. When Lenny was killed, I'd gone out. But I got back in
time to hear everything that happened through the door, and to
see Dimitri leaving."

She told him the story in detail. "Dimitri would have killed me,
too, but I was hiding outside in the hallway. Once I was sure he

was gone, I stepped into the apartment long enough to see that Lenny was dead. Then I left everything and ran for my life."

"You're positive you heard Dimitri say that Lanzoni had sent him?"

"Absolutely."

"And you'd testify to that?"

"Providing I agree to testify."

Halvorsen leaned back in his chair and tented his fingers. "I'm curious. Why are you coming forward now?"

"I thought I'd left the whole nightmare behind me. But this week I came to Las Vegas with my family and discovered that I'd stepped right back into it. Someone's been stalking me, and last night I saw Dimitri at the PBR finals. I'm sure it was him and I'm sure he recognized me.

"Something else—a few days ago, a man identifying himself as Assistant DA Paul Brandt accosted me. He had ID, but after I'd told him my story—everything I've told you—I found out that he wasn't who he said he was. I get the impression he might have been working for Lanzoni. He was tall, sharp dresser, wavy chestnut hair, and bushy eyebrows, about your age."

"Maybe you could identify him from a photo." Halvorsen pulled a manila folder out of a drawer and spread some glossy photos on the desk. The photos were candid shots of Carlo Lanzoni, accompanied by various people, mostly men in suits.

Val scanned them with her eyes. "There"—she pointed to a photo of a tall man standing next to Lanzoni at some kind of party, both smiling, with cocktail glasses raised—"that's him."

"You're sure?"

"I even recognize the jacket—and the Rolex."

Halvorsen scooped the photos back into the folder. "You've just identified Wayne Duvall, one of Lanzoni's top legal eagles."

Val shrugged. "Nothing surprises me anymore. But would you answer one question for me? If Duvall is defending Lanzoni, why on earth would he urge me to testify, when it could put his boss in prison for life, or even get him the death penalty?"

Halvorsen was silent for a long moment, his fingers drumming on the desk. "I'm going to tell you something in confidence," he said. "I'm not authorized to pass this on, but I think you need to know for your own safety.

"An undercover source in Lanzoni's crime organization has informed us that Lanzoni's arrest has touched off a power struggle. Dimitri is trying to take over, and based on what you just told me, I'd say Duvall must've sided with him. They want Lanzoni out of the way—in prison for life or even dead."

"So they actually want me to testify—even Dimitri?"

"It appears that way. But keep in mind, Lanzoni's friends are out there, too. They'll do anything—scare you, threaten you, even kill you—to keep you off the witness stand. And right now we don't have the resources to protect you."

"There's something else," Val said, thinking out loud. "I'm also a possible witness against Dimitri. Even if he wins, I'll still be a threat to him."

"That's right," Halvorsen said. "For now, we're holding off on Dimitri until we can figure out which way the wind is blowing. Before we arrest him, we'll want to make sure we can lock him up so tight that no mob lawyer will be able to spring him."

"You've got Lanzoni. Couldn't he give you that evidence?"

"He could. But he knows he'd be incriminating himself, and that Dimitri would find a way to get to him, even in prison."

"So, in other words, when it comes to Dimitri, I'm on my own."

Halvorsen stirred in his chair, a signal that the interview was coming to an end. "When the time comes, your testimony will be helpful. Meanwhile, all I can tell you is to be very, very careful."

CHAPTER TEN

VAL TOOK A CAB BACK TO THE ARENA, FEELING AS IF SHE'D STUMBLED into a hall of mirrors, like the ones in old-fashioned amusement parks. Mac Halvorsen's card was tucked in her purse, but aside from advising her of the danger, he'd offered nothing in the way of protection. She was on her own, still wondering whether she'd done the right thing.

As she fished her phone out of her purse, her fingers brushed the canvas holster of the pistol. Taking it from the truck had been a good idea, especially given what she'd just learned. But she barely knew how to use it. Maybe Casey could show her. But for that, she would have to come clean about where she'd been and what she'd done. Turning on her phone, she saw his voice message and opened it.

> *Val, I just had a major fender bender in the truck. Nobody hurt, but I'll be a while taking care of things. Damn it, where are you? Call me.*

She sighed, guessing that he'd likely be tied up much of the afternoon. At least he was all right. But she was still debating how much she could safely tell him. With a phone call, she'd be facing questions she wasn't ready to answer. Again, she sent him a text.

All fine. See you at the arena.

Without Casey she felt a sense of something missing. But she couldn't allow herself to need him. She couldn't be clingy and dependent at a time like this. Casey would come when he would come. And after the finals, he'd be gone again. They had no future. They barely had the present.

As the cab pulled into the rear parking lot, Val felt as if she were about to walk into a minefield. When she'd left for the DA's office, she'd told no one where she was going. But that didn't mean she couldn't have been tracked. Both Dimitri's agents and Lanzoni's thugs could be watching her. And Wayne Duvall, likely unaware that she'd learned his real identity, could show up anytime. She'd be jumping at every shadow.

Getting out of the cab, she dodged another long stock trailer unloading more bulls. Tess and Lexie were standing back among the pens, watching. Val willed herself to put on a smile, stay calm, and hide her anxiety. Her sisters had their own concerns. They didn't need to be burdened with hers.

Watching the top PBR bulls come down the unloading chutes and into the pens, Tess felt an excitement akin to seeing movie stars or the star players at the Super Bowl. She knew most of the bulls by sight—world champion Smooth Operator, two-time champion, a huge white bull with specks of black; Chiseled, black and sharp with a tan blaze down his back; Air Support, white and powerful; Big Black, a top performer for years. And coming out of another truck was Sweet Pro's Bruiser, three-time former world champion, a kingly bull, his colors like coffee and cream, his presence owning the arena.

There were more, all magnificent. Watching them, Tess felt goose bumps rise on her arms. Her own bulls were talented buckers with a lot of heart. But these animals had been selectively bred from generations of the best, and it showed. If only the Alamo Canyon Ranch could produce bulls like these.

She remembered last summer, when Lexie had wanted to buy semen from prize bulls to breed their cows. Pressed for time and strapped for money, Tess had opted for borrowing a second-rate bull from a Phoenix ranch. Most of the cows were pregnant now, but the calves would likely be no better than their sire.

She nudged Lexie, who was standing next to her. "You were right," she said. "I was wrong."

"Yes, you were. But that can change." Lexie didn't need to ask what her sister meant. "We've lost this year, but if we start planning ahead now, setting money aside for semen, we can be ready by next breeding season. It'll be expensive, and risky. If the semen doesn't take, you don't get your money back."

"I know," Tess said. "But if we can get one bull like these, let alone more, or even some heifers with great bloodlines, it'll be worth the effort. The only way to build the ranch is to improve our stock."

"We'll need to hire a vet at first," Lexie said. "I learned the basics in college, but I'll need practice. A professional can walk me through the procedure a few times. Then I'll be able to do it myself." She responded to Tess's startled glance with a laugh. "You know, I won't be pregnant forever."

Tess, who wasn't usually that affectionate, gave her sister a hug. Did Lexie's words mean that she and Shane would be staying on at the ranch? What if they decided to take Brock Tolman up on his offer? The artificial breeding program sounded promising, but how could she manage it without Lexie's expertise? And what about the rodeo school that Shane wanted to start, and the bucking horse project he'd suggested?

If Lexie and Shane were to leave, Tess's hopes and dreams for the ranch would go with them.

Val stood to one side, a faraway look on her exquisite face. She'd said little since coming back from her errand, except to mention that Casey's truck had been wrecked. Maybe she was just worried about him. You could never tell with Val. She was as mysterious as a cat.

"They're really something, aren't they?" Brock Tolman had come up behind Tess. Glancing to the side, she saw that Lexie had slipped away, and Val was lost in Neverland. She had no one to come to her rescue.

"They're magnificent," Tess said. "I could look at them all day."

He nodded. "I know what you mean. I've got some fine bulls, good enough to be here, but I look at these beauties and wonder, what does it take? What do I have to do to get a bull in this class?" There was a note of obsession in his deep voice.

"Is that why you've been so keen on getting Whirlwind? He's a great bull, but he's not Smooth Operator or Chiseled."

"No. But he's got amazing flash and spirit. If I could breed him with my cows and get that bloodline . . ."

"That can be arranged for a price, you know," Tess said, wondering why she hadn't thought of it before. "But Whirlwind is a mutt. True, he's like a great, great, grandson of Oscar. But that blood is pretty diluted. Everything else is a mix, a lucky accident. The same with Whiplash."

"I'm not one to discount lucky accidents," Tolman said. "I'm just impatient for one to happen to me. That yearling of yours, the one I ended up buying, could be the one with the magic in him. But I won't know for sure until he's old enough to compete. That's at least two years off."

"You don't strike me as a patient man," Tess said.

He was silent for a long moment, watching the prize bulls settle into their pens. "I'm not the only one who's impatient. I know I'm not your favorite person, Tess, but you and I are alike in a lot of ways."

"Maybe that's why I don't trust you," she retorted. "If you think you can charm me—"

"Charm you? Charming a wet wildcat would be easier." With a raw-edged laugh, he turned and walked away.

The time was coming up on 4:30 when Val saw a black Dodge pickup drive into the parking lot with Casey at the wheel. As he parked and climbed out, she felt her anxiety ease—only to be replaced by a flurry of concerns.

She crossed the lot to meet him, forcing herself to an unhurried walk. After what she'd done, sneaking out that morning and turning off her phone, she could expect him to demand answers. But how much of an explanation did she owe him?

Today she'd stumbled into a rattlesnakes' den of danger and deceit. Did she want to risk involving him, or did she care enough to keep him at a safe distance?

In other words, did she care enough to lie?

He stood by the truck, waiting to speak until she came close. "Damn it, Val, what's going on with you?"

"Nothing that can't wait." She stopped an arm's length from him, the tension between them thickening the air like smoke. "Are you all right?"

"I'll live—after a day that's been like a ride on a roller coaster run by lunatics."

"And the truck?"

"Pretty much totaled. I sold it for parts and bought this one. It was less of a hassle than renting a vehicle and taking it one-way out of state." His gaze narrowed. Val could sense that he was struggling to hold the rein on his temper. "But we were talking about you. Where have you been?"

"Forget it. It doesn't matter."

"The hell it doesn't!" His tight control snapped. "Blast it, Val, if this were a different century, I'd turn you over my knee. I'm here because for some reason I'm idiot enough to care about you. Now talk to me."

"Only if you promise to stay out of the way and let me handle this situation myself."

"No promises. Just talk to me." He opened the truck's passenger door. "Get in. That's an order." He ushered her to the door and assisted her inside.

As Val fastened her seat belt, she couldn't help wondering what he would have done if she'd resisted. Knowing Casey, he would probably have driven away and left her standing there in the windy parking lot. She wasn't ready for that, but she was still torn between her need for Casey and the need to stand alone against the threats closing in on her.

"Have you eaten?" he asked, starting the truck.

"I can't say I've had much appetite."

"Neither have I. But we can't run on empty. There's a place close by with decent pizza. It should be pretty quiet at this hour."

The restaurant was traditional, with candles and red checkered cloths on the tables and country music playing low over the speakers. The few customers in the place were cowboy types, probably grabbing an early bite before tonight's PBR semifinals.

In a quiet corner booth they slipped iced Cokes while they waited for the pizza they'd ordered. "You could've had a beer," Val said, knowing it was what he'd have preferred. "I know you're trying to help me stay on the wagon, but I wouldn't have minded."

"I'm working tonight—no beer for me," he reminded her. "So after sneaking out of my bed and ignoring my calls, now you're being nice?"

"Stop teasing, Casey. I've had a hellacious day."

"*You've* had a hellacious day? It couldn't beat mine. After you've told me your story, I'll tell you about Madge."

"Okay, I'll bite. Who's Madge?"

"She's my new girlfriend. She drives a big red Cadillac. She's on a first-name basis with the cops, her nephew is the mayor, and her brother owns an insurance company. Now, that's my kind of woman."

Val lowered her head to hide a smile. This was a side of Casey she loved. No matter how angry or upset she might be, he could always coax a laugh out of her. And if the shoe happened to be on the other foot, his own dark moods never seemed to last long.

He would have made a great husband and a loving, patient father. But she'd destroyed all that, and now it was too late to go back.

"So, down to business," he said. "I know you got my message about Brandt being fake. But did you get it in time?"

"No, I didn't get it until after I'd met with him. But even before I learned the truth, I was suspicious. He showed up in designer clothes and driving a Jaguar—pretty rich for an assistant DA. Then he not only encouraged me to testify against Lanzoni, he tried to convince me that Dimitri wasn't a danger and should be left alone."

"That should've been a red flag right there, Val."

"It was. But even after I found out he wasn't real, I couldn't understand where he was coming from. If he was working for Lanzoni, why would he want me to testify against his boss?"

She was telling Casey far more than she'd meant to, the words pouring out like water through a broken dam. Maybe she'd needed to tell him. Maybe some instinct was prompting her to share and trust him.

So she told him her story—how, after learning that Brandt was an imposter, she'd gone to the real assistant district attorney's office, spoken with Mac Halvorsen, and learned about the power struggle in Lanzoni's crime family.

By the time she finished, she was shaking. Only now, as she recounted the events, did the full implications sink in.

The pizza had arrived. Untouched, it lay cooling on the table.

"Let me get this straight." Casey spoke calmly and quietly. "If you agree to testify for the DA, and Lanzoni's people get wind of it, they'll be out to stop you any way they can."

"That's right. If I refuse, both the DA and Dimitri's allies will be pressuring me to change my mind. And I won't be safe from Lanzoni's people either. All they'll want is to silence me."

"On the other hand," Casey said, "if you go to court, and your testimony puts Lanzoni away, his thugs will be out to make an example of you."

"Yes, and it gets worse. Once I've testified, Dimitri will have no more use for me—in fact, since I could also give evidence against him, he'd have no reason to let me go on living. If I'm right, he's only holding off now on the chance that I'll nail Carlo Lanzoni for him."

"My God." Casey's face was pale in the candlelight.

Val drew a ragged breath. "Any way this goes, I'm a dead pigeon."

"Can't the DA offer you protection?"

"Halvorsen will only do that if I commit to testify. Even if he does, I know for a fact that Lanzoni has paid thugs on the police force. They'd find a way to get to me. As for the witness protection program, I left my family once. I'd do it again if it would keep them safe. But even that's no guarantee. If I disappear, it could put them in more danger."

"Val, you've got people who love you, people who'll stand up and protect you, including me."

"No, that's exactly what mustn't happen. If I go down, I don't want to take anybody else—you or my family—with me. That's why you need to stay out of this. It's my battle. I have to fight it alone."

"Damn it, you know that's not going to fly. Not with me."

"It has to." She shook her head. "I'm not worth dying for, Casey."

His fists were clenched in front of him on the table. He gazed down at them. Time seemed to crawl before he spoke. "I have a suggestion. It's not a final answer, but it should buy us some time."

"Buy *me* some time," she corrected him.

"No, *us*," he said. "And I won't have it any other way. Do you want to hear me out?"

"I'm all ears."

"Fine. Here it is. You go with the person who has the most to gain by keeping you alive—and the one who has the best means to do that."

Val's heart dropped as she realized what he was implying. "Dimitri."

Casey nodded. "The grand jury hearing probably won't happen for a few more weeks. Hopefully by then we'll have found another way out. If nothing else, it could be our best chance of keeping things under control until the finals are over and your family can go back to the ranch."

"So you're thinking I should string Duvall along without letting him suspect I'm on to him—make him think I'm fine with leaving Dimitri alone?"

"Right. With luck, as long as he and Dimitri think you're willing to follow their lead, they'll protect you and yours against Lanzoni's goons." He reached across the table for her hand. She gripped his strong fingers, holding on for dear life. His plan was the only one that made sense. But she'd be walking a tightrope.

"I'd have to steer clear of the DA's office," she said. "If Duvall finds out I've talked to Halvorsen, I'm in trouble."

"You could always scrap the whole plan and turn yourself over to the DA."

"No, they might put me somewhere safe, but I couldn't count on them to protect my family. And that's who both sides of the mob would go after if they couldn't get to me." She blinked away tears. "Oh, Casey, I'm not brave. I just want to go home. I just want the people I love to be safe."

Casey lifted her hand and pressed his lips to her fingers. "You're braver than you think. And I'll be there for you."

"No, be there for Tess and Shane and Lexie and the baby. I can do this as long as I know they're protected."

His hand tightened around her fingers, almost hurting. "We'll get through this. But tonight, after the event, you're going back to the room with me. Stay around the chutes with Tess, where there are plenty of people. I'll find you after I've changed and cleaned up. And I want you there in the morning. No sneaking out before I'm awake."

Val nodded. She had mixed feelings about the risks of another night in Casey's bed. But she had no resistance left.

He glanced at his watch, then at the table. "We need to be getting back soon. I don't suppose you like cold pizza."

"Not even warmed over." Val's appetite was gone.

"I saw a couple of homeless teens with a dog on our way in. Maybe they're hungrier than we are." He asked the waitress to heat the pizza and put it in a box. As they went out to the parking lot, Casey passed it to the homeless pair, who took it with thanks.

On the way to the truck, he caught her hand. Val held on tight, as if she could draw strength from his warm clasp. Casey was courageous to the bone. Strong and fearless, he was the kind of man who'd rush into a burning building to save a trapped puppy. But Val considered herself a born coward. At any hint of trouble, her first line of defense had always been to run. That wasn't an option now. In the face of deadly enemies, she would have to stand firm and use her acting skills to play a dangerous game.

Even the thought of what she might have to do made her knees quiver. Minutes from now, when she walked into the arena complex and Casey left her, the game would begin. Frightened or not, she would have to be ready.

By the time they parked and walked to the rear entrance, it was getting dark outside. Through the gray murk, the hotels and casinos glittered like towers of dime-store gems. To the west, beyond the arena, the traffic on I-15 streamed steady ribbons of light that flowed southward all the way to the horizon. The twilight air smelled of popcorn, hot dogs, and cotton candy.

Fans were already pouring into the arena. The fourth and semifinal round of bull riding wouldn't start for more than an hour, but the preshow entertainment was already underway. Country music headliners blared cowboy songs from a makeshift stage while the audience clapped, whooped, and sang along. It was cowboy celebration time in Vegas, the biggest and wildest event of the PBR year.

Val felt her blood racing, as much from fear as from excitement as Casey pulled her into the shadows outside the gate and gave her a lingering kiss, so desperately tender that it made her head spin. Despite the anxiety, her body flamed in response. She warmed at the thought of the night ahead, loving him, being close, even though it might be for the last time.

When he spoke, his voice was husky. "Be careful, Val. Stay with your people and don't take chances. I'll meet you by the pens when this is over."

"You be careful, too," Val murmured, reeling from the kiss but also thinking of the danger he would face every time a bull burst out of the bucking chute. She wouldn't take an easy breath until the event was over.

After passing through the gate, they went their separate ways, Casey to warm up and change in the locker room, Val to look for her sisters.

It didn't take her long to find them. Tess and Lexie were standing next to the pen with Whirlwind and Whiplash in it. A glamorous-looking brunette, wearing an ID badge from a local TV station, was doing an interview.

"Isn't it unusual for women to be raising rodeo bulls?"

"Unusual, but not unheard of," Lexie said. "We know of other women who raise bucking bulls. They do fine. So do we."

"But isn't it dangerous?" the woman asked.

"Of course it is," Tess said. "We have to use common sense. When we move our bulls at home in the pastures, we do it on horseback. And you'll notice that here, in the arena, they're driven through a series of chutes and gates to get them where they need to go. The only time they're loose is when they're bucking."

"Some bulls, like Whirlwind here, are easygoing and accustomed to handling," Lexie said. "But he's a powerful animal. He could become startled or angry, or he could even hurt you by accident. And he's dynamite in the arena. We're careful around all of our bulls."

"And the other bull over there? He looks like a rough customer."

"He is," Tess said. "Nobody takes chances with Whiplash. He's *rank*. That's the word for a tough bull."

"I understand Whirlwind will be bucking tonight."

"That's right. José Gilberto—he's in second place so far—will be riding him. We wish him luck, but of course we'll be cheering for Whirlwind."

As the interview dragged on, Val, who'd moved far out of camera range, realized that she needed a restroom. And after passing on the pizza, she was beginning to feel hungry. There would be plenty of people on the concourse. It should be perfectly safe to use the facilities, then visit the snack bar on the way back to the bull pen.

As she climbed the stairs to the concourse level, she felt the weight of the pistol in her purse. What if she had to use it? The only thing she knew about firing a gun was that you pointed it at the target and pulled the trigger. She could probably manage that. But she'd feel more confident if she'd had some practice. Maybe she could ask Casey to help her tomorrow.

But anything could happen between now and then.

At the top of the stairs she came out onto the crowded concourse and found the nearest ladies' room. Finishing, she washed her hands and left. Farther along the concourse, she spotted a concession booth, but there was a line in front. If she wanted something, she would have to wait. Would it be worth the time?

As if in answer, her stomach rumbled, demanding nourishment. With a sigh, Val moved to the rear of the line. She needed energy to get her through the night, but there were at least a dozen people ahead of her. The ones in front were carrying away big orders. She could be here awhile.

"Please don't turn around, Miss Champion."

The annoyingly flat voice came from directly behind her in the line. Val recognized the speaker as Wayne Duvall, alias Paul Brandt. It was time for her performance.

Her pulse was racing, but she willed herself to speak calmly. "I didn't know you were a bull riding fan, Mr. Brandt."

"I find it . . . relaxing." Now that Val knew who he was and what he did, his way of speaking grated on her nerves. "I happened to see you and thought I'd say hello. Is anything new?"

"Not really," she said. "I'm still leaning toward testifying. But I'm worried about Lanzoni's people. They could be anywhere. If any harm came to my family because of this, I'd never forgive myself. Isn't there anything you can do to protect us?"

"I'd have to go through channels. It may take time."

"We haven't got time."

He leaned closer, smelling of the same Cuban cigars she remembered Lanzoni smoking. Had Halvorsen been wrong about his alliance with Dimitri? She could no longer be certain of anything.

"Let me do some checking," he said. "Meanwhile, if there's any problem, feel free to call my cell number, day or night."

"I'll do that. Or I could call you at the DA's office."

"No, not there. Lanzoni has ears everywhere. Just my cell, understand?"

"Yes, I understand."

She waited for him to say more. When she didn't hear, she realized he'd gone.

Without looking around for him, she waited in line. Her legs felt as if they were about to buckle, but there was no place to sit. Had she believed the right people and said the right things, or had she already made some fatal mistake?

The fans flowing around the concourse looked so innocent and happy—families with excited kids, hopeful young cowboys, seniors, couples, groups of women friends, and more. Many were dressed in western gear or T-shirts emblazoned with the PBR flag. Rodeo sports, like bull riding, tended to attract wholesome crowds, folks with deeply held traditions of family, God, and country. That Duvall and Dimitri were slinking among them like venomous reptiles filled Val with surprising anger. It had been a long time since she'd thought of herself as a good person. But why couldn't the world be just and fair? Why did evil have to hold so much power?

Reaching the head of the line at last, she bought an overpriced energy bar and hurried away.

Inside the arena, the entertainment was winding down, the seats rapidly filling for the main event. Whirlwind would be bucking early in the program. He would probably have been moved to a holding pen while his two human mothers, Tess and Lexie, hovered and fussed. Let them enjoy tonight, Val thought. Later she would tell them as much as they needed to know. For now she would stay close enough to keep watch against any possible harm.

As the opening ceremony began—the colors, the pledge and anthem, the prayer, and the presentation of tonight's riders—Val took her place next to Tess, who had already tied Whirlwind's flank strap in place and seen him herded into chute number three. Lexie had gone to join Shane at the press table.

It was an edge-of-the-seat time for the Alamo Canyon Ranch family. But until the last bull had bucked, Val would have her eyes

on just one man—a man who faced death to save others every
time a chute opened.

A man she couldn't help loving.

Casey adjusted his position as he waited for the gate to open.
He'd checked the roster beforehand. First out would be Cannonball, one of Brock Tolman's bulls. An 1,800-pound one-horned
black, he was strong but predictable, a good choice for young
Cody Woodbine, who was still high in the standings.

As Woodbine made the final adjustments on his rope, Casey
risked a glance beyond the chutes. There was no sign of Val's
flaming hair—not that he'd expected to see her. He'd told her to
stay with her sisters, but knowing Val, she could be anywhere. He
could only hope she was safe.

The gate flew open. Clearing his mind of everything but the
bull and the young rider, Casey moved into position with his team.
As Cannonball kicked and spun, Woodbine hung on, arm pumping, back straight, legs forward. Good ride. At the eight-second
whistle, he worked his hand out of the rope and flew free. Then
something went wrong. One instant Woodbine was in the air; the
next he was under the bull, rolling to get clear of the pounding
hooves.

Casey sprang into action, flinging himself in front of the bull to
draw him away from the fallen rider. Cannonball lunged forward,
knocking him into the dirt and butting at him with his single
blunted horn. Casey let his body armor take the blows, protecting
his head until his teammates could drive the beast off him and
out through the exit gate.

Shaken but unhurt, Casey pushed to his feet, retrieved his hat
from the dirt, and checked to make sure the rider was safe. Then
he readied himself for the next bull.

Val had choked back her scream as Casey went down. This was
his job and he did it well. He wouldn't want her carrying on and
making a fuss every time he tangled with a bull. But whenever he

rushed in to save a rider, her heart dropped. She would never get used to watching him.

One more ride, and then it would be Whirlwind's turn. The cowboy in chute number two had already mounted and was adjusting his rope. Val moved with Tess to a spot up front, next to the chutes, where they could get a clear view of their bull's performance.

She knew better than to look up, but it happened without thought. Her gaze traveled to the rows above the chutes—high and to the center. There he was, as cold and grim as a death's head, wearing a black silk shirt and a black leather jacket.

As their eyes made contact—his the color of sea ice—Dimitri nodded and gave her a bone-chilling smile.

CHAPTER ELEVEN

A S HE WAITED FOR THE NEXT CHUTE TO OPEN, CASEY SPOTTED VAL. She was with Tess, the two of them standing just behind the rails. Even from where he stood, he could tell she was distracted. He saw her turn, look up and to her right, then jerk her gaze away.

When he followed what had been her line of sight. It led to a solitary figure in black, standing out amid a sea of denim, baseball caps, and T-shirts.

Dimitri. Casey had never seen him before, but there could be no mistake—and no question that he was stalking Val. Casey felt a jolt of rage. But for now he would have to put it aside. The gate man was pulling the rope to open the chute.

The second cowboy was bucked off his white-faced bull in four seconds. By the time he'd scrambled to his feet, the bull was trotting out of the exit. Some bulls were easier than others, but none could be taken for granted—including Whirlwind, who was shifting and banging his horns in chute number three.

Casey could see his silvery hide through the gate. "Do your family proud, big guy," he muttered under his breath. "We'll all be cheering for you."

Brazilian José Gilberto was in contention for first place, along with McClintock and Cody Woodbine. The son of a Mato Grosso ranch hand, he'd ridden his first bull before he owned his first pair of shoes. Prior to every ride he kissed the crucifix that hung by a silver chain around his neck.

Whirlwind snorted and tossed his head, trying to buck as Gilberto mounted him. A chute man jammed the wooden wedge inside the rails to hold him in place until the rider could get his seat. Cool and focused, Gilberto wrapped his rope handle, checked it, shifted forward, and nodded.

Casey sprang into motion as the gate snapped open and Whirlwind shot out, kicking, bucking, and leaping, never in a predictable way. As a rider, Gilberto was poetry in motion, arm pumping in an arc, the fringe on his chaps flying like wings on both sides of the bull's body. As the seconds whirred past, Whirlwind spun, then changed directions with the high, twisting kick that had dumped most riders into the dirt. Gilberto fought for balance, sliding dangerously to the left as the eight-second whistle ended the ride. Unable to hang on, he let go of the rope, tumbled to one side, and rolled clear. Because he'd been on the bull at the whistle, the ride qualified—forty-six points for the rider, forty-five for the bull—a grand total of ninety-one points. On his feet now, a jubilant Gilberto snatched off his helmet and flung it high in the air.

Casey could imagine the Champion sisters cheering and hugging. He might have given them a congratulatory thumbs-up, but he was still dealing with Whirlwind. Searching for the gate, the bull had become confused. He charged one way, then another, becoming more agitated as the protection team tried to herd him in the right direction. When Marcus stepped in his path, trying to turn him, he flattened the bullfighter and stampeded over the top of him. Casey and Joel rushed to the aid of their teammate as the roper finally got Whirlwind under control. Protected by his body armor, Marcus was helped to his feet. Whirlwind vanished into the exit chute, where Tess would be waiting for him.

"Good boy!" Tess scratched Whirlwind's back as she reached over the rails of the narrow chute to untie his flank strap and pull it away. She could feel him quivering beneath her hand. Two ninety-point rides in a row. The top bulls in the PBR couldn't have done better than that. Of course, Whirlwind had carried two of the best riders in the world, she reminded herself. But not even McClintock and Gilberto could have made those scores without her bull's help.

She was proud of him—but there was more than pride involved. Whirlwind's showing in the world finals would drive up his earning power for the ranch. The silver bull would be in demand as a contender and as a stud.

She followed him back through the gates and saw him safely into the pen he shared with his brother. Whirlwind was through bucking. One more night, with Whiplash on standby as a reride, and the finals would be over. Then they could pack their bags, load their bulls, and head for home the next morning.

For Tess, the week couldn't have gone better. The bulls had performed well, she'd met some important people, and she'd learned a lot about the business of being a stock contractor at the lunch with Brock and Clay Rafferty. But she wouldn't be sorry to leave Las Vegas behind and get back to life on the Alamo Canyon Ranch—a life of fresh air, peaceful mornings, and good, hard physical work.

It would be an even bigger relief to get Val away from the invisible danger that had kept her on edge all week. Maybe once things settled down, they could invite Casey to the ranch for a visit. Perhaps away from the stress of Las Vegas, the magic would happen between her troubled sister and the one man who loved and understood her.

She'd been away from Val long enough, Tess reminded herself. Val had seemed especially nervous tonight. It wouldn't do to leave her alone too long.

How real was the threat? Tess had seen no physical evidence of danger. She knew that her sister was still fragile after her recent stint in rehab. Could Val's mind be exaggerating things she'd seen and heard, like the phone calls to the room that could have been simple mistakes?

But two things argued against that idea. Casey—a rock of common sense and stability—absolutely believed Val. And it was possible that the two of them weren't sharing everything they knew. It stood to reason that they might not want to worry her or distract her focus from the bulls.

For now, Tess resolved, she would give Val the benefit of the doubt and be ready to protect her family.

By the time Tess returned, Val had moved back into the area behind the chutes. She could no longer see the action in the arena, but that suited her fine. Whirlwind's turn was over. She took no pleasure in watching Casey flirt with death. And she couldn't stand being where Dimitri could play with her nerves. He was toying with her, the way a cat might toy with a mouse—and if his game worked, it was because she knew what he was capable of doing. She was terrified.

She couldn't say she knew Dimitri well. But being with Lenny had given her the chance to observe him. Lanzoni's hit man was no dumb punk. Descended from a once-powerful Lithuanian family, he was well educated and keenly intelligent. But beyond an occasional cold smile, Val had never known him to show emotion. No anger. No compassion. No remorse.

It had never occurred to Val that he was ambitious. But now, with the boss in jail, he was moving to take over—and she was part of his plan. He allowed her to live only as long as she served his purpose. After that, she'd be disposed of like a racehorse with a broken leg.

"What are you doing back here, Val?" Tess had come up behind her. "You can't even see what's going on."

"Sorry, I'm not feeling red hot." That much was true. And this was no time to tell her sister about the encounter with Duvall or Dimitri's presence in the nearby stands. This was Tess's moment. She was over the moon with Whirlwind's performance. Let her enjoy it.

"Go on up front," Val said. "I won't be far. I'm just going to look for a chair."

"You're sure you're all right? You're not sick, are you?"

"I'm fine. Just tired."

"You'll tell me if you go anywhere else, okay?" Tess asked.

"Sure." Val bit back a comment about Tess's constant mothering. Her sister was only concerned—and she'd be even more worried if she were to learn what had happened tonight.

Stressed and weary, Val wandered back toward the locker, training, and medical rooms. With luck she'd be able to find a folding chair that she could borrow and a quiet place to sit and wait.

"Sorry, miss, you're not allowed back here."

Startled, Val looked up into the acne-scarred face of the security guard. "Sorry, I'm just looking for a chair," she said. "I thought I might find one in an empty room."

"See that sign? It says AUTHORIZED PERSONNEL ONLY. That means nobody but the riders and bullfighters and the medical staff are allowed past this point. Except for me." He grinned, showing crooked teeth that wanted a good brushing. "I can go anywhere I want to. Wait here. I'll find you a chair."

Val waited while he strode down the hallway, stepped through a side door, and came out with a folded metal chair. "Here you are. When you're finished with it, you can leave it right here."

"Thank you." Val remembered something curious about the young man. "I hope you don't mind if I ask you a question. Every time I come here, whatever the hour, I seem to see you on duty. Don't you ever go home?"

"Easy." He chuckled. "I work a split shift—four hours in the morning and four at night, longer if there's an event on. The money's good, and it gives me time to do other stuff in the daytime, if you get my drift. Not a bad life. Satisfied?" He gave her a wink.

Good grief, did he think she was flirting with him? "Thanks. I'll see that this gets returned." She grabbed the chair and fled. Finding a spot next to the stairs, she settled down to wait.

She couldn't see the arena from where she sat, but the cheers, gasps, and groans of the crowd fed her imagination. Casey was out there, risking his life. And if it scared her, she had to be a big girl and accept that. It was who he was. He loved his job, and he did it as well as any man on earth. When she saw him in the arena, she should be proud, not afraid.

At least her location hid her from Dimitri—though even the thought of those cold blue eyes watching her made her flesh creep. He was a part of her nightmare that would never go away.

But as she thought about him, a spark of anger kindled and grew into a slow-burning flame. Dimitri's being here, making sure she saw him, was about control. He knew that he could manipulate her emotions with a look, or even a thought. He could do it because she let him. And letting him was her choice.

He could kill her on a whim—that much was reality. But why should she allow him to control her thoughts—and her life?

A collective gasp and a roar from the crowd broke her train of thought. Something spectacular had just happened in the arena. The fans were getting their money's worth tonight.

She would have to move her chair out of the way when the stands began to empty, but by then it would be almost time to meet Casey. For her, the minutes couldn't go fast enough until she was with him again, the two of them keeping each other safe and warm for one more night—even though it had to be for the last time.

After showering and changing, Casey found Val waiting by the pens with Tess. She looked frayed and edgy. Having seen Dimitri for himself, he could understand why. The man was straight out of central casting for a B-grade vampire movie.

Casey's pistol was stowed in the gym bag he carried. He'd grown up hunting game on the family ranch, and he was a good shot. If Dimitri threatened Val when he was around, the bastard would be dead meat.

They didn't speak of what had happened until after Tess had left to go to dinner with Shane and Lexie. Only when they were alone did he pull Val close. He held her fiercely.

For the first few moments, she stood rigid in his arms; then she slowly softened against him, her body molding to his. "He was there again tonight," she said.

"I know. I saw him." His lips brushed a path along her hairline. "It's all right. I'm here now."

"But you can't always be here." Pulling back a little, she looked up at him. The fire that blazed in her eyes gave him a glimpse of the wild, fearless girl he'd once fallen in love with. "I did some hard thinking while you were in the arena," she said. "I can't let Dimitri control my fear. I have to find a way to beat him at the mental games he plays."

"His game is death. And you told me that Halvorsen wouldn't protect you. The best you can do is get out of here with your family. Go home to the ranch. Keep a shotgun by the door, and if he shows up on the property, blast him to kingdom come."

"You make it sound so simple. But I'd still have Lanzoni's friends to worry about. And I really should do my civic duty and testify."

"Too bad you can't just tell Lanzoni's goons that Dimitri and Duvall are plotting against their boss. That way, they could take each other out."

"Great idea. But I'm not supposed to know about that. And there's nobody I could trust. If I told the wrong people, they could take me out instead."

Casey sighed. This was going nowhere. "Hungry?" he asked. "How long's it been since you had a decent meal?"

"I had an energy bar." She could barely remember when.

"That doesn't count. Come on. I know where to find a couple of rare steaks with our names on them. And no talking about you-know-who for the rest of the night. Deal?"

"Deal." She gave him her hand and let him lead her to the truck.

By the time they drove back to Casey's hotel room, it was almost midnight. Feeling more relaxed than she had in days, Val sat as close to him as the truck's console would allow, her head resting lightly against his shoulder.

This was just what she'd needed. Great food and easy conversation. He'd told her stories about his career as a bullfighter, the bulls he'd handled and the riders he'd known. In turn, she'd given him a bright-side version of her time in Hollywood, vignettes about the very human celebrities she'd met and the movies she'd made. Leaving out the scandals, the heartaches, the over-bearing men, the wild parties, and the shattered dreams, she'd kept Casey amused until the crème brûlée was finished and the check paid.

They hadn't mentioned Val's troubles with the Las Vegas mob, but after leaving the restaurant, Casey took a long way home, cir-cling blocks and cutting through on side streets. He said nothing, but Val knew he was making sure they weren't being followed.

The hotel room was still chilly, but at least Val had expected it. When she came out of the bathroom, wearing Casey's long, baggy tee, without the panties this time, she saw that he'd laid the extra blanket over the quilt and climbed into bed to warm the sheets for her. The lights were off except for the bedside lamp. Her pulse gave a little skip of anticipation. No games to-night. She wanted him.

Lying back against the pillows, Casey watched her, smiling as she turned off the bathroom light and walked toward the bed. "You don't really need that old shirt," he said. "I can keep you plenty warm, I promise."

Val's heart dropped. She forced a smile. "It's not just that. I'm not seventeen anymore. My body's changed. I'm self-conscious about the way I look."

"I can't imagine you wouldn't look beautiful," he said. "But all right. If you feel uncomfortable, we'll turn off the light." He reached over and switched off the lamp. The room went dark ex-cept for the distant glow of city lights through the trees outside. "All right?"

"All right." Knowing that resistance would only exacerbate the issue, Val slipped off the shirt and dropped it next to the bed, where she'd be able to find it later. She didn't want to worry about her scars. All she wanted to think about was loving Casey.

"Come here." He lifted the covers, giving her room to slide in beside him. The bed was warm, his naked, muscular body even warmer as he held her in his arms. They lay skin to skin, breast to breast, the sensations that flowed between them as old as memory.

They'd been so young, so much in love, but she'd gone away and spoiled it forever. To feel all that again, even for one night, and even if it involved a lie, was more than she deserved. She would pay the price in guilt. But right now, nothing mattered except being here, with him.

He kissed her, taking his time, using his tongue to tantalize and tease her. She felt his heartbeat quicken, felt him rise and harden against her as their tongues played games. When her hand moved down to clasp his solid shaft, his breath caught for an instant. Then he chuckled. "Eager little devil, aren't you? But I'm not in a hurry to give you what you want. I'm going to drive you crazy first."

Rolling her onto her back, he shifted above her. His lips grazed downward, skimming her throat to settle lightly on her breast. Cupping her with a hand, he drew a nipple into his mouth. As he suckled her, the delicious ache triggered a clenching need in the depths of her body.

"Casey—"

"*Sshh* . . ." He paused, then moved downward, taking it slow, his hands skimming her belly, his mouth . . . oh, his mouth . . .

She moaned as spasms shook her body, her head falling back, her fingers raking his hair. At some point he must've added protection, but she was barely aware of it. She was still spiraling back to earth when he entered her, gliding in hard and deep. Wrapping him with her legs, she matched his thrusts, the raw sweetness rising in her to burst into exploding stars that ebbed away until only stardust remained.

Rolling to one side, he spooned her against him. She closed her eyes, completely his, as she would always be in her heart of hearts. But even now she sensed that their time was coming to an end.

"Val?" His voice was a breath in her ear. "Why didn't you tell me you'd had a baby?"

She didn't speak. Couldn't.

"The scars," he said. "I could feel them. You had a C-section. What happened? Where's the baby now?"

She found her voice. "Happy, I hope, with his adoptive parents.

I was young and alone. I didn't want an abortion, but I knew I wasn't equipped to raise a child. I did what I believed was best for my baby. I still believe it was best."

"And the father?"

Her pulse lurched, but she answered calmly. "He never knew. But even if he had, it wouldn't have worked out."

"He was married?" There was an edge to Casey's voice.

"It doesn't matter anymore. It was years ago. I've closed that book. All right?"

"All right." He sighed, pulling her closer, brushing a kiss over her bare shoulder. "I'm sorry, Val. No more questions. I was just trying to understand you."

"Then let me give you a bonus." Val took a breath. Now that he knew about the scars, he needed to know this, too. "There were complications with the delivery. The doctors had to do a C-section to save the baby. Then they had to save me. They did all they could, but the bottom line is . . ." She paused. "I can't have more children. Ever."

He was silent for what seemed like a long time. Then his arms tightened around her. "I'm so sorry, Val," he said. "That must've been awful for you. Do your sisters know?"

"They don't know anything. And I want your promise not to tell them. I've put my past behind me, and I don't want them bringing it up or talking about it behind my back. I only told you because you wanted to know why I can't go on seeing you."

"Well." He nibbled the back of her neck. "You've answered my question, and I'm still here. I don't give a damn about your past. I just want more of the present. Where we are right now seems like a good place to start."

"You don't understand. I'm broken, Casey. More deeply broken than you know."

"I wouldn't mind a chance to help pick up the pieces. But let's go to sleep now. We're both done in. We can sort this out later when we're not so tired."

"Fine." She was already drifting.

"You know I wouldn't stick around if you didn't want me," he said. "I've got too much male pride for that. But you didn't exactly fight me off tonight. That tells me something."

Val heard his words, but she didn't reply. Pretending to be asleep was easier than telling him the whole truth—the truth that would tear them apart forever.

Tess opened her eyes at first light. She'd always been an early riser. Even here in the neon jungle of Las Vegas, that habit hadn't changed. After taking a moment to stretch, she swung out of bed, strode into the bathroom, and splashed her face with cold water. She'd showered and washed her hair last night. All she needed to do this morning was brush her teeth, throw on her work clothes, grab some coffee downstairs, and head for the arena, where her bulls were waiting to be fed.

With her coffee in a Styrofoam cup, she stepped out into the chilly gray morning. The thin light gave the city, known for its glamour, a faded, shabby look. The air smelled of cigarette smoke and diesel fumes. A departing plane from nearby McCarran International Airport roared low overhead and vanished into the clouds. The breeze sent a white plastic bag dancing across the parking lot.

The last time Tess had been in Las Vegas was for the previous year's National Finals Rodeo. That was when Jack had died. She'd hated the city then, and she didn't like it much better now. In spite of the good things that had happened here this season, she couldn't wait to be on the road. But even if Whiplash hadn't been chosen as a reride bull for tonight, they couldn't leave until after the finals. Shane was still working as a commentator and clearly loving it. There was no way they could take the SUV, which was customized for his wheelchair, and drive home without him.

Still sipping her coffee, Tess walked around to the back of the arena, where the bulls were kept. Whiplash and Whirlwind had been left together last night in their pen near the rear of the complex. Their bagged chow was stored in the trailer. She would need to get a new bag out, but first, Tess decided, she would check on the bulls.

At this early hour, the place was quiet. A few people were tending to their bulls with more wandering in. There was no guard at the security gate, but that didn't seem to be a reason for concern.

Even at a distance, however, Tess could see that something wasn't right. Her two bulls were milling in their pen, lowing and banging against the rails as if something had upset them. Lengthening her stride, she passed through the unattended gate and hurried down the row of pens.

Neither Whirlwind nor Whiplash appeared to be hurt. But when she noticed the bloody streak along Whiplash's horn and the crimson spatters on his chest, Tess knew something terrible had happened. Only when she looked over the rails and down into the pen did she see what it was.

Her knees went weak. She fought back a wave of nausea as she reached for her phone. She knew she'd have to call the police. But first she scrolled to Casey's cell number. He answered on the second ring.

"Tess?" He sounded sleepy but came to full alert when he heard her voice. "What's the matter?"

"Something's happened. Get here as soon as you can. Bring Val."

"Can you tell me what it is?"

"Just come."

CHAPTER TWELVE

*B*Y THE TIME VAL AND CASEY REACHED THE ARENA, THE ALARM HAD
been raised. The police were on their way. Two chute men had
been roused to come and move the bulls to a holding pen. Clay
Rafferty had been called. Minutes from now, the place would become a bedlam of activity.

But Val and Casey, arriving uncombed and hastily dressed, had
made it there soon enough to view the scene exactly as Tess had
found it.

Val walked to the rails. The bulls were snorting and blowing,
tossing their heads, and rolling their eyes. She didn't know as
much about bulls as her sisters did, but to her they appeared
more frightened than angry. The smears of blood on Whiplash
made her throat go tight, almost choking off her breath, but she
didn't see the worst thing until she forced herself to look down
into the pen.

Sprawled facedown on the blood-soaked wood chips was a broken body clad in the ripped, stained uniform of a security guard.
The lanky frame, the greasy black hair—even without seeing his
acne-scarred face, Val had no doubt who the man was.

She willed herself to stay calm. She'd seen violent death before.
But she couldn't shake the sick feeling that the body's presence
was meant to be some kind of message—for her.

"I know him," she said.

"I think we all do," Casey said. "His first name was Gary, but I don't know his last name, let alone what happened to him. I can't believe he'd go into the pen on his own. He knew the bulls were dangerous."

"Which means he could've been forced in or killed and thrown in," Tess said. "Let's hope the crime scene people will be able to tell us."

"Are the bulls all right?" It was Lexie, rushing in, out of breath and close to tears. Clad in blue sweats, her blond hair tousled, she'd evidently left Shane in the room. "Oh—oh no!" She pressed against the rails, staring into the pen. "Whiplash has blood on him. Do you think he killed that poor man?"

The others fell silent. The question she'd asked had been on all their minds. But she was first to give it voice.

"We don't know yet." Val put her arms around her sister. Lexie was shivering beneath the thin sweatshirt. "We're waiting to find out what happened."

Two police cruisers and a white crime scene van pulled up outside the gate. By then, the two chute men had arrived. They began rigging the gates to move the bulls out of the pen.

Tess turned away, needing to put food and water in the holding pen before the bulls were moved. "Let me do that," Casey offered. "Since you're the one who discovered him, the police will want to talk to you first."

"Thanks." Tess handed him her keys. "Their food's in the trailer. Take the spare feeder tubs, too. We won't be able to get to the ones they were using in their pen."

The CSI team threw up stakes and yellow tape, leaving a space by the opening to the pen. Someone began shooting pictures with a flash. Still comforting Lexie, now wrapped in Casey's jacket, Val moved out of the way as a middle-aged detective began taking statements.

By the time he'd finished interviewing Tess and Lexie, who'd left to go back to the hotel, the gates had been set up to transfer the bulls. Whirlwind and Whiplash bolted out of the pen as if they couldn't wait to get away from the awful dead thing lying at their feet. Only the two bulls knew the truth about what had happened in their pen last night. They would keep the secret in their bullish memories for the rest of their lives.

Tess watched over them as they were herded into the holding pen. She stayed to make sure they were eating and drinking. Casey had gone to move his truck out of the loading area.

"Have you checked the security cameras?" the portly, middle-aged detective sergeant asked the young woman acting as his partner.

"No luck. They don't cover everywhere. This corner of the compound is out of range."

"Then we won't likely know whether it's a homicide or a damn fool accident until we get him to the medical examiner." He swung toward to the CSI team, who'd moved into the empty pen. "Turn him over. We already know he was a security guard. Maybe we'll learn something new."

Val, waiting to be interviewed, forced herself to watch without flinching as the guard was eased onto his back. His scarred face was battered and bloodied but clearly recognizable.

"I'll be damned," the detective said. "I know that bird. His name's Gary Malfa. He's a part-time runner for the Lanzoni gang. Probably did a lot of his business here in the arena. Take some pictures, then cover him up and leave him for the medical examiner. While we're waiting for him, I want every inch of the pen and the area around it gone over."

Reeling from what she'd heard, Val waited while the body was photographed. Was there a link between the guard's death and her ties to Lanzoni? Finding his body with her family's bulls seemed like more than a coincidence. It could be a threat or a warning. But it hardly seemed reason to kill a man.

She remembered when she'd taken a cab to the DA's office. She'd told the guard to let Tess know that she was going on an errand. At the time, leaving word with him had seemed harmless enough. But if Malfa had been told to watch her, getting the cab's number and tracing its route would've been easy enough. Lanzoni had connections everywhere. Even the cab drivers could've been in his pay. It had been careless of her not to realize that.

But why was Gary Malfa dead?

"I'm ready to take your statement, Miss Champion." The gray-ing detective sergeant, whose ID badge showed his last name as Davenport, had the weary look of a man who'd seen it all.

Could she trust him? But what choice did she have?

"I'm ready," she said. "But is there someplace more private where we can talk? I might be able to offer you some insights into why this happened."

He led her toward the parking lot, stopping next to the empty security station, which was out of hearing, but not out of sight. "This'll have to do," he said. "I need to keep an eye on things. Now what is it you've got to tell me?"

Val kept her story simple, telling the detective only what she thought he needed to know—that she'd been a witness to one of Lanzoni's hired executions and was under pressure to testify to the grand jury. She left out the part about the power struggle within Lanzoni's crime family, which had been told to her in confidence.

"So you think what happened here was meant as a warning against your testifying?"

"It's possible. Lanzoni's people have been stalking me ever since my family got here. I don't know how the guard died, or why. But there has to be a reason his body ended up in the pen with our bulls."

"Would Malfa have known you were a possible witness?"

"I certainly didn't tell him. But somebody else could have."

"So why do you think they haven't tried to kill you?"

"I've wondered the same thing. Maybe the murder of a witness would be too easy to trace back to Lanzoni's people."

Even if Lanzoni's people didn't do it. The thought struck her, leaving a chill. That plan could work for Dimitri—kill her and find a way to pin her death on his rival. She felt the weight of the pistol in her purse. She would need to keep it with her and be prepared to use it.

"Sergeant! Come look at this!" One of the CSI team called Davenport over. Val followed, keeping her distance but staying close enough to hear.

"Look." The CSI technician pointed with a gloved hand. "There on the top rail. It's smeared with blood. What's your guess?"

Davenport examined the smear. "Assuming it's the guard's, I'd guess one of two things. Either his body was lifted and pushed over the rail, already bloodied, or he was in the pen and grabbed the rail trying to climb out. Either way, it's not a pretty picture, and there's a helluva lot we don't know. The medical examiner should be here any minute. Maybe he'll be able to give us some answers."

The holding pen for the bulls was within sight of the crime scene. Val moved back to join Tess. As she came around the corner of the pen, she could see the bulls. Whirlwind was eating, but Whiplash was still spooked—snorting, pawing, and rolling his eyes to show the whites.

Tess was talking with an older man in jeans, a western shirt, and a blazer. Val recognized Clay Rafferty, Director of Livestock for the PBR.

"What if Whiplash killed that poor man?" Tess was on the verge of tears. "Would he have to be put down?"

"I'd certainly argue against it," Rafferty said. "He's a bull. Plenty of bulls I know would attack a stranger who invaded their territory, and even kill them, given the chance. It's like these news stories you read where some idiot walks into the tiger exhibit at the zoo. What they get is what they asked for. It's not the tiger's fault."

"But what about handling Whiplash—and riding him? Look at him. He hasn't even touched his food. Will he be fit to buck tonight—or ever again, for that matter?"

Rafferty took a long look at the agitated bull, his eyes narrowing. "That depends. An angry bull can make for an exciting ride. But if he's been traumatized, that's something else. That might be the case with Whiplash. Let's watch him through the day. If he's not doing better by this evening, I'll take him out of the reride lineup for his own good."

"Thanks," Tess said. "I really appreciate your showing up at this hour."

"Just doing my job," Rafferty said. "Right now, if you'll excuse me, I need to go over and talk to the police. That's part of my job, too. If I find out anything important, I'll let you know. I'm hoping we can keep this out of the press for now."

Casey had come back to stand with the sisters. "Are you two all right?" he asked.

"Fine. Just in shock," Tess said.

"And Lexie?"

"She went back to the hotel to be with Shane. She'll be all right."

"And these boys?" He glanced back at the bulls.

"Whirlwind seems okay, and there's no blood on him. But Whiplash is still out of sorts. If he hasn't calmed down by tonight, there's no chance he'll be bucking. I wish these bulls could talk and tell us what happened."

"Can we hose that blood off Whiplash? The smell might be upsetting him."

"I mentioned that. But the detective wants to wait until they can collect a sample of the blood, to make sure it's the guard's."

"Good luck with that." Casey shook his head. "I'm guessing they'll need some kind of long pole with a swab on the end."

"I hate to think that man was killed because of me." Val spoke up after a brief silence. "But why else would he have been dumped with our bulls? I told the detective enough to put him on alert. But all I really want is to go home. It isn't safe here."

"My vote would be to leave tonight, after the finals," Tess said. "We could go sooner, but Shane will be doing commentary. And if Whiplash is fit to buck, he deserves his chance, too. We can have the vehicle gassed, the trailer hitched, and be ready to load the bulls as soon as the show's over. If we drive all night, we could be back at the ranch tomorrow morning. What do you think, Val?"

Val exchanged glances with Casey, knowing what her answer would mean. Her family's safety had to come first. And spending one more night in his hotel room would only complicate things between them. "You've got my vote," she said. "Now we just need to make sure the plan is okay with Lexie and Shane."

"It will be when we explain the reason." Tess looked back toward the yellow-taped crime scene, where the technicians were still collecting evidence. Val followed the direction of her gaze. A woman in gray coveralls was bent over the body, probing and bagging samples as she spoke with Rafferty, who stood outside the tape line.

After a short conversation, Rafferty turned away and came back to where Val, Tess, and Casey waited by the holding pen.

"Interesting," he said. "The medical examiner says she won't know everything until she gets the body back to the morgue. It does appear that the guard was tossed and trampled by a bull, which would explain the blood on Whiplash. But there was evidence of other wounds—wounds that a bull couldn't have made. He'd been punched with brass knuckles, kicked with heavy-soled boots, and whacked with some kind of metal rod, like a pipe or a crowbar, hard enough to break bones. There were ligature marks on his arms, like he'd been tied. In other words, he'd been beaten to death, or close to it, before he was dumped in the pen with the bulls."

Custom job. The words sent a shudder through Val's body. She knew a man who'd kill like that for a price, or maybe for his own gain. But the question remained—*why?*

"So does that mean Whiplash didn't kill the man?" Tess asked.

"The medical examiner said she wouldn't know the actual cause of death until the autopsy," Rafferty said. "But I don't think anybody's going to blame Whiplash for normal bull behavior. Let's just hope that poor bastard was already dead when his body was shoved over the rail."

Casey slipped a supporting arm around Val's shoulders. Val was scarcely aware of him. As one of the CSI team arrived with a pole rigged to get a blood sample off Whiplash, she felt the contents of her stomach roiling like a miniature tempest.

"I think I'm going to be sick," she muttered, pulling away from

Casey. Feeling the signs, she fled into the building and hurried up the stairs. The nearest women's restroom was on the concourse. Her need wasn't urgent yet, but she could feel it building. If she was going to throw up, she wanted to do it someplace clean and private.

At this morning hour, the concourse was empty except for a few workers giving the place a final cleaning before tonight's event. Clutching her purse, she raced toward the nearest ladies' room. She made it through the door and into a stall just in time.

Once her stomach was emptied, Val began to feel better. She had wiped her face, flushed, and was about to leave the stall when she happened to glance beneath the door. Looking down at an angle, she could just see a pair of legs, clad in the khaki-colored pants the workers wore. This was the women's restroom. But one of the men could have come in, thinking the place was vacant.

"Hello," she said, speaking up. "I'm in here. I'll be right out."

There was no reply. That was when Val noticed something else—the black custom-made kidskin loafers showing just below the pantlegs. Shoes no workman would wear. Shoes she recognized.

Terror flashed alarms along her nerves. She should have known he'd be somewhere nearby, watching people react to his kill. She should have known, as well, that he'd seen her take off alone, and that he would follow her.

Now he had her cornered. Maybe he only wanted to talk. But she couldn't take that chance.

Flushing the toilet again to hide any suspicious sounds, she opened her purse and slipped the small pistol out of its holster. It was Tess's gun. Val had never fired it. But she knew the magazine was loaded and how to pull a trigger. She could only hope she wouldn't have to use it.

With the pistol in her hand, she slid back the bolt and gave the stall door a hard shove.

As the door swung open, Dimitri jumped back, out of the way. But by the time she'd stepped out of the stall, he'd recovered his icy poise. He wasn't holding a weapon, but Val could be sure he had one on him.

Glancing at the pistol, he gave her a slow smile. "Hello, Valerie. Are you planning to shoot me with that little gun?" He had a voice like the purr of a tiger, deep and mellifluous. The sound of it had always raised gooseflesh on her skin.

"I'll shoot you if I have to," she said. "I'd kill you before I'd let you hurt my family."

His tongue clicked with a soft *tsk* sound. "Valerie, Valerie, is that any way to talk to an old friend? You're as beautiful as ever. I always thought so. But you never seemed to like me. You were always hanging on to that loser, Lenny."

"This isn't about Lenny. What do you want, Dimitri?"

"Only to say hello. And to ask you why you went to the DA instead of trusting my friend Duvall."

"Duvall lied to me. He even lied about his name."

"And yet, when you saw him again, you pretended not to know about that. So you were lying, too. You can't be trusted, my darling. And now you know things you weren't meant to know. Too bad."

Val's resolve hardened. She knew now that he intended to kill her. It was just a question of when and how, and whether she could shoot him first.

Dimitri kept himself in superb condition, and his hands were lightning fast. She'd seen him do parlor tricks to show off their speed. An instant's hesitation on her part, and he could snatch the gun from her, leaving her helpless.

Then what? Shooting her, even with a silencer, could attract the attention of the workers. But that wouldn't stop him. Lenny had told her how he'd seen Dimitri kill a man simply by twisting his head to break his neck. Unless her timing was perfect, she was as good as dead.

But every man had an Achilles heel. Dimitri's was his vanity. Get him talking—that could be her only chance to distract him.

"I saw your handiwork this morning," she said. "Very clever. Beat a man to a pulp and then let the bulls finish the job. Only a master could come up with that."

"But what made you think it was me?" Val could tell he was pleased. "Did you find evidence, perhaps?"

"Of course not. You never leave evidence. I know your work. That killing had your technique written all over it. With so many bulls to choose from, why would you pick my family's?"

"Why not?" He shrugged, a smile playing around his thin-lipped slash of a mouth. "That big brindle of yours is a mean brute. I'd seen him in the arena. I figured he could do the job. And of course, we wanted you to know what happens to people who betray us—as you have already done, my lovely."

His words sent a chill down Val's spine. The pistol, small as it was, was getting heavy. Her hand was beginning to quiver.

"What about that poor guard?" she asked. "The detective told me he was working for Lanzoni. He was just a drug runner—a no-body. Why him—and why kill him in such an awful way?"

"Why him?" Dimitri's expression darkened. "He was a cop."

Val gripped the pistol harder to keep from dropping it. Hal-vorsen had mentioned a man working under deep cover, but she would never have guessed the truth. "I can't believe you, Dimitri," she said, deliberately baiting him. "What if you were wrong? What if he was just some poor, dumb flunky?"

Dimitri's expression hardened into a rictus of hate. "He was a *cop*! A dirty, stinking, lying *cop*!" Turning his head slightly to aim, he spat on the floor of the restroom.

Val pulled the trigger.

The gunshot echoed in the confined space. She saw him stag-ger, clutching his wounded shoulder, his features contorted in shock and fury.

Still clutching the gun, she turned and ran out of the restroom onto the concourse. "Help! Help me!" she screamed as she ran. Her voice carried around the curved space. Two burly-looking custodians came running in response.

"A man—he came in to kill me—back there in the ladies' room," she gasped. "Don't go in there. He's wounded, but he might have a gun. Here." She thrust the pistol into the smaller man's hand. "Guard the door. Keep him in there. I'm going to get help."

As the men headed back around the concourse to the rest-room, Val found the doorway to the stairs. It was locked, as it had been a few nights before. She was frantically rattling the bar when the door burst open. Alerted by the gunshot, Davenport, his part-ner, and Casey burst onto the concourse.

"Around there—in the restroom—" Breathless, she pointed them in the right direction. "It's Dimitri. He's wounded. Be careful."

Davenport and the woman, pistols drawn, raced on. Casey paused long enough to catch Val in his arms. "Are you all right?" he demanded.

"I'm fine. I shot him, but I didn't kill him."

For a long moment, she let him hold her, clinging to his strength. "Damn it, Val, you could've been killed," he muttered. "What were you doing with a gun?"

"It doesn't matter now." Pulling away, she caught his hand. "Come on!"

They came around the concourse to find the two workmen standing outside the open door of the restroom. Davenport and his partner had evidently gone inside.

Even before she went in to look, Val knew what to expect. The seconds it had taken for her to find the workmen, and for them to get back to the restroom, had given Dimitri enough time to get away. There was nothing to be seen inside except some scattered paper towels and a crimson smear of blood on the tile floor.

By midafternoon, Whiplash's surly nature was returning. The blood had been hosed from his horn and coat, and he was wolf-ing down his food. After a once-over by the on-site PBR veterinar-ian, Clay Rafferty had pronounced him fit to buck if a reride was needed.

Detective Sergeant Davenport had passed the word from the medical examiner that Gary Malfa—not his real name—had died before his body was tossed into the bull pen. Not that it made much difference, but at least it came as a relief to know that Whiplash hadn't killed him.

The police had used every means to track down Dimitri, including an alert to hospitals and clinics to report any man with a bullet wound in his right shoulder. But Dimitri had vanished like a puff of smoke.

Val wasn't at all surprised. The Las Vegas underground was a world in itself, with access to luxury hideouts, expert medical care, vehicles, private jets, forged passports, and anything else a man of Dimitri's status might need.

Knowing Dimitri, once he was strong enough to travel, he would probably fly to some tropical resort to rest and finish healing away from the law. Val knew better than to think she'd seen the last of him.

Whether she testified against Lanzoni or not, she was still the one witness who could link Dimitri to Lenny's murder. And now she'd heard him confess that he'd knowingly killed an undercover policeman—a capital crime in Nevada, a state that enforced the death penalty.

He had bragged about the crime because he'd been about to kill her.

Not only had she escaped, she'd given him a painful and dangerous wound. For a man like Dimitri, being bested by a mere woman was the crowning humiliation.

For now, Dimitri was gone. But he would be back. And when he returned, he would be coming for her.

CHAPTER THIRTEEN

*I*N THE LOCKER ROOM, CASEY STRAPPED ON HIS BODY ARMOR AND slipped over his head the baggy shirt displaying the logo of the night's sponsor. Not only did the loose-hanging shirt allow freedom of movement, it also provided a larger target for the bulls, who would go for the shirt and be less likely to hook the man inside.

As he bent to tighten his sneakers and double-knot the laces, he could hear a big-name country music band blasting its show over the speakers while the fans swarmed into their seats. Tonight the place would be packed to the rafters for rounds five and six of the PBR World Finals. Only ten riders were left in competition. These cowboys would be riding the best bulls in the world, battling it out for the title and a million dollars in prize money.

As he stretched, preparing himself physically and mentally for the night ahead, Casey struggled to block the memory of what had happened that morning. Val had nearly been killed, and he hadn't been there to protect her. Only her own quick actions had saved her life.

Tonight she'd promised to stay close to her family, but he still worried about her. Dimitri might be gone for now, but there were other threats that could turn up anytime. Even going home to the ranch wouldn't guarantee her safety.

He'd spent part of the afternoon helping Tess and Val shovel out the trailer, replace the straw bedding, gas up the SUV, and make sure the hitch was secure. Their luggage was already in the vehicle. As soon as the event was over, they planned to load the bulls and make the overnight drive back to their ranch in the high mountain valley that bordered the Tohono O'odham reservation.

As a boy, Casey had spent happy times on the Alamo Canyon Ranch with Jack, riding, shooting, exploring, getting into boyish mischief, and slowly falling in love with Jack's fiery sister. He hadn't been back to the ranch since Jack's funeral. Today as they were readying the trailer, Tess had invited him to come for a visit. Casey, who owned a condo in nearby Tucson, had made his excuses. He would have welcomed the chance to visit, but only if Val invited him.

She hadn't done so. In fact, she'd pretty much left him dangling, with no mention of when they might get together again. Even after they'd made love, she'd insisted that they couldn't go on seeing each other, but he'd assumed that he could change her mind. Clearly, he'd assumed wrong.

"Wake up, Romeo!" Marcus, his teammate, snapped his fingers under Casey's nose. "I know you're probably dreaming about that hot redhead I've seen you with. The opening ceremony's started and as soon as it's done, we're on."

As he followed Joel and Marcus out of the locker room and down to the bucking chutes, Casey could hear the strains of the national anthem. It was time to put his personal worries aside and focus on his job.

In an out-of-the-way spot next to the stands, Val waited for the first chute to open. From where she stood, she could see Casey poised and ready to spring into action. Maybe this time she could bring herself to watch him. As the first bull, a 2,000-pound tan monster, came barreling out of the chute like a charging rhinoceros, she had to avert her gaze. When she looked again, the rider had been bucked off and was walking out with his head down. The bull was doing a victory lap around the shark cage with the roper closing in. Casey was untouched, but Val's nerves were in tatters. Earlier in the day she'd stood up to a professional killer and sent him running with a bullet in his shoulder. But when it came to watching the love of her life fling himself into the face of an animal that could kill him with a blow of its horns or hooves, she was fresh out of courage.

Turning away, she headed back toward the pens. She'd scanned the crowd as the arena filled, half expecting to see Duvall, or one of the men she remembered from her time with Lenny, sitting in Dimitri's place. The seat was empty. But Val knew she wouldn't take an easy breath until she, her family, and the bulls had left Las Vegas far behind.

For now, she would go back to the pens, find her sister, and do her best not to let her nervous state of mind rain on Tess's parade.

She found Tess with the bulls. Whirlwind and Whiplash were together in the holding pen where they'd been left earlier. Whirlwind was chewing his cud, but Whiplash was still restless, snorting, pawing, and raking the wood chips with his horns.

"Is he all right?" Val asked.

"He's just letting off steam." Tess knew her bulls better than anyone. "But I hope he settles down before we have to load him in the trailer."

"So you don't expect him to buck tonight?"

"I'd bet against it. I know he's been cleared. But the bulls bucking tonight are pros. They know how to get the job done. There's not much chance of anybody needing a reride."

"And if there is a chance? What if something happens?" Val asked.

"For these final rounds, the rider will get a choice of reride bulls. With a championship on the line, why should he choose a rookie three-year-old who's never been successfully ridden?"

"It could happen. You never know."

"When did you become the queen of optimism? Are you by any chance in love?"

The sudden change in subject rocked Val. She knew the answer to Tess's question. But not all love was reason to celebrate. And not all love stories had happy endings—as Tess herself had learned when her fiancé was killed on deployment in the Middle East.

"When Casey was helping us today, I invited him to come and spend time at the ranch," Tess said. "I thought he'd enjoy it, and that you might, too. But he said he had plans. It sounded like he was making excuses. What's going on between the two of you, Val?"

"Nothing permanent, if that's what you mean. The sizzle is still there—we've proven that. But forget about a happily ever after. There's too much water under the bridge, as Callie used to say." Their stepmother had never hesitated to offer advice. "Casey deserves an uncomplicated woman who'll love him and make him happy. That woman isn't me."

"I'm sorry. I always thought the two of you were perfect for each other."

"There might be some truth to that. The trouble is, we were never on the same page at the same time. When Casey wanted to get married and settle down, I couldn't wait to try my wings. And now we've both moved on. We're not just on different pages— we're in different books."

Val couldn't remember if she and Tess had ever talked like this. They were so different from each other. They'd never been close growing up. They still weren't close. But maybe, given time, that could change.

"What do you really want, Val?" Tess asked.

"To stay alive. To stay physically and mentally healthy. Right now, that seems enough of a challenge."

"I don't mean just now, but for your life. You know you're welcome to stay on the ranch. It's your home. But can you be happy there?"

"I don't know yet." Val paused to think about her reply. "I'll only stay if I can earn my keep, even if it means mucking out the stable. The last thing you need is a nonpaying houseguest."

"What if it isn't enough for you?"

"I suppose I'll cross that bridge when I come to it."

"And Casey?"

Val looked away, in the direction of the arena, where a roar had just gone up from the fans. "That bridge is already crossed—and burned."

Casey dodged sideways, the massive horns coming close enough to catch his shirt. The bull, a black giant named Bombs Away, was new to the finals, and he was rank. After dumping his rider in six seconds, he'd galloped over the top of him, then caught Marcus and sent him flying over his head. As Joel protected the rider, the bull turned back, and Casey slapped his nose to get his attention while the roper got the lariat on his horns and guided him to the gate.

Marcus was already on his feet, but the rider was doubled over on the dirt, clearly in pain. Broken ribs, Casey surmised, having seen enough injuries to recognize the signs. The medical team was rushing into the ring to surround him and carry him out on a stretcher.

Injuries were expected in what was arguably the most dangerous sport on earth. Football was a contact sport. Bull riding was more like a collision sport. Seasoned riders like R.J. McClintock had been taped, splinted, braced, and stapled so many times that they'd probably lost track, but they kept coming back for the rush and the thrill of competition.

Casey's job as a bullfighter was anything but competitive. There was no glory in it, no trophies or over-the-top prize money. But the rush was as potent as a high. When he was in the arena, using his focus and his skill to protect the riders, he was completely in his element. It was the best—almost as good as making love to a beautiful woman.

Almost.

The memory of last night with Val flashed through his mind. But it was only a flash. The next chute was opening. The rider was

José Gilberto on Road Warrior, a nine-year-old yellow bull, one of the great ones, an animal Casey had faced many times. Gilberto rode him masterfully for eighty-eight points, landing the dismount on his feet. Road Warrior, an old pro, swung toward the exit gate and trotted out.

Round five had ended.

After some hijinks from Sam Callahan, the final round would begin. A rider's standing was based on total points earned over the season of premier events, not just his rides here at the finals. A cowboy with a substantial lead going in could buck off and still have a good chance to win. But Gilberto and McClintock were in a near tie for first place, with the twenty-year-old Texan Cody Woodbine in third. With the scores so close, every ride was critical.

Casey guzzled a bottle of Gatorade and doused his face and hair with water. Glancing behind the chutes, he couldn't see Tess or Val. But this round was the climax of the PBR season. Surely they'd be watching it.

Seven riders had scored high enough to survive the previous round. Seven outs wouldn't take long. Then it would be all over but the celebration for the new world champion—the presentation on the shark cage, the silver cup, the solid gold buckle, the giant-size check, the flames, lights, and pretty women in low-cut jeans and skimpy black tops. Casey had seen it all before. This time he would probably miss out. He'd offered to help Tess and Val load the bulls into the trailer and have everything ready to go when Shane and Lexie finished at the press table.

And then what? When the rig's taillights vanished toward the I-15 onramp, would Val be out of his life once more, this time for good?

If she didn't want to see him again, he would respect her wishes. Casey had never chased after a woman in his life, and he wasn't about to start—not even if that woman was Val. But it was going to hurt like hell to see her go. Damn her, why did she have to show up, share his bed, and bring back all the old urges only to leave again? And, damn him, why had he been fool enough to let her?

It was time for the final round to start. Casey slicked back his wet hair, jammed his hat on his head, and strode out to take his place with his team.

This was the moment PBR fans lived for. The best buckers, the best cowboys, the highest stakes, and glory or disaster riding with every opening of the chute. For as long as Casey had been part of the protection team, he'd enjoyed it to the fullest. But this time it was as if the glow had faded. Something was missing. Maybe it was his heart.

The first two rides were buck-offs. With some dodging and herding, Casey's team got the bulls headed in the right direction. Climbing on his bull in chute number three was Cody Woodbine.

Currently in third place, the young cowboy had just one possible chance of a win—a spectacular score for this ride and buck-offs for both Gilberto and McClintock, who'd be riding last.

The odds of it happening were almost zero. But bull riders lived on hope, and Woodbine was no exception.

He had a good bull. Thunderball, an 1,800-pound white-faced black, was a reliable bucker who'd run up some high scores. As Woodbine gave the nod and the chute swung open, Casey found himself rooting for the plucky young man.

The seconds ticked past. Woodbine was riding well, great control, perfect position. Then something went wrong. As Thunderball made a forward lunge, his front leg buckled. He went down on one knee and rolled to the side. Woodbine sprang free in time to save himself. The bull scrambled to his feet and headed for the exit. By then, the red reride flag was out. Woodbine would get his chance on another bull.

Casey didn't expect it to be Whiplash. The other bulls were good buckers, and Whiplash, even though he'd been cleared, was still unpredictable. If Woodbine were to choose him for the reride, he'd be taking a chance, perhaps a dangerous one. Only if the young cowboy felt he had nothing to lose would he make such a reckless choice.

There wouldn't be much time to get the bull in place. The two leaders would ride last, which meant that Woodbine would be riding fifth. Bull number four was already being mounted, with McClintock's and Gilberto's bulls prepped and ready.

The next rider was bucked off, but the bull wasn't finished. He put up a fight before being roped and herded out of the arena. When Casey had a moment to look at the chutes again, he saw an immense brindled shape behind the rails, shifting, head-tossing, and trying to buck as Cody Woodbine lowered himself into the chute.

Heaven help them all, it was Whiplash.

Val had stayed with Tess as Whiplash was rushed into the narrow preparation pen and, with the help of the chute men, fitted with a flank strap. The big brindle was resisting the whole time, snorting and bucking, his horns clattering against the rails.

Tess had given the strap a final check. "This is your moment, big guy," she'd said, patting his side. "Go out there and show them your stuff."

Now, as Val stood up front with Tess, waiting for the chute to open, she could feel her sister's excitement. Tess was focused on her bull's performance and what a spectacular ride could do for the ranch. But all Val could feel was the worry that gnawed at her gut and the sick feeling that something was about to go wrong.

Casey stood with his back toward her, ready to jump into action. Whiplash was slamming the chute, crashing against the sides as Woodbine struggled to mount. The chute men thrust the wooden wedge into place, holding the bull steady long enough for the cowboy to settle onto his back and wind the tail of the tightened rope around the handle. As soon as the wedge was pulled away, he gave the nod.

Whiplash blasted out of the chute, a bucking, flying fury. Whatever he lacked in experience, he made up in raw power as he kicked and leaped, hell-bent on throwing the cowboy off his back. Style and control forgotten, Woodbine was fighting just to hold on. At the sound of the eight-second whistle Woodbine pulled his hand free of the rope. Before he could jump clear, Whiplash kicked high in back, then flowed down forward like a giant wave, sending the cowboy flying over his head. Woodbine landed hard in the dirt and lay there on his side, conscious but too badly hurt to get up.

Whiplash, however, wasn't through with him. Wheeling from a few yards away, the bull lowered his head and thundered toward the helpless young cowboy.

Then, suddenly, Casey was there, throwing himself right into the bull's path, protecting the rider with his own body. Whiplash's massive head smashed into Casey's chest, the horns catching him and tossing him high.

Casey had been tossed before and been fine. He knew how to fall and how to land. Val had seen it. But this time something went wrong. Casey came down on the one part of him that was unprotected—his head.

Striking the earth, he collapsed and lay still.

Val stifled a sob and started forward, but Tess caught her arm. "Stay here, Val. You'll just be in the way. Let other people help him."

As the roper caught Whiplash and herded him out of the arena, the medical staff and several riders who were watching rushed into the arena. Sam Callahan vaulted off the shark cage and raced to help. They swarmed over the two fallen men, so many people that Val couldn't see what was happening. The rider appeared to be awake and moving. Casey wasn't. Was he unconscious? Even dead? Val felt numb all over. She was scarcely aware of the noise, the lights, or the voice on the speaker. Only one thing was clear. Whatever had happened to Casey, she needed to be with him.

Two stretchers appeared. Casey and the young rider were lifted carefully onto them and carried out. Minutes later, the wail of a departing ambulance told Val they were being transported to the hospital.

Tess had gone back to take care of the bull. Val found her at the exit chute untying Whiplash's flank strap. Whiplash was still snorting and showing the whites of his eyes when the gate was opened to let him go back to the pens, but once he was back with Whirlwind, he became less agitated.

Only then was Val able to get her sister's attention. "I'm going to get my bag out of the SUV and catch a cab to the hospital," she said. "If you haven't heard from me by the time you're loaded and ready to leave, go home without me."

"You're sure? We can wait if we have to."

"No, you need to get the bulls back to the ranch, and I need to know you're safely out of Las Vegas. Casey doesn't have any family but ours. Somebody should be with him." *If he's alive.* Val couldn't give voice to her worst fear. "I'll stay as long as I need to. Then I'll find my own way home."

"What about those awful people who are after you?"

"I'll be in the hospital. They won't even know I'm there. They'll think I've left town. Tell Lexie and Shane for me. I don't have time to see them."

Tess gripped Val's hand. "You know we'll worry—about Casey and about you. Whatever happens, promise me you'll keep in touch."

"Of course, I will."

"I mean it, Val." Tess's grip tightened. "If you drop off the edge of the world like you did last time, I'll never forgive you!"

"I promise. Now I've got to get to Casey." With an awkward hug, Val turned away, took a moment to ask one of the chute men for the name of the hospital, and rushed outside to get her bag out of the SUV and flag down a cab.

Casey opened his eyes, then instantly closed them again. The light—so much light—hurt like looking into the sun. And he had a murder of a headache. He struggled to recall what had happened. Then the memory came crashing back—the fallen rider, with Whiplash charging like a juggernaut; then a blow that turned the world black. As his mind began to clear, he tried moving his limbs—toes, feet, legs, hands, and arms. He was sore as hell, but so far everything seemed to work, thank God. There was just the pain in his head. He was lying in a strange bed, attached to lines and monitors. A hospital. Whatever had happened to him, it must've been serious.

"Casey, can you hear me?" He recognized Val's husky Lauren Bacall voice. She was holding his hand. What was she doing here? Wasn't she supposed to be gone?

"Can you open your eyes?" she asked.

He found his voice. "The light . . ."

"I'll fix it." She let go of his hand. He heard her boots clicking across the tile floor. The brightness eased. "There, I've closed the blinds. It was just the sunlight coming in."

"Sunlight?" He opened his eyes. She was bending over him, her hair hanging limp around her face, her green eyes set in pools of shadow. How long had she been here?

"What time is it? What *day* is it?" The words felt as if they were rattling around like loose ball bearings inside his skull.

"It's Sunday morning. You had a bad concussion. You were unconscious all last night." Only now, as she leaned closer, did he notice the salty tear lines down her cheeks.

"I should call the nurse," she said.

"Not yet." He reached out and caught her hand again. "I can't believe you stayed with me. Where's the rest of your family?"

"I sent them on ahead, told them I'd find my own way home. They should be pulling up at the ranch house about now."

"And Cody Woodbine? How's he doing?"

"I haven't heard. But you've got some friends who've been in the waiting room all night. They'll be happy to know you're awake. Maybe they can tell you more."

She left him then, slipping out the door, her footsteps light and quick echoing down the hall. He put up his free hand and touched his head. No bandage, but a concussion was an injury to the brain. He could expect headaches, dizziness, and other symptoms. He must've come down on that packed dirt with the force of a sledgehammer. It was a wonder he hadn't broken his neck or his spine.

"Hey, man!" The door swung open. Joel and Marcus walked in, relief etched on their faces. Val wasn't with them.

"You gave us a scare, buddy," Marcus said. "How're you feeling?"

"Like hell, but I'll mend. How's Woodbine?"

"Pretty beat up," Joel said. "Broken collarbone, cracked pelvis, and a broken femur. But he's young. He'll heal and be back for the spring season. That bull was set on killing him. You saved his life, taking that hit like you did."

"You'd have done the same," Casey said. "So what happened after the lights went out in my head? I barely remember getting tossed."

"The roper got the bull under control, and the medics carted you and Woodbine away. Sam took the rest of your shift, but the last two bulls were easy. Not that much to do."

"So who won?" Casey asked.

"Gilberto. He had a ninety-two-point ride on Chiseled. McClintock bucked off. Woodbine finished third."

"Tough luck for McClintock, but he's had his day. Gilberto's been great all season. He deserved the win." Casey clenched his teeth as a shimmer of pain passed through his head. "Sorry," he muttered. "I'm a little under the weather this morning."

"We won't stay long," Joel said. "That nurse outside keeps coming by the door, giving us dirty looks. Besides, we know you'll be in good hands with that gorgeous redhead. She didn't leave your bedside all night. If you're ever fool enough to turn her loose, I get first dibs on her phone number."

The conversation faded as Val walked back into the room. She'd splashed her tear-stained face, combed her hair, and added a dab of lipstick and blush to her pale cheeks. She always looked beautiful, but it didn't take many touches to make her look dazzling. There was a brief hush as Casey's friends took her in with their eyes.

"So how soon will you be getting out of here, Casey?" Marcus's question broke the awkward silence.

"As soon as they'll let me," Casey said. "I can recover better at home. Which reminds me, could one of you get my keys and gear out of my locker at the arena and bring my truck over to the parking lot? I'll need it to drive back to Tucson."

"We can do that later this morning," Marcus said. "We'll drop the truck off with your gear and bring you the keys. Right now we'd better go and let you get some rest."

"Thanks," Casey said. "And thanks for being here."

"You'd do the same for either of us." Joel motioned Marcus out the door.

Val waited until Casey's friends had gone before she turned toward him with glints of fire in her eyes.

"You're not driving anywhere, Casey Bozeman. Not with a concussion. You could be feeling the effects for weeks. If anybody's going to drive you back to Tucson, it'll be me. And I'll stay there until it's safe to leave you alone."

Casey sighed. The offer was tempting—sharing his condo with Val, watching her sleep, making her coffee and cheese omelets in the morning, driving somewhere to a good restaurant for lunch, snuggling in front of the TV until bedtime. The fantasy was delicious. But real life was more complicated. And bloodier. And dirtier. And he knew better than to push his luck.

"I can't let you do that," he told her. "You need to get back to the ranch and your family."

She nodded, stepping closer to the bed. "I had a feeling you'd say that. But you still mustn't drive after a concussion, and you shouldn't stay alone yet. So here's my plan B. Come back to the ranch with me. I know Tess invited you, so the door's already open. And since we'd be taking your truck, that would give me an easy way home. You could stay in Jack's old room until you're well enough to drive to Tucson. You could even help with the work if you felt strong enough. How about it?"

The idea did have some appeal. He hadn't spent time on a real ranch since his parents had to sell out years ago. But with things so unsettled between him and Val, the strain might be too much for both of them.

"What about the grand jury?" he asked. "Will you be going back to Vegas to testify?"

"Maybe. Halvorsen has my e-mail. He said he'd keep me up to date. What I decide to do will depend on how much they need me and how they plan to keep me safe. Meanwhile, all I can do is get on with my life. So are you coming back to the ranch with me?"

"I'm too muddle-headed to think straight," he said. "Let's put the idea on hold for now. I'll be here for a couple of days at least. We can make a decision when the time comes."

"All right. But there's no way you'll want to be on the road until you've recovered. You could get a dizzy spell and kill somebody, Casey."

"You know right where to jab, don't you?" He managed a feeble smile. "You sound like a woman who needs her morning coffee. Go find the cafeteria—that's an order. I promise to behave myself with the nurses while you're gone."

"Are you sure? Maybe I should warn them about you." Val pulled a playful face, turned away, and walked out the door.

Casey exhaled and sank back onto the pillow. Damn it, but he loved her.

Val found the cafeteria, then ordered a large black coffee and a supersize chocolate chip cookie. She needed the sugar fix, her go-to since rehab. At least it wasn't alcohol. Some women had to watch their weight after they got clean. But for her, that hadn't been a problem.

Only after she'd found a quiet table by the window and collapsed onto the chair did she realize how exhausted she was. Yesterday had been hell from beginning to end, and she'd sat up by Casey's bed most of the night, holding his hand and listening to him breathe. But this morning the sun was out, the sky was clear, and Casey had finally opened his eyes. He appeared to be all right, thank heaven—a good start to what she hoped would be a better day.

As she drank her coffee, she could feel the caffeine seeping through her system. How long had it been since she'd last checked her phone? She fished it out of her purse and powered it on.

There were two text messages from Tess, one sent last night from somewhere outside Las Vegas, the other this morning from Ajo saying they were about to take the mountain road to the ranch and wanting to know about Casey. Cell phone service at the ranch was spotty at best. A satellite dish made e-mail a more reliable option.

Val tapped out a quick e-mail saying that Casey was awake and she'd be in touch later. Then, after checking her in-box and finding nothing worth her attention, she put the phone away. Sipping her coffee, she willed herself to breathe and relax.

A man at a nearby table had finished his coffee. His chair scraped the floor, drawing Val's attention as he got up to go, leaving a newspaper, barely opened, on the table.

Val waited until he'd gone before she took the paper. Maybe Casey would enjoy reading about the PBR finals on the sports page. But first she would check the local headlines. Detective Sergeant Davenport had mentioned wanting to keep the guard's murder and Dimitri's shooting out of the press. But news had ways of leaking out. She could only hope her own name hadn't been shared with the public.

She scanned the national headlines and moved on to page 2. So far so good. She saw nothing about yesterday's events at the arena. But then an item near the bottom of the page caught her eye.

LANZONI'S LAWYER FOUND DEAD

Wayne Duvall, head of the defense team for alleged crime boss Carlo Lanzoni, was found shot through the head in his car late last night. The killing appears to confirm rumors of a gang war between factions of

Lanzoni's organization. Lanzoni's case is slated to go
before a grand jury early next month.

There was more. Val's hands shook, blurring the print, as
she read it. Duvall had been playing both sides of the deadly
power game. Either side—Lanzoni's or Dimitri's—could have
killed him.

But what did this mean for her?

Was she next in line to die?

CHAPTER FOURTEEN

*T*HE AC IN CASEY'S NEW TRUCK WAS WORKING, BUT VAL DROVE WITH the side window partway down because she liked the wind in her hair. The day was pleasantly cool, the traffic sparse on Highway 93, which cut through the high, scrubby desert from Henderson down to Wickenburg and continued to the outskirts of Phoenix. From there, if she could navigate the maze of exits and switchbacks and pick up State Highway 85, it would be a straight shot south, through open country, all the way to Ajo, then a climb over the mountain road to the ranch.

Allowing time for navigation, rest stops, and slowing down after dark, the drive from Las Vegas took about nine hours. She and Casey wouldn't be arriving at the ranch until almost midnight. But Val was in no mood to complain. The most welcome sight she'd seen all week was Las Vegas in the rearview mirror as they passed beyond the city limits.

Casey had reclined the passenger seat and fallen asleep with his head on a pillow. He was still having headaches and occasional waves of dizziness, but the hospital had released him after two days with a bottle of high-dose ibuprofen and orders to rest until the symptoms went away. Recovery would take time, the doctor had said. Weeks, if not longer.

Val knew how it frustrated him that he couldn't bounce back to his regular life. He hated being cared for and fussed over, even by her. But at least the PBR was on seasonal break. He wouldn't be missing work.

She glanced over at him, reining in the urge to reach out and brush back the lock of hair that had tumbled over his forehead. She'd often accused Tess of mothering her. At least she understood how Casey must feel when she tried too hard to take care of him.

She was grateful that he'd agreed to go to the ranch with her. The outdoor air, tasty food, and active lifestyle would be good for him. And having her family there would lessen the awkwardness if she had to make it clear that there could be no happy ending for them—no matter how much she might want it.

"Where are we?" Eyes open, he raised the seatback and sat up.

"A few miles out of Wickenburg. Are you hungry?"

"I can wait. How about you?"

"We can eat later then. Maybe when we get to Phoenix. How are you feeling?"

"Fine." It was what he usually said. There was silence between them for a mile or two. Then he spoke again. "So what about that mess back in Las Vegas? Are you going to testify?"

"I don't know. It depends on what I hear from the DA. Halvorsen has my e-mail."

"And Dimitri?"

"He's probably off in some plush hideout, nursing his wound and plotting revenge." She hesitated, knowing the story was bound to come out. "Wayne Duvall is dead. Shot in his car. I read about it in the paper while you were in the hospital."

"And you didn't tell me?"

"You had a concussion. You didn't need anything else to worry about."

"I've got you to worry about. That's enough for any sane man— if sane is the right word." He gazed out the window, watching the mesquite-covered desert slide past the dusty glass. "Does anybody know who shot Duvall?"

"Not that I've heard. There was no more about it in the papers."

"Going on what you've told me, it appears the man was batting for both teams."

"So either side—Lanzoni's or Dimitri's—could've killed him, and for a whole list of reasons."

"They could kill you, too." He turned to look at her, pain glinting in his narrowed eyes. "Don't go back, Val. Just don't. You don't owe anybody your testimony, let alone your life."

Val slowed the truck to steer around a pair of ravens feasting on a road-killed coyote. They flapped upward, then settled again as the truck passed. The country was beginning to look like home. "That's probably wise advice," she said. "But I've done so many wrong things in my life. Maybe it's time I did something right for a change."

"They've already got Lanzoni on racketeering and extortion charges. He'll go to prison even if it isn't for murder."

"Will he? Those mob lawyers are pretty sharp."

"I understand that Lanzoni ordered your boyfriend killed, and Dimitri carried out the hit. But is getting justice for him worth your life?"

"You can't imagine how many times I've asked myself that question. Lenny made so many foolish mistakes that it was almost as if he had a death wish. It was just a matter of time. But isn't everybody entitled to justice? How can I turn my back when I could make a difference?"

"You can make a difference by staying alive and being happy, Val. You could've gone the same way as Lenny, but you didn't. You escaped and turned your life around. Don't let all that effort go for nothing."

His argument made sense but only in a way. Hooking up with Lenny had been one of the worst mistakes of her life. She couldn't say she'd loved him, but the codependency they'd formed had gone deep. It had taken his death to break the bond. How could she ever admit that Dimitri had done her a favor? And how could she pass up her only chance to see justice done?

"Did you hear me, Val?" Casey asked when she didn't answer.

"Every word." But she hadn't known how to reply.

"Blast it, Val, don't do this!" His patience exploded. "I lost you once. I can't stand the thought of losing you again."

Val's heart sank. He'd said them, the words she'd both yearned and dreaded to hear—the words that crossed the line. She couldn't allow those words to take root and grow.

"There's more than one way to lose someone," she said. "Especially someone who isn't yours to lose."

A beat of silence passed before he spoke. "Message received and understood," he said. "We can stop to eat anytime you're hungry. You choose the place."

"Fine." She kept her gaze on the road. "It won't be long now."

Val slowed the truck, watching the road signs as they neared Phoenix. The country was becoming more populated. Billboards, housing tracts, and strip malls were strung along both sides of the road. She pulled up at a Taco Bell, where they settled for burritos and Cokes, eaten fast with no more conversation than necessary. Tension simmered between them as they walked back to the truck.

"You've been driving a long time," he said. "If you need a break, I can spell you. There's not much traffic on that long stretch down to Ajo."

"I'm doing fine and you just got out of the hospital. No way are you taking that wheel. There may not be much traffic, but you could still veer off the shoulder and roll the truck."

He shrugged. "Let me know if you change your mind. Meanwhile I feel another nap coming on." He climbed into the passenger side. As Val started the engine, he levered the seat to its reclining angle, adjusted the pillow, and settled back with his eyes closed.

Val knew he was shutting her out, and she couldn't blame him. Casey was a proud man and she'd wounded him where it would hurt the most. But she hadn't asked him to find her again. She hadn't asked him to make love to her or protect her.

Then again, she hadn't resisted.

But hadn't she warned him that they couldn't stay together? Hadn't she made that clear time and time again?

Yes, and then she'd stayed with him in the hospital. Now she was driving him home to be with her family. What else was he to think?

By the time she'd picked up the freeway at Sun City and navigated her way to the Highway 85 off-ramp, the sun was low in the sky, streaking the clouds with the first golden glints of sunset.

As the altitude changed, the twilight air grew warmer. Saguaro cactuses towered against the sky, casting long shadows across the desert floor. Spines of teddy bear cholla glimmered like diamond needles in the slanting light. A roadrunner sprinted along the roadside, springing to catch a lizard in its long, sharp beak.

The sunset blazed with ribbons of blood and flame, then faded to the colors of a dying bonfire. The branches of paloverde trees fluttered like lacy fans in the evening breeze.

Val had switched on the truck's headlamps and rolled the window all the way down. She loved nightfall on the Sonoran Desert, when the air cooled and creatures that slept through the day stirred to life. This was one of the few times and places where she felt as if she belonged—as if she'd been a night creature on the desert, a fox perhaps—in some earlier life. If she were to wake Casey to share the night, would he understand? But she would never know. He was sound asleep and needed his rest.

She touched the brake as a burrowing owl flashed through her headlights and vanished into the dark. A mile down the road, she slowed the truck to steer clear of some javelinas, small wild pigs, foraging in the barrow pit. Everything she saw and heard and felt brought her closer to home.

Strange how, years ago, she'd been so wild to leave that nothing could have stopped her, not even Casey. But that was before she'd learned how empty and cruel the world could be. It had taken this week's nightmare return to Las Vegas to remind her how lucky she was to have a peaceful refuge with supportive people who cared about her.

She was thankful to be going home. But Thomas Wolfe had been right—you can't go home again. Places changed. People changed. And for her, there could be no going back to what she'd had with Casey. Some things, once broken, could never be right again.

* * *

By the time the lights of Ajo appeared in the distance, Casey was awake and sitting up. The pain in his head had eased, and he was feeling more alert, but he knew better than to ask Val to let him drive. The final leg of the trip involved a climb up a winding road to a low mountain pass, then an even more perilous descent along a series of switchbacks. He was in no condition to handle it safely, especially at night.

As Val drove, he stole glances at her profile, etched in silhouette against the moonlit window. With her flawless face and wind-blown hair, she looked like the perfect movie heroine. If she hadn't made it big in Hollywood, it wasn't due to any lack of beauty. And it wasn't due to any lack of courage. Going off to face the dog-eat-dog world of moviemaking, giving up a baby, and still fighting for her dream had taken guts. But she'd been too young, too innocent to handle the lifestyle. Hollywood had chewed her up and spit her out, leaving her vulnerable to the lies of a scumbag like Lenny Fortunato. She'd caused Casey lasting pain, leaving the way she had. But the person she'd really hurt was herself.

He loved her, but he knew better than to trust her. Once on his family's old ranch, his father had trapped a fox. Caught by one leg in the cruel jaws, the beautiful animal had chewed off its trapped limb and escaped—wounded, vulnerable, and in terrible pain, but free. That was Val. It was as if there were a wild animal inside her, trapped and frantic to escape. That was her nature, and it wasn't likely to change.

Ajo was a place Casey knew well. A former mining town, it had faded with the end of the copper boom. In recent years it had sprung back to life as an art colony and retirement mecca, retaining the look of a company town with its small, uniform houses, vintage buildings, and central plaza. Tonight the streets were dark, the businesses closed.

"We'll need to stop for gas," Val said. "There's an all-night station on the road out of town. We can stretch our legs and take a break before we drive up to the ranch."

"I know you think I'm still a patient," he said. "But I can at least handle gassing the truck."

She gave him a tired smile. "I'll trust you to do that while I visit the ladies' room. And I'll be getting some coffee to keep me awake going over the pass. Do you want some, too, or anything else?"

"I'll be fine. I had a good rest while you drove. I owe you big time for this, Val. I hope you'll give me a chance to repay you."

"No need. You already have." She vanished into the convenience store. By the time she came out, Casey had gassed the truck, washed the windows, and was waiting for her in the cab. Pulling away from the pumps, they headed south on the highway, toward the place where a graveled road cut off through the cactus-dotted foothills and up to the pass.

Val kept the lights on high beam and the truck's speed slow to avoid the jackrabbits that bounded across the road as if playing chicken with oncoming traffic. At least some things hadn't changed.

"I haven't set foot on the ranch since Jack died," Casey said, making conversation. "I understand there've been a lot of changes since then. Your dad's gone, Lexie's married and expecting—and Callie. Lord, I can't believe she's gone. The ranch won't be the same without her."

Bert Champion's second wife, the longtime stepmother of his three girls, had been murdered this past summer. The neighbor who'd killed her was serving a life sentence in the state prison.

"I didn't know about her death until I came home," Val said. "What a shock. I barely remember my real mother, but Callie was always there to take care of us and Dad."

"And her cooking—Lord, that's what I remember. The meals, the pies and cakes, the biscuits . . . It takes love to cook like that."

"Callie put love into everything she did. We still miss her. Tess hired Ruben's daughter, Maria, to cook. She does fine, especially with Mexican food. But she isn't Callie. She and her husband, Pedro, moved their trailer from the reservation to the ranch. He helps with the work and with the driving when the bulls go out to rodeos."

"And what's your job at the ranch?" Casey asked her.

Her laughter was edgy. "That remains to be seen. I filled in as a cook before Maria came. And I refurbished the house for Lexie's wedding. But if I plan to stay long, I'll need to pull my weight. I was never a cowgirl—you know how I always hated the smelly, noisy beasts. But I can ride. I suppose I could learn to handle a rope and a branding iron."

"So are you planning to stick around?"

"It's home. Right now that sounds pretty good to me. If it's not what I want, I'll know when the time comes."

They had come to the turnoff where Val and her sisters had caught the school bus for years. Val swung the truck left. The coarse gravel crunched under the tires, the sound stirring Casey's memories of driving to pick her up for a date and to deliver her home.

"I'm sorry I couldn't make it for your dad's funeral," he said. "I was working and couldn't get away. He was a good man."

"If you say so. We never got along. I think I reminded him too much of my mother. For what it's worth, I didn't make it to the funeral either. I was in rehab. And I figured that sending flowers would be too little, too late."

"You sent flowers for Jack. Two dozen red roses, I remember."

"Actually, there were twenty-eight roses, one for every year of his life. Not enough years. Jack would've made all the difference—for the ranch, for my father and my sisters. Even for me."

"For me, too. He was my best friend."

"And you were there in the arena with him. I know." She reached across the console and rested her hand on his for a moment before taking it away.

They fell into silence as the truck climbed the steep road toward the pass. The night sky was clear, the moon full and bright, the stars like spilled diamond dust across the sky. Casey recalled the night they'd stopped the rusted ranch pickup at the top of the pass after a movie date, spread an old sleeping bag in the open bed, and lay there looking up at the stars.

That was the night they'd made love for the first time.

They crested the top of the pass and started down the other side. The road, a series of steep, hairpin turns, demanded Val's total concentration. For the life of him, Casey couldn't imagine how the ranch's drivers could maneuver a trailer loaded with bulls around the switchbacks without slipping off. But if there'd been any accidents, he'd never heard about them.

Looking down from the road, he could see the rambling Spanish-style ranch house. The lights were on inside. Val must have called from the gas station to let someone know they were coming.

Minutes later they rolled into the yard and came to a stop. Two people were waiting on the porch. Casey recognized Tess and Ruben Diego, the ranch's longtime foreman. An elder of the Tohono O'odham tribe, whose reservation bordered the ranch, he was stocky, muscular, and as tough as any man Casey had ever known. In his younger years he'd ridden bulls without any modern safeguards such as vests and helmets. Old injuries, some badly healed, showed in the way he moved. But there was energy in every step as he strode out to meet the truck.

"Tess told me you were coming, Casey." He extended a leathery hand. "It's been too long. Let me get your bags." Before Casey could protest, Ruben had opened the rear door of the club cab, slung a bag from either hand, and headed into the house. That was like the man, always looking out for what needed to be done. He had watched the Champion girls grow up and he treated them like his own daughters.

Tess had come off the porch. Val hurried around to greet her. "How was the trip home with the bulls?" she asked. "Did they do all right?"

"Whiplash was wound pretty tight at first," Tess said. "But after a while, they both went to sleep. They're in the pasture, doing all right. We can talk about them more in the morning."

"And how about you?" Tess turned to Casey. "How are you feeling?"

"Fine, thanks to Val. She did the driving. All I did was nap."

"But you'll both want to rest," Tess said. "You know your way around, Casey. You'll be in Jack's old room. His workout machines are in there for Shane, but the bed's made up for you."

"A bed's all I need. And I plan to help with the work. I didn't come here to be treated like an invalid."

"We'll see about that in the morning. Shane and Lexie are asleep. They'll see you at breakfast."

"I'll be up for chores," Casey said. "It's my head that's messed up. The rest of me is fine."

Val had headed for the house. Casey was about to follow her when Tess stopped him with a hand on his arm. For a moment she studied him, the moonlight casting her intelligent gray eyes in shadow. "How are you really?" she asked.

"I'm fine. Just a nagging headache and occasional dizzy spells. That's why Val wouldn't let me drive. The doctors told me the symptoms were normal and should go away. So no worries."

Tess glanced toward the porch, where Val had just gone inside. "And the two of you? You know I've always wanted you in the family. How's that going?"

Tess had never been one to beat around an issue. Casey shook his head. "We're taking it one day at a time. Val's been through some rough patches. She's got a lot of healing to do."

"Don't I know it? She hasn't told me much—maybe she never will. But I know broken when I see it. I suspect that messy business in Las Vegas was just the tip of the iceberg."

"And I suspect it's past your bedtime, Big Sister." Casey wasn't about to betray more confidences. He'd gotten himself in enough trouble for that. "I'll see you bright and early. Thanks again for inviting me."

"Thank you for coming, Casey. Having you here will do us a world of good."

Tess lingered by the truck after Casey had gone into the house. She'd spoken the truth to him. Casey's solid common sense and good nature tended to have a calming effect on people around him. She was going to need that in the days ahead.

Leaning back against the hood of the truck, she gazed up at the sky. In Las Vegas, the stars had been invisible, their light drowned by the blinding glare of the city. But here, on the ranch she loved, the night sky was as glorious as she remembered from her childhood, when she used to lie on a blanket with her sisters and make up names for the constellations they could see—the mermaid, the horse, the cougar, and so many others.

Would there always be starry skies above the Alamo Canyon Ranch? Would her family be here to see them?

The truck hood was dusty from the road. Brushing off her jeans and jacket, she walked up the slope to the stout fence that separated the ranch yard from the rolling grassland that was divided into large pastures. At the far end of the nearest pasture, a dozen bucking bulls clustered under the scraggly oak tree that had been planted by Tess's grandfather. Another pasture held the cows and calves, a farther pasture the younger bulls, still being tested. The farthest and largest pasture was reserved for beef cattle, the sale of which paid the bills and helped support the bull-raising venture that had been Bert Champion's dream.

Half the pastureland lay fallow, to be fertilized with manure and rotated to use when the grass grew in. But the rains had been little more than showers this year, and the grass was sparse everywhere. The surplus beef cattle had been sold in the fall, leaving only the breeding stock and the bucking stock. But the grass would not feed even this smaller number of animals. The ranch would have to buy hay from the farm that shared one end of the mountain valley. And no thanks to Brock Tolman, part owner of the company that had bought the land, the hay wouldn't come cheap.

Brock had made a show of being nice to her at the finals, introducing her to Clay Rafferty and giving her chances to spend time with the PBR livestock director. But Brock Tolman never did anything without a good reason. Behind that polished smile was a greedy, conniving bastard who'd do anything to get his hands on her bulls and the ranch.

Leaning on a fence post, Tess watched the bulls drowsing in the moonlight. She loved them, and she loved the land even more. In the years since Mitch's death, weeks before the wedding they'd planned, the Alamo Canyon Ranch had become her life. She'd promised her father, as he lay dying of cancer last spring, that she would preserve the land and protect it for their family.

She'd made that promise in good faith, confident that she'd be able to keep her word.

But now there was this.

While the family was in Las Vegas, Pedro had picked up the mail in Ajo and brought it home. Mostly bills and junk, he'd left it in a pile on the office desk.

Tess, Lexie, and Shane had arrived home exhausted from the all-night drive with the bulls. It was the next day before Tess had gotten around to sorting the mail. Most of it had gone straight into the trash or the basket where she kept unpaid bills. But one official-looking envelope, from a Tucson mortgage company she'd never heard of, had caught her attention. Probably just an ad, she'd told herself. She would give it a quick look.

A cold premonition had crept over her as she tore open the envelope, slid out the single page, and began skimming the text.

To: Mr. Bert Champion
Alamo Canyon Ranch
P.O. Box 444
Ajo, Arizona 85321

Dear Mr. Champion:
This letter is to inform you that payment for equity loan #3348890, which you took out on your property January 10 of this year, will come due on December 31. Since you opted for a single balloon payment, the full amount will be due at that time:
Principal: $100,000
Interest and penalties: $22,050

Total due: $122,050
*If the amount is not paid by the due date, be advised that we will
institute foreclosure proceedings immediately.*

Yours truly,
Bentley R. Lamb, Loan officer
Patrick and Packard Mortgage and Insurance Co.

Numb with disbelief, Tess had read the letter again. Her father
had said nothing about owing a large sum of money. She'd assumed that, aside from seasonal operating costs, the ranch was
free of debt. An even more troubling question was why had Bert
Champion taken out that huge loan? And what kind of company
would lend that kind of money—at that exorbitant interest rate—
to a man who might not be in his right mind?

Toward the end of his life, Bert's reason had become flawed.
Had he believed that after he died the lender would be unable to
collect? Had he known what he was doing when he signed away
his ranch as collateral?

Wouldn't the loan have been insured?

Was the whole business a scam from beginning to end? If it was
real, what had happened to the money?

Tess had told no one about the letter. She needed to know
more before she shared it. Maybe it was only some scammer's
clumsy attempt to extort money. But if it was real—and she could
guess who might be behind it—her family was six weeks away
from losing the ranch.

CHAPTER FIFTEEN

*T*HE NEXT MORNING, CASEY WAS OUTSIDE BY CHORE TIME. THE LIN-
gering headache was still there, but the pain had dulled. And
being out in the crisp morning air, watching sunrise flame above
the Tohono O'odham reservation to the east, was the best medicine he could imagine.

He had saddled up, along with Ruben, Pedro, and Tess, and
ridden out to take care of the stock. Shane, who was up as well, set
out in his hand-powered wheelchair to clean the stable, a job he
claimed to enjoy because it gave him the chance to smell like a
cowboy again.

While Pedro and Ruben rode to the lower pasture to take care
of the remaining beef cattle, Casey followed Tess's buckskin horse
along the fence line to check on the bucking stock. The air was
filled with bird calls—the piping of a cactus wren, the cries of foraging quail, and the drumming of a woodpecker on a saguaro.
On the hilltop, a golden eagle lifted off a creosote bush and soared
into the dawn.

How long had it been since he'd sat a horse? Too long, Casey
decided. When he thought of his Tucson condo, what came to
mind was the traffic jams, the crowded parking lots, the smell of
molten asphalt, the fake-looking palm trees, and the wail of police sirens in the night. Maybe down the line, he could sell the
condo and get some land out of town, with a house and a few animals to care for. Would Val go for that?

But what was he thinking? Val didn't know her own mind from one day to the next. And she'd never said yes to him. She hadn't even said maybe.

"Take a look at the grass," Tess was saying. "It's grazed off here, and the reserve pastures aren't much better. I just wish we'd had the money to put in sprinklers. If it doesn't rain soon, we'll be in trouble."

"And here I was thinking that this place felt like heaven," Casey said. "Forgive me. I can imagine how much work and worry it's taken for you to hold it together after losing Jack and your father."

"One day at a time," she said. "Like you and Val. Come on, let's check out the bulls."

She unlatched the pasture gate, and he closed it behind them as they rode in. Most of the bulls, accustomed to being approached on horseback, paid them little heed until Tess began filling their feed tubs with bull chow from the bag she carried. Then they lumbered over to eat, while Casey filled their trough with fresh water from a hose connected to a tap.

Whiplash, the biggest of the herd even at his young age, snorted and pawed the ground but didn't try to charge. "How is he doing?" Casey asked Tess.

"As you see, he's still aggressive." She turned her horse back toward the gate. "I'm a little worried about him. He was traumatized by that awful incident in his pen. I know the sport demands a bull with a lot of fight, but I saw how he went after Cody Woodbine and then you. He might be too dangerous for the arena."

"Give him time," Casey said. "He's got so much potential as a bucker. It would be a shame to waste it."

They fed and watered the white cows, most of them looking pregnant. Then they checked the younger bulls, about twenty of them, waiting to be tested in the spring. The Alamo Canyon Ranch was a small operation. Some of the breeders, like Chip Harris and Brock Tolman, had more than a hundred bulls on their ranches. But just one great bull, even from a small ranch like this one, could make all the difference in a stock contractor's reputation.

As they rode back down toward the house, Tess waited for Casey to catch up with her horse. "There's something worrying me," she said, taking an envelope out of her jacket. "I haven't shared this with anybody else, but I'd like you to take a look at it and tell me what you think."

She drew a letter out of the envelope and passed it to Casey. By now the sun was coming up, giving him enough light to read. Stopping her horse, she waited until he'd finished. "Well?" she asked.

Casey scanned it a second time. "Is this for real?"

"You tell me. It was waiting when I got home. Dad never said a word about it. Do you know anything about these people?"

"I've never heard of them," Casey said. "But since I want to make myself useful, let me check this out for you—do some Internet searches, make a few phone calls. You've got to get to the bottom of this, Tess. If it's real, you need to act. If it isn't, somebody belongs in jail."

"Will you promise not to tell the family? If it turns out to be nothing, I don't want them to panic."

"All right, if that's what you want."

"Then thank you for this." She handed him the envelope. "One more thing?"

"Name it." Casey folded the paper and slipped it back into the envelope.

"If Brock Tolman is involved in any way, I want to know."

"And if he is?"

Her mouth tightened. "Then it's war."

As they neared the house, the aromas of coffee, bacon, and fresh biscuits teased Casey's hunger. Val's bedroom door had been closed when he'd left earlier. Maybe he'd see her at breakfast.

On awakening that morning, he'd lain still for a few breaths, imagining her asleep in the next room, her eyes closed, her fiery hair tangled on the pillow. No woman could look more beautiful in sleep than Val did. But he had too much respect for her family to invade her room and wake her with loving. That—if it happened—would have to wait for a better time and place.

Pedro, a sturdy man in his forties, was waiting to take their horses. They washed their hands at the tap and went inside to find the dining room table set for breakfast. Shane and Lexie were already in their places. There was no sign of Val.

As Casey was taking his seat, she popped out of the kitchen with a plate of hot biscuits that she set on the table before going back, then coming out again with a platter of bacon and scrambled eggs. She looked rested and happy this morning, dressed in jeans and a flannel shirt, her hair tied back and her face bare of makeup. Casey gave her a smile as she took a seat and passed him the plate of biscuits. "I made these myself," she said.

"Showing off your domestic talents, are you? We'll see." He took a biscuit, split it, and spread the halves with butter and a dab of saguaro fruit jam from the Tohono O'odham reservation. Since other people were already helping themselves, he took a bite.

"Wow, this is delicious," he said, meaning it.

She raised an eyebrow. "I may not be much of a cowgirl, but I can cook. I'm trying to talk Maria into letting me help the women pick the fruit and make the jam next season."

"Don't you have to be Tohono O'odham to do that?"

"Maybe. But at least I'm a woman, and there's a first time for everything. I haven't given up." She turned aside to say something to her sisters.

As he was pouring his coffee from the carafe in front of him, Casey noticed the three other places at the table. He remembered Callie's custom of including the hired help in family meals. Nice that it hadn't changed, he thought, as Ruben and Pedro came in through the front door and sat down at the table. Maria, who was Ruben's daughter and Pedro's wife, joined them from the kitchen. Plump and pretty, she was about her husband's age. Casey remembered Ruben saying that they had grown children.

Surrounded by good food and good people, Casey found himself thinking about the letter Tess had given him. Hopefully, it was
nothing more than a con. He could almost believe that, given
that the alleged lenders weren't even aware that Bert Champion
had died. But what if it was real?

In one of their last conversations, Jack had mentioned that he
was worried about his father's mental state. Bert could have gotten some sales pitch in the mail and contacted the lenders, who
recognized a dying man and saw the chance to get their hands on
a valuable property for less than ten cents on the dollar.

There could be other explanations, but for starters, he would
go with the worst-case scenario and assume the letter was legiti-
mate.

Casey gazed around the table, thinking of the generations that
had taken their meals here, the people who had lived, loved, and
died in this house.

He remembered the anguish of his own parents when they'd
lost their family ranch and had to spend their last days in a rented
cottage in Ajo. For the Champions to suffer the same fate, to lose
their family home, as well as their livelihood, was unthinkable. He
would stop at nothing to help put things right.

When breakfast was done, he made sure that neither Tess nor
Shane would be using the office. After mentioning to Val that
he'd be busy doing some work for Tess, Casey shut himself in and
began his search.

He started with the filing cabinet, which, it appeared, hadn't
been purged in years. If Bert had taken out a loan, surely he
would have filed a copy of the agreement.

Unless he hadn't wanted his family to know about the loan.

Casey spent more than an hour going through the file drawers,
finding nothing. With that search at a dead end, he sat down at
the antique desk and powered up the computer.

Patrick and Packard did have a website. As far as Casey could
tell, the business appeared to be real. The site included photos of
Mr. Patrick and Mr. Packard, two slick-looking younger men in
cheap suits. There was a shot of the office, which appeared to be

a front in a Tucson strip mall, and the usual link to a map with directions. The site also included phone and fax numbers and an e-mail address.

A shoestring operation, most likely. When he checked the Better Business Bureau, he found no record of any complaints.

He didn't have a good feeling about this, but it was time to let Tess know what he'd found.

After shutting down the computer, he left the office to find her. She wasn't in the house, but she'd said something about observing the young bulls and taking some notes.

He stepped out the front door to find Val sweeping the porch. At breakfast he'd sensed an awkwardness between them, as if, with the family around, they were unsure of how to behave. They needed some serious time together.

"I see you're earning your keep," he said, knowing the remark sounded lame.

"Maria has extra work with all the people here. I'm just trying to help out." She kept on sweeping.

"You mentioned you'd refurbished the house for Lexie's wedding," he said. "I was noticing how much better it looked than when I used to come here. New paint, new covers on the furniture, new cushions, everything scrubbed and polished. Did you do all that?"

"I did. I was just out of rehab and I needed something to keep me from climbing the walls. It helped." She stopped sweeping and looked up at him. "So Tess has put you to work. What is it she's got you doing?"

"Just some research. If it amounts to anything, she'll let you know. I'm looking for her now. Do you know where she is?"

"She took the ATV and went up to the east pasture. She said to tell you she'd be back soon." Val frowned. "What's going on between you two?"

"I'm helping her with a project. That's all. If you want to know more, you'll have to ask Tess." In the distance he could hear the sound of the ATV coming back. Casey knew he couldn't leave things like this with Val. "If you're free late this afternoon, I was hoping we could take horses and ride up that canyon we used to enjoy. The one with the waterfall. How does that sound?"

Her expression brightened. "Fine, but it'll probably be too chilly for skinny-dipping."

"I think we can find other things to do." He stroked a thumb down her cheek as the four-wheeler roared into sight, bouncing over the rough dirt road. "Later, then," he said to Val.

"Later." She gave him a playfully raised eyebrow, then went back to her sweeping. Casey strode out to meet Tess as she stopped the ATV alongside the house.

"Let me show you what I found," he said. "Then you can decide where to go from here."

After seeing the website, Tess agreed with Casey that the only thing to do was contact Patrick and Packard. Casey composed an e-mail, explaining that Bert Champion had died and he was representing Mr. Champion's family. He requested a copy of the loan disclosure and signed contract by return e-mail.

"If this is real, you'll want to talk to a lawyer," he told Tess.

"The ranch can't afford a lawyer. We can barely pay our bills as it is. Did you find out whether Brock Tolman had an interest in the company?"

"Not yet. I'll need to do more digging. But a one-horse outfit like this one isn't Tolman's style. I'd bet against it."

Casey checked his e-mail for a reply. Seeing none, he put the computer in sleep mode. "The ball's in their court now. If they can't come up with a genuine contract, you should be all right."

"And if they can?" Tess sighed. "If Dad really took out that loan, there's something else I need to know. What did he do with the money? It certainly didn't go into the ranch account."

"The bank might be able to help you," Casey said. "He could've opened a new account."

"Or he could've had a secret family or a gambling habit we never knew about. At this point, I'd believe anything. Blast it, Casey, life is hard enough. I don't need this problem. My family doesn't need it."

"Let's wait until we hear back from the loan company before we jump to conclusions," Casey said. "But I do think Val needs to know about this."

"Val wasn't here for Dad's illness or even his funeral. Why should she be involved?"

"Because she's your sister and she deserves to know. She's already wondering what we're up to. Tell her, Tess. If you don't, I will. Then the two of you can decide when to tell Shane and Lexie. Damn it, you can't carry a burden like this by yourself."

"So, did Tess talk to you?" Casey asked Val as they rode their horses out of the yard and up the road.

"She did." Val adjusted the angle of her Stetson to keep the late-afternoon sun out of her eyes. "I told her I'd have her back, but aside from knowing a few people in Vegas who'll twist arms and break legs for a price, there's not much I can do to help. I don't have that kind of money. Hell, I don't have *any* money. I might have to go back to waitressing."

She brushed a fly off her chestnut gelding's neck, sensing Casey's gaze on her and knowing what it meant. "I did suggest to Tess that, assuming this business is real, we could sell some land and pay off the loan," she said. "I even suggested a ready buyer."

"Tolman." It wasn't even a question.

"He already owns the hay farm through that investment firm. I'm sure he'd be happy to buy the strip of pastureland that runs alongside it."

"I can imagine what Tess thought of that idea," Casey said.

"Oh—you should've heard her. It was as if I'd dropped a bomb. She said she'd cut off her arm before she'd sell an inch of the Alamo Canyon Ranch, especially to *him*—and I won't even repeat what she called the man."

Casey chuckled. "I'm not surprised. Tess is too proud for her own good. And she's never had anything nice to say about Brock Tolman."

"Do you want to hear something funny? That day in Vegas,

when we were with the bulls and he came by to talk to her—I caught some definite vibes. I think he's got a thing for her."

"What kind of thing? You mean like the thing I've got for you?"

"You know what I'm talking about. Come on! I'll race you to the trail!" Val kicked her horse to a gallop and tore up the road toward the spot where a narrow pathway branched off to the left. The horse's mane whipped her face as she leaned forward like a jockey in the saddle. She didn't want to talk about Tess or the ranch's problems. She didn't want to think about the chaos she'd left behind in Las Vegas or what could happen tomorrow. All she wanted was to forget everything but being with Casey for however much time they had left.

She could hear his horse thundering up the road behind her. As she reined in the horse where the trail branched off, he caught up with her. Moving his horse in close, he reached out, seized her waist, and pulled her against him. His hungry kiss devoured her, almost bruising in its intensity. A rush of heat burned through her body, lighting a fire of need between her thighs. Her free arm caught and held him, fingers gripping his shirt.

As she began to slide, he let her go and pushed her back into the saddle. When he spoke, his voice was thick with need. "Let's ride," he said.

The trail cut a level path across the brushy slope that overlooked the ranch, then wound around the far side on its long descent into a rocky canyon. In the very depths of that canyon, a waterfall from a hidden spring cascaded into a sheltered pool.

It had been their place when they were young, a place to swim, lie on the rocks, and sometimes make love on hot summer days. Painted figures on the cliffside suggested that this spot had been sacred to ancient native people. But as far as they could discover, no one else had come here in a long time.

The November day was cool, and they had no plans to swim. Driven by other, unspoken needs, they urged their horses down the winding trail.

Clumps of prickly pear and brittle bush, with its turquoise leaves, grew along the trail. Two ravens circled overhead, scolding with their hoarse voices. Partway down, Val, who was in the lead, pointed silently to a rugged cliff on the far side of the canyon where bighorn sheep climbed among the rocks.

Except for the splashing of water and the bubbling call of a wren, their place was as quiet as the last time they'd been here, years before. They dismounted and dropped the reins of their mounts. Standing still, he let her come to him, crushing her close as she plunged into his arms. Their kisses were frantic with need, their hands roaming over each other's bodies, touching and groping, hips thrusting and straining through their clothes. They hadn't brought a blanket, but a flat rock, the size of a small bed, lay tilted at an angle at the foot of the cliff. He laid her back against it, jerked open the fastenings of her jeans and pulled them, with her panties, off over her hips. Freeing his erection, he parted her and buried it in her moistness. She welcomed him with a cry, wrapping him with her legs, pulling him deeper inside her, meeting his thrusts until every part of her felt the shattering response. They had made passionate love, but not like this, with a raw, brutal hunger, as if it might be the last time.

It was almost as if he knew.

Three more days passed with no word from the loan company. Then, just as Tess's worries had begun to ebb, the message appeared in the ranch e-mail—a brief note with an attached file.

It was Shane who saw it first, but he left the file for Tess to open. When she scanned the pages and saw the name on the borrower's line, her heart sank. The unique signature, with the looping tails on the *h* and *p* and the last letters trailing off into a scrawl, was definitely her father's. And he'd initialed each of the terms—$100,000 to be repaid in quarterly installments or, with penalties and interest, in full, at the end of the year. The interest rate was one that only a desperate man would accept; the collateral, the entirety of the Alamo Canyon Ranch.

"But look at this." Casey had joined them. "The lender was supposed to take out mortgage insurance on the loan. Maybe that's what Bert had in mind—take out a loan and let the insurance pay it off after he died."

"Isn't the borrower supposed to do that?" Shane asked.

"Maybe," Tess said. "But Dad knew he had terminal cancer. He was uninsurable. So maybe the loan company decided to bend the rules and take it out themselves."

"Or make him think they were," Casey said. "I'm betting that what they wanted was for Bert to default on the loan so they could go after the ranch."

"Or maybe the insurance did pay and they just kept the money," Shane said. "It wouldn't hurt to consult a lawyer."

"Enough!" Tess threw up her hands. "Tomorrow I'm going to Tucson to see the loan company and our bank. I'm not coming home until I know what Dad did with the money and whether we really owe that sleazebag loan outfit."

"If you need backup, I'm available to go with you," Casey offered. "Just ask."

Tess knew that Casey was recovering well. He'd mentioned that the dizzy spells had stopped. He'd done some driving and was already talking about returning to his condo. She would miss his advice and support. But she knew what would happen in Tucson if she were to show up with a man. People would assume that the man was in charge.

"Thanks, Casey," she said, "but I need to do this by myself. I'll be leaving first thing tomorrow morning. If you want to help, you can take over my chores for the day. Just wish me luck."

Val was aware of the situation with the loan, and she was worried about it, but there was little she could offer in the way of help. Tess appeared to be handling it on her own, with some assistance from Casey and Shane. But Lexie, who was too often left out of the circle because of her so-called delicate condition, was in need of company. Today, with Tess off to Tucson and Casey working, Val was helping her younger sister make a wish list of items for the online baby shower the bull riders' wives were planning. The two of them were seated on the front porch, Lexie with her laptop and Val sitting close enough to see the screen.

"I can't believe how many things a baby needs," Lexie said, "or how much they cost. I can't ask those women to buy me a crib or a stroller. And even those packs of diapers—good grief, they really add up. And all the other little things—clothes, blankets, bottles, a high chair, and one of those little slings that lets you carry the baby in front of you—what's it called?"

"I think it's called a Snuggle," Val said, although she couldn't recall how she knew.

"And the hospital—we have a little insurance, but not enough. And now—" She shook her pretty blond head. Val knew what she must be thinking. If the worst happened and that unexpected loan crisis couldn't be resolved, the whole family could end up looking for a roof over their heads.

Lexie hesitated, then took a deep breath. "Oh, Val, I've got to tell somebody. Just promise you'll keep this to yourself. You know that Shane lived with Brock Tolman for a long time."

"Yes, I know that."

"And you know how much our family hates the man, especially Tess."

"I know that, too."

"Shane and Brock did a lot of talking in Las Vegas. He wants Shane and me to come and live on his ranch. We'd have a home, the best rehab treatment for Shane that money could buy. The best schools for our kids, whatever we need. And if it all works out, we'll inherit the ranch when Brock dies."

"I have just one question," Val said. "Why are you still here?"

Lexie gazed down at her growing baby bump. "It's not that simple. Shane left Brock in the first place because he was so controlling. He says he'd be giving up his independence if he went back. For me, it's family. How often would I get to see you and Tess? Would you even get to spend time with the baby? And Tess—she's got all these plans for the ranch, and she needs Shane to help her. If we leave, the only family she'll have here is you—and maybe Casey if you two get married."

"Trust me, honey, that isn't going to happen."

"But why? You and he are so great together."

"Too many complications. Let's leave it at that. As for the future, whether you go or stay, you and Shane need to do whatever's best for your little family and nobody else. You two take care of each other and your little one. The rest of the world can take care of itself."

"But what if we lose the ranch? Shane and I would be okay. So would you, I think. You've been on your own for years. But what about Tess? This ranch is her whole life."

"Don't count Tess out, or the rest of us either. We've only begun to fight." But Val was genuinely worried. She'd suggested to Tess that they sell off part of the land. But thinking about it since, she realized that if the entire ranch had been put up as collateral, they'd have no right to sell any of it.

Dad, you fool, how could you do this to us? You must've been out of your mind!

Tess walked in the front door at dinnertime, dropped her briefcase on the couch, and sank into her place at the table. One look at the drained, defeated expression on her face was enough to prepare Val for bad news.

"Well, I found out where the money went," she said. "Over the years, Dad had taken out a series of smaller loans from the bank. The payments and interest were adding up. In January, the day he got the money from the loan company, he went in and paid them off."

"And the loan company?" Shane asked.

"I met Patrick and Packard. What a couple of little creeps." Tess shook her head. "They claimed to have acted in good faith—showed me evidence that they'd purchased mortgage insurance, filed a claim when Dad died, and been turned down. But I think they knew what they were doing all along."

"Wait," Val said. "If they knew Dad was deceased, why was the payment notice addressed to him?"

"I asked that question. They had a new secretary who didn't know the score. When the due date came up on her calendar, she sent out the notice. Actually, she may have done us a favor. I think her bosses were planning to wait until the loan was in default before they swooped in. The notice gave us six weeks to come up with payment—not that there's any way we can."

"You asked the bank?" It was Casey's question.

"I did. I begged. Too risky, Mr. Heart of Stone said. So I made the rounds—same answer from every bank I asked."

There was silence around the table. Maria scooped an enchilada out of the pan on the table and laid it gently on Tess's plate. "You still need to eat," she said. "Don't worry, I will ask the Holy Virgin. Something good will happen. You'll see."

But something told Val it was going to take a lot more than Maria's faith to save the family's beloved ranch.

CHAPTER SIXTEEN

*T*HE HOUSE WAS DARK, THE NIGHT QUIET EXCEPT FOR THE RUSTLE OF wind in the dry grass along the pasture fence. Even the dog, who tended to stir at the slightest sound, slept peacefully on the porch, hind legs twitching as he chased a rabbit in his dreams.

Unable to sleep, Val wrapped Jack's old flannel robe over the tee and leggings she wore as pajamas, slipped her feet into worn leather loafers, and wandered outside.

The dog raised his head as she stepped past him. After a pat and a word from her, he settled back and closed his eyes.

Casey's truck was parked in the yard, alongside the ranch pick-up, Shane's custom SUV, and the aging Toyota Corolla used for light errands. Val had long since sold the red convertible she'd driven home from LA. She'd used the money—not much since the engine was almost shot—to pay her share of the bills.

Soon there would be one less vehicle in the row. Now that Casey was well enough to drive, he'd be leaving in the next few days for his condo and his old life—the friends she didn't know, the places she'd never seen, and maybe the women he'd never told her about. He needed to go, and she needed to let him, no matter how much it hurt.

Reaching the pasture fence on the far side of the yard, she stood leaning against the rails, watching ragged clouds blow across the waning moon. The wind was dry, the pale grass grazed almost to the ground by hungry animals. At the distant end of the pasture, she could see the bulls, dark hulks, like massive boulders in the moonlight. Soon they'd be moved to another pasture, where the grass was parched, brittle, and not much more nourishing than here.

During her time away, Val hadn't missed the ranch. But now, thinking about the news Tess had brought home, Val felt a grief bordering on love. It was as if the Alamo Canyon Ranch was dying and she was helpless to save it.

"I thought I saw you come out here." Casey's voice startled her, but only for an instant. Turning around, she stepped into his open arms. Closing her eyes, she let him hold her. He was safety. He was protection. But only for now.

"What are we going to do about the ranch?" she asked. "I've been racking my brain. Our family has put its lifeblood into this place, and just like that, because Dad was foolish enough to trust the wrong people, those awful men can steal it."

Casey's arms tightened around her. "The fight isn't over, Val. I won't be here much longer, but I still plan to be involved. From Tucson, I can actually do more—talk to people, use any connections I might have to get your family some help. There's money out there. We just have to find it."

"I know you need to go," Val said. "But it's been nice having you here. I don't suppose we'll be seeing much of each other after this."

"What are you talking about? We've hardly had any serious time alone here. When I'm in Tucson, you can stay with me. We can go out on real dates, snuggle in front of the TV, wake up in the same bed. It's going to be fine. Or if you'll hear me out, I've got an even better idea."

Val felt it coming—in the tightening in her chest, in the sudden painful pounding of her heart. The words, yet to be spoken, were like a bomb falling out of the sky, and her reply, the only one she could give, would be the explosion that would end everything. She'd let herself enjoy loving him, pretending this moment would never come. But now it was here. She had to face it.

"Val, are you listening to me?"

"I'm listening."

"Then listen good. I know things aren't perfect for us. Maybe they never will be. We're not perfect people. But I've never stopped loving you, and after all this time, I know I never will. We're good together, and we make each other better." He took a breath. "Marry me, Val Champion. I want us to be whatever kind of family we can make. I want to spend the rest of my life taking care of you and making you happy. I didn't plan this for now, and I don't have a ring, but I hope you'll say yes."

As she looked up at him, she could almost feel her heart ripping itself into pieces. "I can't marry you, Casey."

Shock passed across his face. His arms released her. "I don't understand. You've never said the words, but if you don't love me, you've been putting on a damn good imitation of it."

"This has nothing to do with love."

"What is it, then? More secrets? Tell me the truth."

"I will." Val had to force the words. "But when you hear it, you won't want to marry me. You won't even want to look at me."

"I'm waiting." His expression had hardened, but Val could tell he hadn't guessed the truth on his own. It was time to shatter his heart. She took a deep breath.

"The baby I told you about," she said. "The little boy I gave birth to and gave up for adoption—he was yours, Casey."

He'd gone rigid. Cold. His mouth tightened. "Go on."

"I'd been in California almost two months before I found out I was pregnant. I wanted to have the baby, but I knew I wasn't ready to be a mother. My father had disowned me. I didn't have any money or any kind of support. And I had my heart set on a career. What kind of mother could I be? What kind of life could I offer him? I did what I thought was best—and believe it or not, I did it out of love."

"Out of love?" His voice emerged as a rasp. "You could've come home and married me, Val. We could've been a family. Or hell, you could've just left him on my doorstep and gone. I'd have

raised him myself, maybe found a good woman to help me. But you gave my son to strangers and never even told me he existed." His eyes glittered with cold rage. "For God's sake, say something!"

"There's nothing to say." Actually, there was—how she'd wanted to come home and why she hadn't. But he was better off not knowing. It was easier to let him hate her for what she'd done. "I can't go back and change the past. That's all there is to it," she said.

"But now—you came back to me, you let me love you, knowing all the time what you were keeping from me. How could you do that?"

"I didn't go back to you," she said. "I came home to heal. And I didn't ask you to love me. But I couldn't deny what I still felt for you. I knew I needed to tell you, but the right time never came— maybe because there was no right time." Her voice broke. "At least I know better than to ask your forgiveness."

He took a step back, away from her. His expression could have been chiseled from ice, but she could imagine the anguish behind it. "Val, I would have forgiven you for almost anything," he said. "But I can't forgive you for this. I'm going inside to get my gear. When I come back out to my truck, I want you out of my sight. I don't want to see you again, not even to say goodbye."

Behind her closed bedroom door, Val listened to the roar of Casey's truck driving away. She willed herself not to cry. What she'd done to Casey didn't even deserve the relief of tears.

At least he'd be able to move on now—find a woman who could give him the family that her own selfish ambition had denied him. Casey would make a wonderful father, just as he would have made a wonderful father to the boy she'd given up.

She'd been so young and scared. And she'd never meant to come back here. How could she have known that life would take her back home and back to Casey?

The adoption had been a closed one. Her only chance of seeing her son again would come if, after he came of age, he chose to see the record. Casey's name was on his birth certificate. But their baby was still a young boy. The only chance for a reunion with his father would be years away.

And now, she needed to move on, too.

As the sound of the powerful engine faded, she left the bedroom, walked back outside, and sank into one of the rocking chairs. Roused from sleep, the dog trotted over and thrust his nose into her hand. She scratched his ears as the truck's red taillights disappeared over the top of the pass. She fought back a surge of emotion. Casey was gone—and there was no other way this could have ended.

"What are you doing out here?" Tess, in pajamas and robe, had come out onto the porch.

"Couldn't sleep."

"Neither could I." She gazed up at the road, where a long cloud of dust was still settling in the moonlight. "I heard Casey's truck start. Why would he leave at this hour? Did he have some kind of emergency?"

"We broke up," Val said. "For good."

"Oh, no, I'm sorry." Tess sank into the chair next to Val's rocker. "I had such hopes for you two. What happened? Or should I mind my own business?"

"The truth happened. A truth that neither of us could live with."

Tess settled back in her chair. "If you need to talk, I'm a good listener," she said. "I'm also a good secret keeper."

Val gazed up at the sky, the only thing in her life that didn't appear to be changing. Maybe she should talk to her sister. Maybe the pain would ease if she were to share it.

"How much time do you have?" she asked.

Tess laid a gentle hand on her arm. "All the rest of the night, if you need it."

Where the ranch road joined Highway 85, Casey braked and looked both ways before pulling out onto the asphalt. The fact that his emotions were out of control didn't give him the right to endanger other people's lives.

Val's revelation had left him in shock—partly because of the way Val had deceived him, but mostly because of the discovery that he was a father.

He had a child—a young son, his own flesh and blood. And even though he might never see the boy in his lifetime or even know his name, he was astonished by the surge of love he felt. Never again would he go to sleep at night without thinking about his son. And in the years ahead, if he were to have more children, the secret thought in his mind would always be that they had a brother.

What Val had done to him, giving away their child, was monstrous. But when he thought of the scars on her body, he remembered that she'd gone to the brink of death to bring her baby into the world. She could have ended the pregnancy. But she'd chosen to give him life.

That, at least, was in her favor, Casey told himself. But not loving him enough to let him know his son—how could he forgive her for that? He'd asked her to marry him, thinking love would help them work through their differences. But now, how could he even look at her without remembering what she'd done?

At a spot in the road, inexplicably called Why, the highway forked. One branch cut south to Mexico. The other would take him across the Tohono O'odham reservation and all the way to Tucson. Casey had never minded this long stretch—the open desert, its rolling hills covered with an army of towering saguaros, broken by stands of bright green creosote or gnarly patches of cholla. At night, the desert had a haunting quality, a shadowy beauty that Casey usually enjoyed. But tonight the darkness only weighed on him.

By first light he would be back in Tucson. He would park his truck in the crowded lot, unload his gear, and take the stairs to his plain, two-bedroom condominium with its thin walls and its balcony view of the strip mall across the street. Only then would reality hit him. Since walking out of the condo less than two weeks ago, on his way to Vegas, his life had changed so much that he barely recognized himself. He was a stranger, going home to a strange place.

Val sat in the rocker on the front porch, wrapped in a quilt from her bed. Her sleepless eyes gazed across the yard at the long shadows cast by the glow of dawn. She was alone. Even the dog had trotted off in search of an early breakfast at the kitchen door.

How long had she been here? She'd come outside in the dark, after a dream had shaken her so badly that she was afraid of going back to sleep. Kept awake by the chilly night air and the calls of prowling coyotes, she'd huddled in the quilt to wait for dawn.

Since Val's return to the ranch her nightmares had become less frequent. She'd even begun to hope that they'd go away. But now, in the nine days since Casey had left, they'd come back, different, but more terrifying than ever.

Even now, she couldn't stop the dream from replaying in her head.

She was running barefoot in the dark through a black maze of tunnels and alleyways, drawn on by the plaintive cry of a baby. Bony hands reached out from nowhere. Small creatures scurried across her path, clawing at her feet. Overhead, a lightning bolt split the sky, releasing a deluge of rain. She ran on. She had to get to that baby. Sometimes the cry sounded mere inches away, or its cry would grow so faint she feared it would stop. Driven by desperation, she plunged ahead through the downpour.

As she ran, she heard footsteps pounding behind her. Was it Casey? Her heart leapt with hope. But no. More lightning revealed a hulking shape looming behind her. An evil smile flashed in the blue-white light.

Dimitri.

Suddenly a wall blocked her way. Cornered, she turned and

prepared to fight for her life. As Dimitri closed in, his echoing
laugh drowned out the baby's cry . . .

She'd awakened in a tangle of legs and bedding, her heart flail-
ing against her ribs like a trapped bird. It had only been a dream.
But she'd been too afraid to go back to sleep. So here she was, sitting on the porch, wrapped in a blanket, waiting for the safety of
sunrise.

She'd had enough therapy to understand that dreams of that
kind sprang from unresolved issues—like coming to terms with
giving up her baby, the wrong she'd done Casey, and the situation
she'd left behind in Las Vegas.

But the dreams weren't the half of it. When Casey had driven
away, she'd told herself to grow up, accept what she couldn't
change, and move on. But the sleepless night hours, interspersed
with those dreams, had taken their toll. She was losing weight and
had trouble concentrating. Worst of all, she'd begun to crave the
numbing effects of alcohol. There'd been moments in the past
week when, had it been available, she'd have sold her soul for a
shot of vodka or even a beer.

Talking with her sister had made Val feel less alone. But even
Tess had questioned the decision she'd made to give up her baby.
"But why didn't you let us know? We'd have welcomed you home
or at least sent you money. And if you didn't want to get married,
we'd have helped you raise him. Callie would have loved a little
baby."

"I couldn't. I wrote to Dad. I told him I was pregnant and
needed help. He wrote back saying he'd washed his hands of me."

And that wasn't the half of it. She'd been tempted to burn the
letter. But thinking she might need it someday, to support what
she'd done, she'd sealed it in an envelope and hidden it away.
She'd never wanted to see that letter again. But the words had already been burned into her memory.

Don't you dare show up here with that big belly and no husband
to show for it. I'll be damned if I'll tolerate a bastard brat on the

place. And the sonofabitch who knocked you up is guilty of sex with a seventeen-year-old. That's statutory rape. If I find out who did it, he's going to prison."

She'd never told anyone about that letter, not even Casey. But she hadn't sent flowers to her father's funeral, and that was the reason.

Val hadn't told her sister about the heightened alcohol cravings either. Tess had enough worries. She and Shane were still searching for a lender to stave off foreclosure. Casey, who remained loyal to the family, was making calls from Tucson. Val had tried to do her part by contacting the few friends she had left in Hollywood. But the effort had been little more than a gesture. Times were tough all over. So far, nobody was interested.

"What are you doing out here? It's cold." Ruben had come around the corner of the house, the dog at his heels. Now in his sixties, the Tohono O'odham foreman had been part of the ranch family since Val was in pigtails. He treated the Champion girls as if they were his own daughters. That included looking out for their welfare.

Val shrugged and pulled the quilt more tightly around her body. "I couldn't sleep," she said.

He planted himself in front of her, his sturdy figure blocking the pale dawn light. "I've been watching you," he said. "You don't look so good."

"I'm fine." She sounded like a surly teenager, Val thought.

"You are not fine. You're not eating and not sleeping. You are starting to look like a ghost."

Without being asked, he sat down in the chair next to her. "Among my people, we have something called the staying sickness. It happens when a person's spirit is out of harmony with the world around him—with the animals, with the plants and the earth, with his family and his neighbors. It causes him to be unhappy, and sometimes to act in bad ways.

"Only the Tohono O'odham can have the staying sickness. But

when I look at you, I think that maybe other people can have something like it. People like you."

The good man's earnestness touched Val. He couldn't expect her to share his beliefs, but at least he was trying to understand and help.

"So how do you treat this staying sickness?" she asked.

"Some people choose the new ways now. But in the old days, it was done with singing," Ruben said. "A shaman would make a ceremony with smoke and special plants. With the sick person lying on a blanket, the shaman would sing a special song to drive the sickness away."

"And does it work?"

"As a boy I saw it work many times. My grandfather was a shaman. He knew the song. It took a long time to sing it all. And because our language had no writing, it had to be learned by ear and sung from memory."

"That's amazing." Val shook her head. "It's too bad there's no one around who could sing it over me. It might do me a world of good."

"What if I told you that I know somebody who could do it? Maybe it could help you. Would you be interested?"

"I might be." Val felt a tingling sensation that was part disbelief, part hope, and part fear. "Who is it that you know?" she asked.

"My mother. She was never taught the song, but she heard it so many times, growing up in her father's house, that she came to know it by heart. She is old now, but she still lives on the reservation. I visit her every time I go home."

"Is she a shaman?"

"No, but she's a gifted healer. She inherited her father's abilities. If she'd been a man, she might have been a great shaman."

A woman. A healer. Val found herself warming to the idea. What if this old woman could end the nightmares and cravings and give her peace? She was ready to try anything. "But I'm not Tohono O'odham," she said. "Would your mother do the ceremony for someone like me?"

"It would be her choice. I would tell her that you are like a daughter to me, so she would see you as a grandchild. But one thing you need to understand. For the ceremony to work, you must believe that it will. Can you do that?"

"I think so." If wanting was believing, then yes, she could do it. She'd tried different therapies in rehab, including hypnosis. If they'd worked, it was because the real healing had come from inside her.

"I can take you to her tonight," he said.

"Thank you. Should I plan to pay her?"

"Not money. But a gift, like a blanket or a warm sweater, something she can use, would be a kindness."

"I'll find something nice. And thank you again, Ruben."

Val kept busy during the day, helping Maria in the kitchen, pulling the dead plants from the vegetable garden, and making a run into Ajo, in the Toyota, to pick up mail and a few groceries. She used her personal credit card to gas up the small car. Ruben had mentioned that the distance to his mother's village was about fifty miles, a drive of more than an hour each way, over unpaved roads. If the old woman agreed to perform the ceremony for Val, Ruben would stay and drive her home in the morning.

When she'd shared her plan with Tess, her practical sister had shrugged. "I've never put much faith in native superstitions, Val. But I know you could use some help. If you want to try it, what have you got to lose?"

Among the boxes that had been moved outside to a storage shed, Val found a light blue woolen blanket, an unused gift, still in its original packaging. New and soft and pretty, it would make a fine present for Ruben's mother.

Later in the day, finding the office empty, she'd used the desktop computer to check her e-mail. There was nothing from Casey—she was learning to accept that. But at least she'd hoped to hear something from Mac Halvorsen about the Lanzoni case. Had the grand jury hearing been set? Was she still expected to testify? Had there been any news about Dimitri?

When she failed to find any word from the assistant DA, she dashed him off a quick note asking for an update. That done, she left the room and went to the kitchen to help Maria with supper.

They left at sunset, the sky aflame behind them as they drove east across the rolling desert that made up much of the reservation. Cactus and scrub dotted the dry hills. Here and there, century plants cast their towering blooms toward the sky.

Small villages and single dwellings, mostly prefabs and trailers, with a few adobes, rose from the land. Some places had cars and trucks parked next to them. Some had sheep or goats behind fences made of cactus ribs. Scruffy-looking dogs chased after the car as it passed.

Ruben wasn't much of a talker, but he'd told Val what to expect. His mother, Juanita, was eighty-four years old. She was mentally alert, but she spoke little English. Spanish and the Tohono O'odham language were her native tongues. If needed, Ruben would be there to interpret. If she declined to do the ceremony, they would thank her politely, leave the gift, and go home.

The sun had gone down by the time they reached a scattering of homes surrounding a well with a windmill. The soft glow of lamplight flickered in windows. Some places on the reservation had access to electricity, or those who could afford one might buy a generator. But the modern age appeared to have left this quiet place by the wayside.

They pulled up to a small adobe house with a cactus fence. From next door, an unseen pair of dogs set off a cacophony of barking. Ruben climbed out of the car and spoke a word to quiet them.

Carrying the blue blanket, which Ruben had advised her to unwrap before presenting, Val accompanied him through the gate and up the walk to the house. A lantern hung alongside the porch. In its light a tiny, white-haired woman, dressed in a long skirt and wrapped in a shawl, stood waiting. Her arms reached out to embrace her son. They spoke in their native tongue for a few moments before Ruben turned to introduce her to Val.

In the flickering light, her child-size face was furrowed like a
walnut. But her dark eyes were sharp with intelligence. Reuben
had mentioned that she liked to be addressed by her first name—
Juanita.

"Welcome to my home," she said in halting English.

"Thank you, Juanita. This is for you." Val held out the blanket.
The old woman took it. Her work-worn hands brushed the soft
fabric. A smile deepened the creases under her eyes. "It is good,"
she said. "Thank you."

Ruben spoke to his mother again. Val couldn't understand the
words, but by the way Juanita kept glancing at her, she knew they
were talking about the healing ceremony.

"My mother wishes to know if you are one of those people who
will write about the ceremony to make money," Ruben said.

"No." Val shook her head. "Tell her I am only a troubled woman
wanting peace."

They spoke a few moments more. At last the old woman nodded. Ruben turned back to Val. "She will do it, even though she is
old and the long singing will make her tired."

"I understand," Val said, speaking directly to Juanita. "And I am
grateful." She spoke to Ruben. "Do you think it might be too
much for her?"

"She wants to do it. And I will be here in case she needs to stop.
She also wants you to understand that because she is not a true
shaman, and because you are not Tohono O'odham, the ceremony might not work for you."

"I understand," Val said. "But if it works here"—she touched
her forehead—"and here"—she put a hand to her heart—"that
will be enough."

"Come inside." Taking the lantern, Juanita led the way through
her neat little house. There was nothing extra here. Nothing out
of place. A few pots and dishes sat on a shelf. Bundles of herbs
hung drying from the ceiling. A large woven basket held what appeared to be her clothes.

She paused to lift a worn and faded blanket off her bed. "My father's. For the healing." Handing the blanket to her son, she picked up a basket of small items and led the way out the back of the house to a garden area, where remnants of corn stalks and the dried vines of beans and squash lay pale against the darker soil.

She pointed to a spot of bare ground and said something to Ruben. He spread the faded blanket on the packed earth. "My mother wants you to lie down here and close your eyes," he said. "Before the song begins, I'm to cover you with the new blanket to keep you warm. Don't talk. It's best for you to be quiet."

Val did as she was told. Excitement, hope, and a little fear quickened her pulse. But she closed her eyes in complete trust of the people beside her. She wanted this ancient ritual to work. She wanted the power to calm her troubled spirit and ease the ache in her heart.

She heard the hiss of a match lighting and, a moment later, smelled fragrant smoke passing over and around her body. Reuben covered her with the new blanket to warm her against the night chill. She took slow, deep breaths as the chanting began, punctuated by the shake of a gourd rattle.

Juanita's singing voice was surprisingly powerful. With Val's eyes closed she found it hard to imagine that much sound coming from a tiny, aging woman. Val understood nothing of the language but the rise and fall of the song; the repetitive patterns and intricate phrasing seemed to lull her into a waking dream. She let the song carry her to a silent, peaceful place. Lying still, breathing to the cadence of the chant, she lost all track of time.

When the song ended, Juanita roused her with a nudge. The night was still dark, but the thin crescent of the waning moon had crossed the arc of the sky, so Val knew that several hours must have passed.

Rising, she felt energized and at peace—everything she'd wished for. She could only hope the feeling would get her through the challenges she had to face in the weeks ahead.

"Thank you so much. I know you helped me." She gave Juanita a grateful hug.

Juanita returned her embrace. "Now you are my granddaughter," she said, making an effort to speak English. "Come back soon."

Val drove all the way back to the ranch, allowing Ruben to get some sleep. They pulled up to the ranch house as the sky was paling with the first light of day.

Tess would already be outside doing chores. Later today they'd be moving cattle to the unused pastures. All hands would be needed to help, even Val, who found herself looking forward to the work. For now, she would have some coffee, check her e-mail in the office, and give Maria a hand with breakfast. For the first time in more than a week, she felt hungry.

Coffee in hand, she sat down at the desk and brought up her e-mail on the computer. She wasn't expecting much—a few sales and solicitations, maybe a bill from her credit card company.

She scrolled down the list of messages, deleting some, opening others, before she saw the reply from Mac Halvorsen. It was probably nothing, she told herself, just a polite response to her earlier message telling her there was no news. Still, as she opened the message, she could feel the tension creeping through her body. Her pulse jerked as she read the message.

Dear Ms. Champion:

Forgive me for not getting back to you sooner. I'll get right to the latest development. Carlo Lanzoni was found stabbed to death in his cell three days ago. It's assumed that someone working for Dimitri was behind the killing, but so far we have no killer and no proof. The grand jury hearing has been cancelled, as has any need for you to testify. However, if we can arrest Dimitri for the murder of our undercover man, your testimony will be critical in getting him the death penalty he deserves. Please keep us informed of your whereabouts.

Yours truly,

M. Halvorsen

Val sat frozen in the chair, staring at the message. As she struggled to make sense of what she'd just read—and what lay between the lines—three facts jumped out at her.

Lanzoni was dead, almost certainly on Dimitri's orders.

Dimitri was back and in command of the organization.

As the witness who could tie him to the murder of the undercover policeman, she would need to be eliminated. And knowing Dimitri, he wouldn't trust anyone else to take her down.

He would be coming for her himself.

CHAPTER SEVENTEEN

*T*HIS WAS NO TIME TO PANIC, VAL TOLD HERSELF. NOW, OF ALL TIMES, she needed a clear head. She would use the sense of peace Juanita's ceremony had given her to keep herself calm while she made her plans.

With Dimitri on her trail, there was no safe place. The ranch's location was public record. If she were to leave or go into hiding, he would harm her family. Keeping them safe—even at the cost of her own life—had to be her first concern.

At least Casey was clear of this mess. If she were to ask for his help, he would give it because that was Casey's way. But he didn't deserve to be put in danger on her account. No matter what happened, she wouldn't involve him.

As for the rest of the ranch family, she would have to make them aware so they could be alert. But if they chose to stand and fight to protect her, Dimitri was capable of slaughtering them all. Val couldn't let them take that risk.

There was just one way to protect her loved ones. She would have to face him alone.

Taking time to think, she gazed past the monitor and out the window. The office gave her a view of the ranch yard and the pasture beyond, where the mature bucking bulls grazed in the morning sunlight. She'd never cared much for the huge, smelly, dangerous animals. But being at the finals in Las Vegas had given her a new appreciation of their strength, their beauty, and their value to the ranch. She looked forward to being on horseback later today, helping move them to the new pasture.

She was coming to love her life on the ranch. But now, that life and the life of the ranch itself were under threat. She couldn't just sit back and let it all happen.

What were the odds that Dimitri would kill her? Certainly not in her favor. She wanted to live—but so had that young undercover cop. So had Wayne Duvall. She would fight Dimitri with everything she had. But in case she lost, she wanted to know that she'd left something good behind. That meant doing two things. She would do them today, while she could.

Going back to her room, she rummaged under the lining of her suitcase and lifted out a medium-size plain manila envelope. The envelope had been in her purse the night Lenny was killed. She'd taken it back to LA, kept it through rehab, and brought it home with her to the ranch.

She carried it back to the office and sat down at the desk. The flap on the envelope was sealed. She didn't bother to open it. She knew what was inside and what it would do to her emotions if she were to look. But whatever might be in store for her, Casey deserved, at long last, to know the truth.

The address of his condo was in the online list Tess had compiled. Val copied it onto the envelope and put the return address, along with her name, in the upper left-hand corner. There was no message. When Casey saw the contents of the envelope, he wouldn't need an explanation.

It would have to be mailed from the post office in Ajo. Val had other business there as well. She could take care of everything in one trip.

After checking with Maria for any needed groceries, she took the keys and her purse and went outside to find Tess, who was just coming out of the stable.

"You're going to town again?" Tess asked. "You went yesterday. And you were up most of the night on that visit to Ruben's mother. How did that go, by the way?"

"She was amazing. I feel like a new woman. But I really do need to go to Ajo again. It'll be a quick trip. Don't worry, I'll be back in time to help you move cattle this afternoon. Is there anything you need?"

"Not a thing. Just don't fall asleep at the wheel."

"I'll be fine. We need to talk later." Val climbed into the car and headed up the gravel road. The manila envelope lay on the seat beside her. She found herself picturing Casey's face when he opened it and saw what was inside. Would he finally understand what she'd done? Whatever the answer to that question, she couldn't expect it to change anything. She and Casey were finished—for good.

She told herself thinking about him was a waste of precious time. She needed to focus on Dimitri, his possible plans, and how she might counter them.

Just getting here would be a challenge for him. The drive from Vegas would take the better part of a day. The nearest commercial airport was in Tucson, more than two hours away. He would need a vehicle.

The only practical way to drive to the ranch was over the pass. But Dimitri was a pro. He wouldn't announce his arrival or make himself a target by driving down the road on the near side, especially with headlights on. He'd be more likely to park short of the top and walk down the steep hillside, invisible in black. The waning moon, soon to be completely dark, would argue for trying it in the next few nights.

But what would he do after that? He could lie in wait and pick her off sniper fashion, or even put an explosive device under her car. But that wasn't Dimitri's style. He would want her looking at him. He'd want the satisfaction of seeing her terror before she died.

What if she could find a way to use that?

Was she just fantasizing, thinking she could outguess a master criminal like Dimitri—a man who'd spent his adult life hunting people down and killing them, efficiently or, for an extra fee, with embellishments? She'd wounded his body and his ego, and the fact that she was female made her an ideal candidate for an "interesting" death.

She was coming into Ajo now, passing the long row of mine tailings from the old days. The post office was off the central plaza. She felt a twinge of self-doubt as the postmaster stamped the manila envelope and tossed it into a bin that was being carried out for pickup. Maybe she was making a mistake, sending its contents to Casey. But it was too late to change her mind.

Her second errand involved a visit to the in-home office of a local insurance agent. Twenty-five minutes later she left with a three-month term insurance policy, the $500,000 death benefit payable to her sisters. She wouldn't tell them about it, of course. But she would leave the paperwork where it would be found in the event of her death.

In the event of her death. The words chilled her as she drove home. Val was prepared to fight for her life. But if Dimitri succeeded in taking that life, at least she'd be leaving something good behind.

Something to justify a selfish, wasted existence.

As promised, Val arrived home in time to wolf down a beef sandwich for lunch and saddle up to move the cattle. Tess was in charge, with Ruben, Pedro, and Val helping. Lexie had insisted on helping, too, even though her sisters and husband had protested against it.

"I'm not even five months along, and the doctor says I'm fine," she'd insisted. "I've always helped move cattle, and I'm sick of being treated like a porcelain doll. I'm mounting up with you, and that's that."

"Fine, but you'll keep to the outside," Tess had ordered. "If things get dicey, I don't want to worry about you getting butted or thrown."

They started with the beef stock—white-faced Herefords, mostly pregnant cows whose last batch of calves had been sold earlier that fall. Tess, Ruben, and Pedro moved the bulk of the small herd, with Val and Lexie riding the outer flanks to head off any animals that might take off on their own.

The sun was warm, the weather calm and clear. Flocks of migrating birds heading south to Mexico etched V's across the sky.

The hooves of the cattle and horses stirred up whorls of dust and occasional clouds of white butterflies. Val sat easy in the saddle as long-buried skills came back to her. Growing up, she'd hated moving cattle—the dust, the sweat, the bawling animals, and the soreness after hours in the saddle. Today she found herself enjoying the work—the warmth of the sun, the sure movements of her horse, the camaraderie among the riders. She would savor each moment of this time—as if it might be the last.

She kept an eye on Lexie, but she needn't have worried. Her sister appeared to be riding comfortably and staying out of danger. Now she was laughing at something Pedro said, her face radiant and joyful.

Val remembered her own pregnancy, how helpless she'd felt after receiving her father's letter. She'd had no money, no way to take care of the tiny, precious life growing inside her. The reputable agency she'd gone to had offered her shelter, food, and medical care in exchange for her consent to the adoption. Desperate, she'd made the choice for her baby's future. She could only hope it had been the right one. She hadn't been allowed to meet the couple who took him away. She didn't even know what they'd named him.

With the beef cattle secure in their new pasture, they set about moving the bucking stock. This part of the operation was riskier. The cows were fiercely protective of their calves and would charge if they felt threatened. But it was this ferocity that made them so valuable as breeders. From what Val understood, bucking bulls inherited their size and strength from their fathers. But it was their mothers who passed on the fighting spirit and that vital tendency to buck. The most fiery cow on the ranch had been the mother of Whirlwind, Whiplash, and the yearling bought by Brock Tolman. Unfortunately, she'd died last year, leaving only three sons to carry her bloodline.

Lexie was getting visibly tired. At Tess's insistence, backed by Val, she left the pasture and rode back to the barn, where Shane was waiting for her. The remaining riders had their work cut out for them with the protective cows and their calves. By the time they'd herded them through the gates into their new pasture, everyone was perspiring.

The bulls, accustomed to being herded into chutes and trailers, were the easiest to move. Only Whiplash put up any resistance. Tess had to rope him when he tried to charge Pedro's horse. The new pasture, up slope from the old one, was dotted with clumps of mesquite, which ought to be cleared. But for the winter, the bulls would enjoy the extra cover.

"I'm worried about Whiplash," Tess confessed to Val as they put away their horses. "I was hoping he'd calm down once we got him home, but he seems more aggressive than ever. If nothing changes, he might be too dangerous for the arena."

"We could still breed him, couldn't we?" Val asked.

"Yes, but he'd be more in demand, and could command bigger fees, if he had a solid record in the PBR. Right now, I don't see that happening."

"Maybe Brock Tolman would buy him."

It was the wrong thing to say. Tess, who'd just put up her saddle, spun around to face her sister. The anger, worry, and frustration she'd held back exploded in one outburst.

"Don't you ever mention that name to me!" she snapped. "Never again! Do you hear?" Turning away, she stalked out of the stable. Val waited, giving her sister a chance to calm down, before she followed her to the house.

Tess was under pressure from all sides. Unfortunately, Val's news would cause her even more worry. And that news couldn't wait past tonight.

Val's original plan had been to confide in Tess before telling the rest of the ranch family about Dimitri. But rather than lay one more burden on her sister, she decided to break the news to all of them at once, over dinner that night.

Everyone at the table knew about Val's last encounter with Dimitri and how she'd shot and wounded him. There was no need for backstory or any reference to her scandalous past. All that mattered now was the present danger.

"Dimitri's back, and he'll be coming for me," she said. "Even if

I were to leave, he'd come. All I want from you all is to be alert, keep your distance, and stay safe. Dimitri doesn't leave witnesses alive. If he knows you've seen him, he'll try to kill you."

"So you're saying we need to either kill or disable him before he can do any harm." It was Shane who spoke up.

"Not *we*," Val said. "Me. I have to face him alone. If I go down, I don't want any one of you going down with me. Your lives are too precious for that."

"Don't be ridiculous, Val," Tess said. "We're family. We protect each other. You're not standing up to this monster alone."

"You girls are my family, too," Ruben said. "I may be getting old, but I'm still good with a gun. You can count on me."

"And me," Shane said. "We've got plenty of guns and ammo, and I'm a good shot."

"Me too," Pedro said. "But we should keep Lexie and Maria somewhere safe.

"Shouldn't we call the police?" Maria asked.

"It wouldn't help. If there's trouble, even if we could get through to them, they'd never get here in time. We're on our own." Tess glanced around the table. "So is everybody on the same page here?"

"Wait, no!" Val said. "I told you, I want to face him alone. I don't want any of you exposed to danger because of something I did."

Tess shook her head. "Think about it, Val. You're assuming he'll come alone, just looking for you. But what if he shows up with friends, planning to set the place on fire and massacre us all? This isn't just about you. We're all in it together. Now let's make some plans."

Casey usually looked forward to the break between the PBR finals and start of next year's season. Last year, he'd taken advantage of the free time to go sport fishing in Mexico and skiing in Utah. This year, so far, he'd divided the week he'd been home between watching pro basketball on TV and gazing at the beige walls of his condo, wondering if he should paint them or just sell the damned place and move away. With a job that took him all over the country, he could live anywhere. Why stay in Tucson?

The Pacific Northwest might be nice. Lots of green there year-round and nothing to remind him of Val. He had loved her for almost as long as he could remember. He would probably love her for the rest of his life. But after what she'd done, he never wanted to see her again.

The phone call from Marcus, inviting him to lunch at 2:00, had come as a welcome distraction. Joel, who lived in Santa Fe, was in town for a couple of days. It was always a pleasure to get together with his teammates and enjoy a good meal away from the pressures of work. All three were bachelors. Joel had a steady girlfriend. Marcus enjoyed a variety of women. Only Casey, the oldest of the three, seemed to suffer from an unsettled love life. He'd begun to hope that might change. But he should have known better.

They'd planned to meet at a steakhouse downtown. Casey had cleaned up and was on the way to his truck when he passed the bank of mailboxes at the entrance to his building. The box key was on the ring with the truck keys. He'd been expecting a bonus check from the PBR. If it had arrived, he could deposit it on the way home.

Using the small key, he opened the mailbox. The only thing inside was a manila envelope with Val's name and return address in the upper left-hand corner. He felt the slight thickness. Probably just some old photos and other mementos. She could've saved herself the trouble. He wasn't interested in looking at them and wallowing in the past. A trash receptacle stood next to the mailboxes. He was tempted to toss the envelope into it. But no, it made sense to take a look, at least. He could always put the photos through the shredder. That might prove cathartic.

Since he was on his way out, he replaced the envelope and closed the mailbox. He would take it inside when he got home and open it when he was in a mood to punish himself.

Good food and good friends. That was just the medicine he needed, Casey told himself as he polished off a cut of prime rib and ordered apple pie for dessert. They'd caught each other up on their plans for the break and the prospects for next season. Remembering Tess's situation with the loan on the ranch, he'd asked his friends to keep a lookout for anyone who might be willing to lend the money. Not that he expected anything to come of it. He truly wanted to help the Champions out. He'd even looked into securing a loan for them with a second mortgage on his condo. But he'd only had the place a few years and didn't have the equity to qualify.

Putting his concerns aside, he switched his attention back to his friends. Joel mentioned that his girlfriend was pushing to get married, and Marcus offered a glowing description of the new woman in his life. Casey braced himself for the question he knew was coming.

"Say, what happened to that gorgeous redhead you were with at the finals?" Joel asked. "You two looked like the real thing to me."

"We broke up," Casey said. "It happens."

"Is that all you can say?" Marcus shook his head. "A man would fight like a tiger to hang on to a woman like her. What happened? Did she dump you?"

"Let's just say we dumped each other."

"But why?"

"She was keeping secrets. Things she hadn't told me. And that's all I'm going to say, so no more questions."

"Okay, man," Marcus said. "But if I had a woman like that, she could keep all the secrets she wanted to."

"My girl has a friend who works as a legal assistant here in Tucson," Joel said. "Classy blonde. Her name's Amber. I could introduce you while I'm in town."

"Thanks, but right now I'm not fit company for any woman. I need some downtime. And speaking of time"—Casey glanced at his watch—"I just remembered someplace I need to be." He slipped two $20 bills out of his wallet and laid them on the table. "That should cover my share of the bill. Nice seeing you two. Keep in touch."

He left the restaurant. His friends would see through his subterfuge of having someplace to go, but they would forgive him. And having been through their own romantic ups and downs, they'd understand that he didn't want to talk about Val. But they wouldn't understand how deep the pain was, or how personal.

There was a game on TV. He couldn't remember who was playing, but it didn't matter. He could pick up a six-pack of beer to sip while he watched it. And maybe if he drank enough to take the edge off, he would open the envelope from Val. Or maybe he never would.

The countdown of days until the ranch was due to go into foreclosure was like the slow drip of blood from a fatal wound. With less than six weeks to go, the Champions were no closer to a way around the problem than they'd been on the day Tess opened the letter from Patrick and Packard.

Three nights after moving the cattle, Val came out onto the porch to find Tess slumped in the rocker with her face buried in her hands.

Ruben, Pedro, Tess, and Val had spent a grueling two days hauling manure from the pile behind the barn, loading the spreader, and scattering it on the empty pastures in the hope that the rains would wash the vital minerals down to the roots of the grass. Whether those rains would come was anybody's guess.

But what did it matter? That was the thought that none of them dared to voice. They had tackled the hard, dirty work as if they were going to be here forever. But they all knew better.

Val took a seat next to her sister. Tess had always been the strong one, the unbreakable one. But now her shoulders shook with dry, silent sobs. "How can we keep doing this?" she muttered. "I've tried everything to save this damned piece of ground. I look around at the place, all the backbreaking work that's gone into it, and I ask myself, why? Why not just give up, sell off the stock, and let the land die?"

Shane and Lexie had come outside in time to hear Tess's last words. All four of them, including Lexie, were armed with loaded pistols, and there was a double-barreled shotgun propped behind the door. But with no sign of Dimitri or his thugs, the focus of worry had swung back to the ranch's money troubles.

Lexie walked over and laid a hand on Tess's shoulder. "Don't give up, Tess," she said. "I know you're tired of fighting. We all are, but this isn't over. We're going to stick together, and we're going to win. You'll see."

Looking up at her, Tess tried to smile. "How could I forget that you were a cheerleader in high school? You sound just like one."

"I'm not cheerleading," Lexie said. "There's got to be a way to save the ranch, and we're going to find it."

Tess shook her head. "Thanks for the encouragement, honey, but I've tried everything. I even talked to a lawyer who advertised a free consultation. He said that if we can't pay the money, those people can take the ranch. And since we can't pay the money, we all need to face reality. This isn't that old Christmas movie where the angel gets his wings. This is life, and sometimes life isn't fair."

Lexie and Shane exchanged glances. Val noticed, but Tess didn't seem to.

"You need a break, Tess," Val said. "There's a good chick flick playing in Ajo. The three of us could make it a girls' date tomorrow, go to the matinee, pig out on popcorn and sodas. We'd be back before dark. What do you say?"

Tess sighed. "Sorry, I'm not in the mood. I'd only be a drag. If you and Lexie want to go—"

"No," Lexie said. "It wouldn't be the same without you, would it, Val?"

"We'll make it another time, when we can all go," Val said.

Tess stretched her legs, stood, and yawned. "I don't know about the rest of you, but I've had a long day and I'm beat. I'll see you all in the morning."

"Sleep tight," Val said. "Don't worry, Pedro has the watch, and I'll be listening, too." She settled back in the chair as Tess went inside, leaving Shane and Lexie on the porch with her.

Val fixed her gaze on them. "I saw the way you looked at each other when Tess said we'd be losing the ranch. What kind of scheme are you cooking up?"

"Scheme? What scheme?" Shane made a poor show of looking innocent.

"Come on, you can't fool me," Val said. "What's going on?"

"We can't tell you," Lexie said. "So please don't try to guess."

"I take it you haven't mentioned anything to Tess."

"No, and we don't plan to," Shane said. "Call it plan B. It's a backup in case everything else fails."

"But that's all we're telling you." Lexie looked tired. It had been a long day.

"Get some rest, you two," Val said. "I'm going to sit up for a while and help Pedro keep an eye on the place. I'll see you in the morning."

"Not a word to Tess, understand?" Lexie held the door for her husband's chair.

"I understand." Val settled back in her seat. A moment later she heard a thud and a little cry.

"What is it?" She sprang up and raced into the house. Lexie was using an arm of the sofa to pull herself to her feet.

"It's all right." She forced a smile. "I'm just clumsy, that's all. I should've looked where I was going." She turned to Shane, who'd been too far away to catch her. He looked worried. "Hey, I'm fine," she said. "Come on. Let's go to bed."

Val gazed after them as they disappeared down the hallway. When she'd first stepped into the room, she'd seen Lexie's face. What she'd glimpsed there, before her sister smiled, was pain. Whatever Lexie had done, it had hurt.

Vaguely worried, Val went back outside and sat down in the rocker. She'd had a long, tiring day, but any urge to sleep had fled. She was wide awake now, alert to the slightest sound—the yelp of a coyote, the grunt of javelinas foraging up beyond the pastures, the call of an owl. The bulls were farther away in their new pasture, but she could still hear them snorting and lowing in the dark. They seemed more restless than usual, but maybe that was because they were in a new place.

A few minutes later, when Pedro came around the house with a flashlight and a pistol, she stopped him. "Get some rest, Pedro. I'll keep watch for a while. If I get tired, I'll wake you."

"You're sure?"

"I'm sure. Go on."

He handed her the flashlight and went back around the house

to his trailer. Val turned off the light, drew her pistol from its holster, and laid it across her lap. The dog, who'd been following Pedro, came up on the porch, curled up next to the chair, and went to sleep.

The house was silent. Val gazed up at the thin sliver of the waxing moon—not even enough light to cast a shadow. The night seemed peaceful enough, but she couldn't shake the vague, gut-level sense that something was wrong.

She wasn't sure how much time had passed, but she'd just gotten out of the chair to stretch her legs when the light in the master bedroom came on. The next thing she heard was the sound of Lexie sobbing.

The bedroom door was open. With Tess behind her, Val burst in to find Lexie huddled on the edge of the bed and Shane, in sweats, getting into his wheelchair.

"She's got some bleeding," he said. "Not too much yet, but it could get worse. We need to get her to the hospital."

Lexie's doctor was in Tucson—a long drive. But there was a small hospital in Ajo. Even that was an hour away, but no better choice was available.

"I'll drive." Tess was already grabbing her clothes. "We'll put that spare cot in the back of the SUV and lay her on it where you can watch her, Shane. Val, get us a pile of clean towels and pray we won't need them. We'll need you to stay here and keep an eye on things. If you can get a phone signal, call the hospital, and maybe even the Highway Patrol and let them know we're on our way."

Val ran to get the towels. She hadn't prayed in so long that she'd almost forgotten how. But she prayed now. Of all the things that could go wrong, the most tragic would be for Lexie and Shane to lose their baby.

She helped Tess load the camp cot into the back of the SUV. Lexie, wearing a warm robe, was helped onto it and covered with blankets. She looked pale and scared.

The custom lift moved Shane's chair in beside her. He held her hand as Tess closed the doors and climbed into the driver's seat.

Ruben, Pedro, and Maria had come around front. They stood with Val as the powerful SUV drove out of the yard and up the road to the pass, watching the red taillights vanish over the top.

"You might as well go back to bed," Val said. "There's nothing we can do but wait and hope. Don't worry, I'll keep watch and let you know if I hear anything."

Maria squeezed Val's hand. "I will pray to the blessed Virgin to protect her baby," she said.

"Thanks. We'll need all the help we can get." Val gave her a hug before the three went back to their trailers. When, after several tries, she failed to get a phone signal, she went outside and sat down. This time she took the shotgun with her and propped it next to the chair. If Dimitri showed up tonight, she'd be ready for him.

Leaning forward, she gazed into the darkness. "Come and get me, you murdering bastard," she muttered. "I've waited long enough. Let's get this over with."

CHAPTER EIGHTEEN

THE TV BASKETBALL GAME HAD BEEN DISAPPOINTING, AND HE'D barely finished two beers. Feeling the need to move, Casey had stashed the rest of the beer in the fridge and gone to the gym. He hadn't given his body a full workout since the concussion, and he was overdue for a good sweat session. It might be the seasonal break, but it was essential that he stay in shape—even more so now that he was pushing thirty.

After more than an hour of lifting weights and pumping the machines, he'd hit the well-lit outdoor track around the fitness complex and run three miles. After that, he could've used some time in the hydrotherapy pool to ward off muscle soreness. But he'd had enough. All the strenuous exercise he could do wouldn't be enough to get his mind off Val.

After what she'd done, and the way she'd kept it from him, he'd had every reason to walk out on her. But he couldn't shake the awareness that he'd left her in a dangerous situation. Sooner or later Dimitri would be back, and he'd be coming for her. It wasn't a matter of *if*. It was a matter of *when*.

By the time he got home, worry was gnawing at his gut. When he walked into the condo and turned on the light, the first thing he saw was Val's envelope lying on the kitchen counter where he'd tossed it. Maybe it was time he dealt with whatever was inside. But first he wanted to check something on his computer.

The laptop sat open on the kitchen table. Powering it up, he found the site for the *Las Vegas Review-Journal.* There was nothing about the Lanzoni trial or the grand jury in the current edition, but a search for the name led him to a headline that chilled his blood.

CARLO LANZONI KILLED IN JAIL STABBING

According to the story, the killer hadn't been identified. But the murder was assumed to be related to Lanzoni's alleged mob ties. No mention was made of Dimitri. But it didn't take a genius to figure out who'd arranged the hit. With Lanzoni dead, Dimitri would almost certainly be the new boss. And once he firmed up his organization, the next step would be to eliminate the witness who could put him away for life and probably land him on death row—the woman who'd shot him and forced him to run.

Val wouldn't leave her family unprotected. She'd be with them on the ranch, where Dimitri would have no trouble finding her. And when he did, her only allies would be her two sisters, one of them pregnant, a brave man in a wheelchair, a loyal but aging foreman, and his hired relatives.

Dimitri wouldn't hesitate to kill them all.

Did Val even know what had happened to Lanzoni? The man at the DA's office might have notified her. But there was no guarantee of that. Her family could be going about their lives, unaware that a killer was stalking them. At the very least he needed to let her know and to make sure she had help.

He tried her phone. Nothing. The signal had always been spotty at the ranch. All he could do was wait a few minutes and make the call again.

After the last bitter words he'd said to her, she might not even answer a call from him. But he had to keep trying. He would send her an e-mail, then try the phone again a little later. If she didn't answer, he would try Tess.

Meanwhile there was the envelope lying on the counter as if challenging him to open it and look inside.

Forcing himself to move, he picked up the envelope, used a kitchen knife to open the sealed flap, and dumped the contents on the table.

He stared down at what the envelope had held.

He'd expected maybe a few prom photos, school pictures, and mementos like concert tickets and the inexpensive friendship ring he'd bought her. What he saw instead, at first glance, was some kind of certificate, two photos, lying facedown in a plastic sleeve, and a sealed business-size envelope with something inside.

He picked up what appeared to be a photocopied birth certificate from the state of California. His throat tightened as he studied it—the date, the time, the name of the hospital. There was no name for the baby. But Val was listed as the mother. And in the space for the father was his own name. In the lower corner, next to the doctor's signature, was a tiny, perfect footprint.

Casey traced the footprint's outline, brushing each little toe with the tip of his finger. He clenched his jaw to hold back the rush of emotion. This was his son, all he would ever know of him. And Val had given him away.

Hand shaking, he turned over the plastic sleeve that held the photos. Taken under harsh hospital light, one showed a baby sleeping in his bassinette. A beautiful boy with Val's red hair. What would the baby have of him? Casey wondered, blinking away a tear. Who would he look like now?

The other photo showed Val propped in a hospital bed, holding her baby, perhaps for the last time. She looked pale and drawn, her thin face streaked with tears. Her arms were clasped tightly around the tiny bundle, her eyes fierce, as if daring anybody to take her baby from her.

It must have been agony, handing her little one over to strangers. Only after seeing this picture did he realize how hard it must've been for her.

But then, why had she done it? She could have come home. She could have married him. They could have raised their son together. Had the drive to succeed in Hollywood been so strong that she would give up her child for it?

Only the plain white envelope remained to be examined. Casey tore off the end. A smaller envelope fell out, this one stamped and sent to Miss Valerie Champion at a Los Angeles address. The return address bore the name of Bert Champion, Val's father.

The envelope had been opened. Folded inside were two hand-written pages. Flattening them on the table, Casey began to read.

"*When you left for the bright lights, I warned you that no good would come of it. So now you're pregnant and want to come home. That sure didn't take long. But don't expect any welcome from me. You've made your bed. Now you can lie in it.'*"

So Val had asked to come home. And her father had said no. Things were beginning to make sense, but not in the way Casey had imagined. He read on.

"*Don't you dare show up here . . . I'll be damned if I'll tolerate a bastard brat on the place. And the sonofabitch who knocked you up is guilty of sex with a seventeen-year-old. That's statutory rape. If I find out who did it, he's going to rot in prison.'*"

The rest of the letter was more of the same—a father's vitriolic rejection of his daughter. Feeling vaguely sick, Casey crumpled the letter in his fist. So there, at last, was the truth. Val had wanted to come home. With her family's support, she probably would have kept her baby. But when Bert had refused her and threatened to have the baby's father jailed, she'd been forced to make a heartbreaking choice.

He couldn't even imagine how hard it must have been.

So why, when she'd told him about their son, hadn't Val given him the whole story? Casey already knew the answer to that question—he hadn't let her. He'd said unforgivable things to her and gone storming off into the night. Lord, what a fool he'd been.

Picking up his cell phone, he tried her again. Either there was no signal from the ranch or Val had turned off her phone. Growing more worried by the minute, he scrolled to Tess's number.

To his surprise, she answered on the second ring, her voice coming through with perfect clarity.

"Casey? What's happening? Is Val all right?"

"That's why I'm calling you. I can't get her on the phone. But you're coming through fine."

"I'm in Ajo, at the hospital. Lexie was having trouble with the baby—some bleeding. Shane and I just got her here. The doctor's examining her now."

"So Val isn't with you?"

"We left her at the ranch with Ruben and Pedro."

"Does she know that Lanzoni is dead and Dimitri could be back?"

"She knows." Tess paused, as if hearing something. "Got to go. Lexie wants me. I'll keep you posted."

The call ended. Casey put down the phone and strode to the closet to get his pistol, a box of ammo, and his jacket. The ranch was more than two hours from Tucson by daylight. In the dark, on the narrow roads, the drive would take longer. Until he got there, he could only pray that Dimitri wouldn't show up first. If Val refused to speak to him, he would accept that. All that mattered now was keeping her safe.

Val had kept her phone with her on the porch, hoping for news about Lexie. But she didn't really expect a call. When she'd checked for a signal, there was none. For now, the phone was useless. She'd lost track of the time that had passed since her sisters and Shane had left for Ajo. But they should be at the hospital by now. Hopefully, Lexie was stabilized, the baby safe. A miscarriage would break all their hearts.

She couldn't help thinking how different things might have been with her own baby if her father had welcomed her home. There would be a young boy growing up on the ranch, loved by everyone. Or maybe she would have married Casey after all. But there was no point in brooding about the past—not when so much was at risk in the present.

The night sky had clouded over, hiding the moon and shrouding the landscape in darkness. On the hillside where the road zigzagged up to the pass, the grunts and squeals of the rummaging javelinas had ceased. Only the bulls, restless in their new pasture, made enough noise to carry to the porch, where Val sat.

The house was dark, as were the two trailers. Everyone asleep. Everything peaceful.

Then the dog growled.

Val's pulse lurched. "Quiet, boy." Val laid a hand on the back of his neck. The hair was bristling. She fumbled for his collar to hold him, but he tore it out of her hand and shot off the porch, barking as he vanished into the dark.

Standing, she listened as the barks faded with distance and then abruptly stopped. Dead silence ruled the night—as dead as the dog probably was. Gooseflesh rose on Val's arms.

He was here.

Dimitri—or whomever he'd sent—appeared to have done what she'd expected—parked his vehicle short of the pass and come down the slope on foot. But was he alone? So far, there was no way to tell.

She glanced back at the two trailers. No lights had come on in the windows. She could only hope that the dog's barking hadn't roused Ruben and Pedro. If the two good men came rushing out to help her, Dimitri would almost certainly kill them.

Still on the porch, she hesitated. The direction the dog had run and where the barking had stopped gave her some idea of the killer's location. But he wouldn't be there anymore. He'd be moving, probably closer to the house.

Would he try to shoot her? There was no cover on the porch. The ranch truck was parked out front, a dozen yards away. The near side of it would give her some protection. And she would take the shotgun. Her aim wasn't the best, but if she could lure him close enough, a blast from a twelve-gauge shotgun could literally blow a man in two.

She chose to leave the flashlight behind. Turning it on would only give her presence away. Her eyes had adjusted to the dark. She could see a little up close, but nothing far away.

The pistol was in her hand. She slid it into the holster, picked up the loaded shotgun, sprinted silently for the shelter of the truck, and stopped behind the front wheel. Keeping low, she balanced the double barrel of the heavy shotgun across the hood, which would steady her aim. Then she waited.

Seconds, then minutes crawled past, the silence broken only by the faint snorting and lowing of the bulls in the upper pasture. Something was bothering them, maybe the unfamiliar scent in the air.

Nerves crawling, Val waited for something to happen. She was tempted to call out—something like, *Here I am, Dimitri, come and get me!* But that would be foolish. Dimitri had the patience of a spider. He would wait for her to come out of cover and expose herself. Then he would strike. Her only hope was to use the advantage of surprise.

From somewhere beyond the pastures came the wail of a coyote. Val kept still. The urge to move and stretch her legs was becoming unbearable. So was the growing sense of dread. Dimitri was playing her, and it was working.

Just when she thought she couldn't stand it any longer, she heard a sound from beyond the truck—a subtle click, like the dropping of a pebble. She waited, her finger on the first trigger of the shotgun, her eyes straining to peer into the darkness.

Another pebble sound. She strained forward, listening and looking, her senses screaming danger. Where was he?

Only then, as a powerful arm looped her neck and the cold muzzle of a gun pressed against her temple, did she realize her mistake. Distracted by the pebbles he'd thrown, she'd failed to realized that he had come up behind her.

"The shotgun, Valerie." Dimitri's voice grated as he dragged her backward. "Let go of it. Let it fall. Then your pistol. Drop it on the ground."

With his arm threatening to choke her and the steel muzzle cold against her skin, she did as she was told. "Go ahead and kill me, Dimitri." She spat out the words. "I'm not afraid to die. Just get it over with!"

His laugh was pure evil. "That would be too easy, you little bitch. I'm going to kill you, all right. But it's going to happen someplace where I can take my time. Before I'm finished having fun, you'll be begging me to kill you."

Ironically, the first thought that struck Val was that if he were to take her away, kill her and dispose of her body, her sisters would have to wait seven years for the money from her insurance policy. The second, more natural thought was that anything would be better than being tortured. If he was going to kill her, it would have to be here.

He dragged her across the yard, stopping at the fence. "Face-down on the ground. Hands behind your back. Isn't that how the cops do it?" He shoved her forward and down, replacing the gun in his shoulder holster while he anchored her with his knees and bound her wrists with double plastic ties. There was nothing sexual in the way he handled her. Dimitri wasn't about sex. He was about pain.

Fighting terror, Val struggled to remain calm. Her hands were bound, but she still had her legs and her head. And she knew the ranch well enough to find her way around in the dark. Whatever advantage she had, she would have to use it. But first she had to get away.

He pushed to his feet, leaving her lying facedown on the ground. Planting his foot between her bound arms to hold her there, he took his cell phone out of his pocket. He probably had a driver waiting at the pass and would be calling for him to come down and help load Val into his vehicle. He was about to discover there was no signal.

He fumbled with the phone, then swore. In this flicker of distraction, Val saw her chance. Raising her bound arms to trap his foot, she rolled hard and fast. Aided by the slope she was lying on, she pulled his leg off balance. The phone flew out of his hand and vanished in the dark as he went down, cursing.

Fighting for her life, she managed to untangle herself from him and scramble to her feet. Before he could grab her again, she was running up the slope along the steel fence that bound the empty bull pasture. At the top of it, along the same fence line, was the new pasture, where the bulls had been moved.

She could hear him coming behind her, cursing and stumbling in the dark. She was gaining on him and might have gotten away if the clouds hadn't parted at that instant, allowing the traitorous moon to spill its faint light over the slope.

Val heard the pistol shot at the same time she felt it ripping into her shoulder from the back. The pain was so intense that she almost passed out, but she had to keep going. Visible in the moonlight, she'd be an easy target if he chose to shoot her again. Her only chance lay in reaching the bulls.

At last she passed the corner post that anchored the steel fence around the new bull pasture. Head swimming with pain, she dropped to the ground and rolled under the lowest rail, into a patch of tall, dry weeds on the other side.

Heart pounding, she lay still. She had taken refuge in the most dangerous spot on the entire ranch. But for her, it could be her only hope of safety.

The bulls were on the far side of the pasture. Beyond the scattered clumps of mesquite, she could hear them snorting and pawing, which they wouldn't do unless something had disturbed them. Had they caught her scent? If they were to attack her, she'd be too weak to get away. She could feel the blood from the wound, flowing in thin streams down her back. With her hands tied, all she could do was lie against the ground to create what little pressure she could.

Seconds behind her, Dimitri was coming up the slope, breathing hard. Had he seen her go under the fence? Clouds were drifting over the moon again, casting thready shadows across the pasture. The mesquites stood dark against the pale grass. On the far side of them, the bulls had bunched together in a defensive mass.

The dry weeds, mostly foxtails, were prickly against her skin. In wetter times, they had sprouted out of a shallow ditch that ran along the fence line between the pastures. Dragging herself forward, Val rolled into the ditch, pressing her wounded shoulder into the bottom. Partly hidden by the overhanging foxtail heads, she lay still, scarcely daring to breathe. Pain swam in her head, threatening to pull her under.

Dimitri stopped by the fence, not far from where Val lay. "Where are you, you little bitch?" he muttered. "When I get my hands on you, you'll curse the mother that gave you birth."

Raising her head slightly, Val could see him climbing between the rails of the fence, pistol in hand. At any moment now, he would see her, and her life would be over.

But no—he was heading toward the mesquite. But it wouldn't take him long to discover that she wasn't there.

Where she lay, the weeds gave her scant cover. But farther down the ditch, the growth was denser. Maybe, while Dimitri's attention was on the mesquites, she could get there. She had to try.

Jaw clenched against the pain, she pushed herself forward with her feet, inching along the bottom of the ditch toward a place where a thick tangle of weeds and grass obscured the view of the depression. The pressure on her wounded shoulder was agony, but she had to keep moving. Her life depended on it.

She'd almost reached the spot when a covey of startled quail burst upward, almost in her face. With whirring wings and cries of alarm, they scattered in all directions.

"There you are!" Dimitri spun toward her, his pistol aimed at her hiding place. "Come on out, Valerie. It's time to finish our little game."

He took a step toward her. That was when Val saw the massive, dark shape bulldozing through the mesquite thicket, coming up hard and fast behind him. A sliver of moonlight flashed on a brindled coat. It was Whiplash.

Dimitri screamed as the horns caught his back and tossed him high. He screamed again and again, his cries fading away as Val sank into blackness.

When Casey reached the pass and saw the rusted black Cadillac sedan pulled off the road, his throat jerked tight. Had he arrived too late? He was tempted to drive on by, but what if Val was in the car?

There was no activity around the vehicle. Taking his pistol, Casey approached from the back. The driver appeared to be asleep. Shooting him might be the smart thing to do, but Casey wasn't a murderer. Staying to one side, he tapped his pistol on the window. The driver started awake. He looked young and scared. A kid. At Casey's nod, he rolled down the window.

"Don't shoot me," he said. "I'm just driving."

"Where's Dimitri?" Casey demanded, keeping the gun leveled.

"Down there somewhere." The kid's voice shook. "I'm waiting for him to call me."

"Open the trunk." Casey had to make sure Val wasn't inside.

The trunk popped open. Empty.

"Please don't kill me, mister," the young man begged. "Dimitri said he'd give me two thousand dollars to drive him here and to pick him up when he called me. That's all I know."

"Have you got a weapon in there?" Casey could see that the passenger seat was empty, but he needed to make sure.

The boy shook his head. "Please. I just needed the money, that's all."

"Listen, kid, I know about Dimitri." Casey kept the gun pointed at the driver, alert for any sudden move. "He went down there to kill a woman. And he doesn't leave witnesses. That includes you. Once he's done, you'll be dead meat. I'm betting he'll leave your body in this junk car and set it on fire. Take my advice. Start this car now, get out of here, and don't go back to Vegas. Otherwise, I might have to save Dimitri the trouble and kill you myself."

The last threat was a bluff, but it worked. The young driver started the car and pulled onto the road. The bald tires spat gravel as he made a sharp U-turn and shot down the steep grade toward the highway.

With no time to wonder whether he'd done the right thing, Casey sprinted for his truck and sped down the road to the ranch, screeching around the hairpin turns.

He arrived to find the porch light on and Ruben, Pedro, and Maria in the front yard. Both of the men were armed.

"We heard a shot from up the hill by the pastures," Ruben said. "We were headed that way when we saw your headlights and decided to wait for you."

"Come on." Casey charged up the slope, shouting Val's name. It made sense that they'd waited for him to avoid confusion in the dark, but even seconds might make the difference in saving Val's life.

Casey and Pedro both had flashlights, so it was easy enough to follow the trail along the fence to the upper pasture. The first thing they saw was Whiplash standing in the open with a crumpled, mangled figure sprawled at his feet. Sick with dread, Casey directed the beam of his flashlight onto it. No red hair, thank God. The hair and blood-smeared clothes were black. It had to be Dimitri. Even from a distance, Casey could tell beyond a doubt that he was dead.

But where was Val? When Casey shouted her name, there was no answer.

"Here!" Ruben called. There's a blood trail going under the fence. It leads to that drainage ditch. She must've crawled in there to hide." He called Val's name. There was no answer.

As Ruben climbed through the fence rails, Whiplash's head went up. Wild-eyed, he bellowed a challenge, pawed the ground, and lowered his horns to charge. Ruben had to retreat fast, climbing back through the fence. Whiplash had killed one man. Adrenaline was still surging through the bull's body, driving him to attack anything that moved.

To Casey, nothing mattered but getting Val to safety—if she was still alive. "I'll hold him off," he said. "You and Pedro go in and find her."

Casey climbed through the fence. He had his gun, but only a very lucky pistol shot could stop a 2,000-pound bull. And Casey didn't want to kill Whiplash, let alone wound him, except as a last resort.

Taking off his jacket, he whistled and waved it in the air. "Here I am, big boy. Come and get me."

The bull's head swung toward him. His eyes were white-rimmed, his nostrils dripping. Casey could see the bloodstains on his horns and legs. He could see Dimitri's savaged body lying in the grass, a grim reminder of the damage a huge, angry animal like Whiplash could do.

"Come on, boy. I know this mess isn't your doing. You were just following your nature."

Whiplash snorted, lowered his head, and charged.

Casey sidestepped, the bull coming close enough to catch his jacket with a horn. Casey let the jacket go, backing off as Whiplash tossed the jacket and trampled it into the grass. He prayed silently that Ruben and Pedro had found Val, but he couldn't risk a glance. He had to keep his eyes on the bull.

Suddenly Whiplash's attention swung back to the two men at the far end of his pasture. Pivoting away from Casey, he charged in their direction.

Desperate to stop him, Casey flung himself into the bull's path, slapping his nose and pulling his horn to turn him. The massive head struck his chest, knocking him off his feet. He hung on to the horns as Whiplash turned, dragging him across the pasture.

"We've got her! We're out!" The shout penetrated Casey's awareness. Unable to hang on any longer, he let go of the horns and rolled to one side. He shielded his head, expecting to be trampled, but Whiplash thundered on past him. In the next instant, Ruben was there, helping Casey to his feet. Together they raced for the fence and dove between the rails.

Val lay on the grass. In the beam of the flashlight, her face was pale, her eyes closed. Casey felt for her pulse. It was there, but weak. He had to get her to the hospital as fast as possible.

Ruben had already cut the plastic ties that bound her wrists. Lifting her in his arms, Casey carried her to the truck and laid her across the backseat. There'd be no time to dress the wound. Every second was critical. Shedding his shirt, he pulled off the clean, white tee underneath and pressed it hard against the back of her shoulder. "One of you come with me and hold it on her while I drive," he said.

"I'll do it." Ruben climbed in beside her, supporting her head in his lap and applying pressure to the wound.

Casey sprang into the driver's seat and drove like a demon all the way to Ajo.

CHAPTER NINETEEN

THE FIRST THING VAL BECAME AWARE OF WAS A HAND CRADLING hers—a big hand, warm and strong and comforting. She clung to that hand as her mind swam toward consciousness. It was solid and real, as nothing else seemed to be.

Little by little her senses woke to other things—a raw pain that seemed to be everywhere in her body. Some kind of clip on her nose, something attached to her arm, a low, steady beeping sound coming from somewhere above her, and suddenly a voice.

"Val, can you hear me?"

She opened her eyes. Casey was sitting next to her bed, holding her hand. His eyes were sunk in weary shadows, his cheeks and jaw rough and unshaven. But he was smiling. "Welcome back to the world," he said. "Do you know where you are?"

She glanced around her, the sterile-looking room, the monitors overhead, the IV drip attached to her arm. "That's a dumb question," she said, pulling her hand out of his. "And what are you doing here? When you said you never wanted to see me again, I took your word for it."

"I got the things you sent, Val. And I read your father's letter. If you never forgive me for judging you, I'll understand. But when I heard Dimitri was back, I knew I had to be there for you."

"Oh? I don't recall seeing you when Dimitri was dragging me across the yard or chasing me with a gun."

"Only because I couldn't get there in time. How much do you remember?"

"Enough. Dimitri grabbed me and tied my hands. I got away from him and ran up along the fence. He shot me. I crawled into a ditch . . . and Whiplash killed him. Whiplash saved my life."

"I know that much. I saw Dimitri's body."

"Oh!" She suddenly remembered. "What about Lexie? Is the baby all right?"

"They're both fine. But Lexie will need to take it easy. No more playing cowgirl. The doctor kept her here yesterday, and Tess drove her and Shane home last night."

"So you—wait!" Val stared at him, the sleepless eyes, the unshaven stubble. "How long have I been here? How long have *you* been here?"

"Ruben and I brought you in here Tuesday night. It's Thursday afternoon. It took three pints of blood to get you stabilized. After that, we just let you sleep."

"And you've been here the whole time?"

"Val, I know I said some awful things to you. But even before I knew the truth, I cared. I still do."

The truth shouldn't have made any difference. Val wanted to fling the words at him. But what good would it do? She'd known as soon as she saw Casey again that she still loved him—and that he would never forgive her for what she'd done.

She wasn't sorry she'd sent him the photos and the birth certificate. Casey had a right to those. But the letter from her father cast doubt on everything. Wasn't love supposed to be unconditional? If that was true, why would the letter make it suddenly all right for Casey to love her again?

"Tess was here when we brought you in," he said, changing the subject. "She waited until she knew you were going to be all right. Then she took Ruben home and stayed to deal with the police. I talked with her when she came back to look in on you and take Lexie home."

"The police came?" But of course they would.

"According to Tess, the county sheriff and his deputy got there first. They took statements from Ruben and Pedro, but they had orders not to touch the body or the crime scene until the Las Vegas crew came in by helicopter. They processed the scene, bagged the body, and left. I'm sure you'll be hearing from them."

"How did they get around the bulls?"

"Tess and Ruben and Pedro herded them back into the old pasture."

"And Whiplash? Was he all right?"

"As far as I know." Casey hesitated, and Val sensed some bad news coming.

"Tell me," she said. "Whatever it is, I can take it."

"They found the dog. His neck was broken. Tess buried him by your father."

"I'm truly sorry about that. He was a good old dog, and he died warning me. Is that all?"

"No." Casey cleared his throat. "It's Whiplash. He won't be bucking in the arena again. Clay Rafferty ruled that he's too dangerous."

Val was disheartened but not surprised. If a bull was involved in an accidental death, such as Jack's, which had happened when he fell under the hooves, that bull was usually allowed to continue. But there was no place for a bull who'd deliberately killed a man, even if it wasn't in the arena.

"There's more," Casey said. "The sheriff is recommending that Whiplash be put down. It's Tess's decision, and she's thinking about it."

"No!" Val sat up so abruptly that it ripped at the dressing on her wound, triggering a searing jolt of pain. She bit back a cry. "They can't do that, Casey. Whiplash saved my life. He killed a terrible man."

"And he could do it again, Val—attack and kill someone. Only this time it could be Ruben or Pedro or Tess—or even you."

"But it's not his fault, the way he is. Look at what happened to him—having that dead man dumped into his pen and then being bucked before he'd had time to recover. He was traumatized. Anybody would be. I won't stand for it. You can tell Tess—"

"Tell her what?" Tess walked into the room. She was dressed in fresh jeans and a black sweater, her curly hair still damp from a shower, but the strain of juggling multiple crises showed in her face. She looked exhausted.

"So tell me," she said. "And by the way, I'm glad you're awake and recovering. I brought you some clean clothes to wear when you leave. You'll be needing them. Now, what's on your mind?"

"Casey just told me that Whiplash might be put down," Val said. "That bull saved my life, Tess. He's a hero. If you kill him, so help me, I'll—"

"Whoa," Tess said, pulling up a chair. "First of all, no decision's been made. I'm still weighing my options."

"*Your* options? What about mine? And Lexie's? It's our ranch, too. Equal shares—I know, if Dad had made a will, he'd have left me out of it. But since he didn't, I'm as much an owner as you are. So why do you get to make the decisions?"

Tess glanced at Casey. "You look all in, Casey," she said. "I'll bet you could use some coffee and a meal. Why don't you take a break and give us a chance for some girl talk?"

He stood, a tired half smile on his face. "I can take a hint, Big Sister. You take it easy, Val. I'll be back in a bit."

"Girl talk?" Val raised an eyebrow as Casey walked out. "I thought we were talking about the ranch—and Whiplash."

"All right, that first," Tess said. "I know you're part owner of the ranch. But I seem to be the only one who understands that it's a business. It has to make money. And our bulls aren't children. They're assets. Are you with me so far?"

"Yes, but it sounds colder than hell frozen over."

"Whiplash isn't just a danger. He's a liability. He won't be allowed to buck anymore, so there goes any money he could earn at PBR and rodeo events. And a 2,000-pound bull isn't cheap to feed."

"What about breeding? He's got a good bloodline."

"Yes, but if you've talked with Lexie, you know that we can't breed him with our own cows. They're too closely related. And with his reputation as a killer bull, nobody's going to want him on their ranch. Oh—and don't even talk to me about semen. You can't get that from a bull who's wanting to murder you."

"But this can't just be about money, Tess. Whiplash didn't ask for the things that made him so mean. He deserves a chance to live. Maybe, with time and good treatment, he could even calm down and be a good bull."

Tess sighed. "I can see your heart's in this. But you know that we could be about to lose the ranch and if we do, we'll have to sell off the animals, including the bulls. But I couldn't in good conscience let anybody have Whiplash. He could hurt somebody else, or maybe get sold out of the country and end up being abused. If we lose the ranch, I'll have no choice."

"So what's the bottom line?" Val asked.

"Until we know what's happening with the ranch, he can stay. In turn, I want you to promise that if he does have to be put down, you'll be an adult about it. Do we have a deal?"

"I guess so, if that's your best offer." Val remembered Shane and Lexie's so-called plan B. Maybe it had just been wishful thinking. Nothing was certain these days. But at least she'd bought Whiplash some time.

"You said we could talk about Whiplash first, so what else is on your mind?" Val asked.

"The 'what else' is what just walked out that door," Tess said.

"You mean Casey?"

"Good guess." Tess pulled her chair closer to the bed. "I know you might not want to hear this, but it's time I talked to you like a big sister."

"As I told you, we broke up. I confessed about the baby, and he said he never wanted to see me again. I took him at his word. As far as I'm concerned, nothing's changed."

"Listen to me. I was here when he brought you in. You were almost dead from blood loss. He practically bulldozed his way into the ER and wouldn't leave until the nurses hustled him out so they could hook you up to the IV and clean the wound. After they moved you to this room, he didn't leave your side. He sat there holding your hand and talking to you, telling you how much he loved you and asking you to forgive him."

"Tess—"

"No, just listen. Do you know how rare it is to be loved that much by a man? Most women never get to find out what it's like. I was one of the lucky ones. But I lost my love, and I've never found anything to compare with what we had.

"Now it's your turn. And if you throw this chance away, you'll regret it forever. You'll end up settling for less with another man—or other men. Or maybe you'll end up like me, living your life alone because nothing could ever be as good as what you had before."

Val blinked away a tear. "But how can I saddle him with a mess like me? I'm an alcoholic and an ex-mob girl. I've broken laws, I've bought and sold drugs. I gave away the one baby I had, and I can't have any more. I'm damaged goods, Tess. Why would any man want me?"

Tess seized Val's hand, her strong fingers gripping hard. "Casey loves you—crazy baggage and all. And I know you love him. But if you throw this miracle away out of pride, it'll be the stupidest mistake you've ever made—and sister, you've made some doozies!"

Brock Tolman nudged the lifeless body of the yearling bull with his boot toe. Rotten luck. Even with good care, animals died, sometimes for unexplained reasons—a hidden defect, a poisonous plant, a sudden blockage or infection. He wouldn't know until his vet had examined the carcass. But why did it have to be *this* calf—the one born on the Alamo Canyon Ranch, the one whose fiery bloodline carried the hope of producing a top bucker?

Brock cursed out loud. Damned shame, and just when everything else seemed to be going so well.

For years he'd been coveting that sweet little ranch in the grassy mountain valley. Now, thanks to a blunder by the late Bert Champion and the avarice of a fly-by-night loan company, he was about to get a piece of it.

It was Shane Tully who'd contacted him out of the blue—Shane, who'd come of age on Brock's ranch and left after a misunderstanding, was the closest thing to a son Brock would ever have. Their relationship had thawed since their parting, but since he'd married Lexie Champion, Shane's loyalties were with his wife's family. Brock knew that Shane was only trying to help them. But that didn't mean Brock couldn't turn things to his own advantage.

Shane had told him about the mortgage on the Alamo Canyon Ranch and the two shysters who'd taken advantage of a dying man. Brock could pay off the mortgage—the amount would be pocket change for him—rescue the ranch, and put himself in a position to negotiate with Tess Champion for whatever he wanted.

Tess was on the ropes, an image Brock found highly entertaining. The prickly female needed taking down a few pegs, and he was just the man to do it. There was another way he wouldn't mind taking her down, as well. But that would have to wait. Right now, this was about business.

Brock had researched the situation and was ready to move forward with his plans. Then one of the hired hands had radioed him about finding the yearling dead in the pasture. The discovery had put a black cloud over the day. Brock had held high hopes for that calf—the last full brother of Whirlwind and Whiplash. Now just two bulls carried the bloodline, and Tess had sworn that she would never sell either of them, especially not to him.

He was walking back to his sprawling, glass-sided house, surrounded by pristine native desert, when his cell phone rang. The caller was Clay Rafferty.

"Clay? What's up?" Brock was caught off guard. Even though the two were casual friends, it wasn't usual for the PBR Director of Livestock to phone him.

"Earlier I spoke with Tess Champion. They've got a situation at Alamo Canyon Ranch that I needed to know about." Rafferty gave a brief account of what had happened—how Whiplash had killed a man who invaded his pasture. "Since you know the Champions, I was thinking you might be able to offer some help. Whiplash won't be allowed to buck anymore, and the sheriff is pressuring Tess to put him down. That seems a shameful waste of such a fine animal. I thought, if you're interested, you might come up with a way to save him. Just letting you know."

"Thanks, Clay, I'll think on it." They ended the call.

Brock whistled under his breath as he continued back to the house. Maybe the day hadn't turned out so bad after all.

After Tess had left, Val lay back on the pillows, exhausted. All she'd done was open her eyes and talk for a few minutes, but she felt as if she'd run a marathon. Recovering her strength was going to take time.

Tess's words came back to her as she lay there. Everything her sister had said rang true. She knew that Casey loved her. And she knew that she loved him. But would that be enough? What if, after all she'd put him through, she couldn't make him happy?

What if they both got tired of him doing the giving and her doing the taking?

Maybe one day he'd meet someone else—someone fresh and uncomplicated who could give him the children he wanted. Maybe he'd just get tired of her insecurities and want to leave.

Maybe sending him away now, before things got ugly and disappointing, would be a kindness.

She needed time to think. Maybe he did, too.

When Casey came back into the room, she knew what she had to say—even though the sight of him made her want to hide in his arms until all the doubts and nightmares were gone.

"I want you to leave for now," she said. "You've been through a lot with me over the past couple of days. You need a break. And I need to rest."

His eyes remained on her, but something guarded had slipped into his gaze. "Fine. I won't call you because I won't want to disturb your sleep. If you need anything, Tess brought your cell in and I made sure my number was on it. Will you still be wanting a ride back to the ranch?"

"Yes, and I'm holding you to it. But it'll be a few days off. I still feel like I've been run down by a freight train." She faked a teasing smile. "So get on your horse, cowboy, and ride off into the sunset for a while."

"Got it." He leaned over and brushed a kiss on her forehead, then turned and walked out of the room.

Even then she was tempted to call him back. He would have come and stayed as long as she wanted him to. Casey was a rescuer, a protector, who would always be there when she needed him. But maybe that was the problem. Maybe, for this to work out, she had to know he needed her, too.

Val stayed at the hospital for three more days. Most of the time was spent sleeping or watching mindless TV as her body healed. Tess checked on her by e-mail on her phone, and Ruben came by once when he was in town. But Casey didn't call her, and she didn't call him. She needed time to rest and think. She could only hope that he was thinking, too.

The morning of her release, she called him. "I'll be there around noon," he said. "Do you want to get lunch somewhere?"

"No," she said. "I just want to go home."

She was waiting when he arrived. On the drive back to the ranch, most of the conversation was awkward small talk. She was holding back. So, she sensed, was he.

Some rain had fallen while she was in the hospital. The desert was coming to life again, the brown, grays, and yellows already beginning to green. On the ranch, new grass would be sprouting in the pastures.

The tension mounted between them as they left the highway and started the climb up to the pass. At the place near the top where they'd watched the stars and where they'd made love for the first time, he pulled the truck off the road and stopped.

"We need to talk," he said.

"Yes, we do."

"You first," he said. "Just make it short."

Val had prepared a long monologue about how he needed to respect her independence and how she still needed to find herself and be strong on her own. But the words wouldn't start. Instead, she just looked at him.

"Oh, Casey," she said.

He reached across the console, pulled her close, and kissed her long and deep. "Blast it, Val," he muttered. "You know we'll never get this a hundred percent right, you and me. Neither of us is perfect. We never will be. So why not just say to hell with it and go with what we've got? If you ask me, what we've got is pretty damned good. So what do you say?"

She looked up at him—the boy she'd adored since she was in pigtails, the man who'd taught her to love, fathered her child, and saved her life. He was right. It would never be perfect. But what they had was irreplaceable. What they had was love, crazy and wild and completely real.

"Kiss me again, you fool," she said.

EPILOGUE

Thanksgiving Day, the same month

*T*his year's Thanksgiving dinner had been a bittersweet affair, Tess reflected as she carried the last dessert plate back to the kitchen.

True, the traditional turkey meal, with Maria's special mole, hot rolls served with saguaro fruit jam, and Val's made-from-scratch pies, was even more delicious than usual. And there were reasons to celebrate. Lexie and her unborn baby, a boy, were doing well, and the threat against Val was finally in the past. She and Casey were making plans for their future—plans that seemed to change almost daily.

But the specter of losing the ranch hung over them all. Tess was already looking for ways to delay or prolong the foreclosure, in the hope of finding the cash—or some other solution—to save the only home she'd ever known.

This year, there'd been an unspoken agreement to make Thanksgiving a happy day with no talk of past or impending losses. But looking around the table as dinner was served, Tess hadn't been able to keep from remembering the faces that were missing from last year. Jack, her brother, had died less than two weeks after Thanksgiving at the National Finals Rodeo. Her father passed away from cancer and grief a few months after that. And Callie, her beloved stepmother, had been murdered that sum-

mer. The neighbor who'd killed her had also been a guest at their
table last year. Sentenced to life, he had recently died in a prison
yard brawl.

All of them gone. This year there were new and welcome faces.
Pedro and Maria had joined the ranch family, as had Shane and
now Casey. And Val was back, after years of bitter absence. Life
continued, the good with the bad.

The day was winding down now. Ruben, Pedro, and Maria had
gone back to their trailers. Val and Lexie were finishing cleanup
in the kitchen. Shane and Casey were watching football on TV.
Maybe this would be a good time to go back to the office and
catch up on some paperwork, Tess thought.

She was crossing the living room to go down the hall when the
front doorbell rang. Startled, Tess hurried to answer the door.
The family hadn't expected any visitors today. But what if this was
some kind of emergency?

She reached the door and opened it. Standing on the porch
was the last person she'd expected to see today.

"May I come in?" Brock Tolman asked.

Tess took a step back. "Certainly," she said. "But if you're here
for dinner, you're too late. We've finished eating."

"I didn't come to eat, and don't worry, I won't be staying long.
I just brought you a present of sorts, and a business proposition."
He stepped inside, closing the door behind him. He was dressed
in jeans, a leather jacket, and a gray alpaca sweater. His looming
presence seemed to fill the room. "We can talk in your office if
you'd rather keep our conversation private," he said.

"No." Tess was still taken aback. "There's no business that can't
be shared with my family. Please have a seat." She indicated an
oversize armchair. "Can I get you anything to drink? We don't
keep alcohol around, but if you'd like some coffee or a Coke . . ."
She was rattling on, she realized.

"No, I'm fine, thanks." He sat down. Shane and Casey had
turned off the TV. Lexie and Val had come to stand in the entrance to the dining room. Tess perched on the arm of the sofa
where the men were sitting.

"Actually, I have two matters of business," Tolman said. "I'll address the simpler one first. Clay Rafferty tells me you have a situation with Whiplash."

"Word gets around," Tess said. "And yes, we have a situation. I certainly don't want to put him down, but it may need to be done, especially if we lose the ranch."

"I have a better solution," Tolman said. "Let me take him off your hands. I have plenty of land for him to run on with other bulls, and it shouldn't be a problem to breed him with some of my good cows."

"So you want us to give him to you? Just like that?" Tess spoke through a surge of anger. The man would take advantage of his own grandmother. But what he was proposing was a way to save Whiplash's life. She had to listen.

"I was thinking more of a trade," he said. "I have some surplus bulls. They're young and healthy, good buckers, and potentially good breeders. You could have your pick of them."

Tess glanced around the room. "What do you think?" she asked her sisters.

"It would be a way to save Whiplash," Val said.

"And a good, new bull would give us a new bloodline," Lexie added. "If the bull could buck, that would be a bonus. We'll want a look at the pedigrees, of course, but the plan's got my vote."

"All right, then," Tess said. "It looks like you've got a deal. Go ahead and arrange transport for him. But we won't have any place to put a new bull if we lose the ranch. The way word gets around, I'm sure you're aware of that."

"I am." Tolman drew a folder from under his jacket and handed it to Tess. "Open this. Take a look."

Tess's hand trembled slightly as she took the folder. Brock Tolman never did anything without a good reason. What was she about to see?

"Go on," he prompted her. "It won't bite you. Open it."

Tess opened the folder. She recognized the loan disclosure statement from Patrick and Packard. It was stamped PAID IN FULL.

Tess stared at him. "You paid off the loan! But why?"

He smiled for the first time. "I had my reasons."

"While you're here we can set up a repayment schedule," Tess said. "Believe me, I intend to pay you back every cent plus interest if it's the last thing I do!"

His smile broadened. "Pay me back? There's no way I'm going to let you do that."

"But what—?" Dumbfounded, she groped for words.

Brock Tolman rose and extended his hand. "Tess Champion, meet your new partner."

ACKNOWLEDGMENTS

Special thanks to Jeff and Wendie Sue Kerby Flitton of Bar T Rodeo for their gracious hospitality and invaluable help in researching this story.

Don't miss Janet Dailey's heartwarming new holiday novel,
Santa's Sweetheart.

Love is the only cure for the holiday blues . . .

Sheriff Sam Delaney is shouldering a lot as the lone lawman in
the small Texas town of Branding Iron—and the widowed
single father of six-year-old Maggie. Especially since Maggie's
determined that what her daddy needs this holiday season is
a girlfriend. Suddenly Sam is hustled off to a meeting with
Maggie's schoolteacher—and surprised to discover the demure
Grace Chapman is unexpectedly alluring. Then he's roped into
playing Santa at the annual Christmas ball, with the pretty Miss
Grace by his side. It's enough to make Sam even grumpier than
usual—if not for the feelings sweet Grace stirs up inside . . .

Grace only wants to heal after her broken engagement. So
why is she so charmed by the slow smile—and the surprising
tenderness—of the town's sheriff? Maybe because Grace is
discovering that beneath Sam's gruff exterior lies a heart as big
as Texas, especially when it comes to the women in his life—like
little Maggie. And now her... Which only has Grace hoping
she'll be Santa's sweetheart for many seasons to come . . .

CHAPTER ONE

Branding Iron, Texas
Thanksgiving Day, 1996

*T*HE MICROWAVED TURKEY TV DINNERS WERE THE BEST THAT SHERIFF Sam Delaney could manage this year. His six-year-old daughter, Maggie, hid her disappointment with a brave smile.

"It's all right, Daddy," she said, clearing the foil trays off the table. "Next year I'll be big enough to cook dinner myself, with a real turkey and everything, just like Mommy used to make."

"I'm sure you will, honey." Sam hugged her close, fighting the rush of emotion that threatened to bring tears to his eyes. Bethany, his wife and Maggie's mother, had died in a car accident a year ago, just a week before Thanks-giving. After it happened, Sam had sent Maggie to stay with her grandparents until after the holidays, while he struggled to cope with loss and grief. This year would be their first holiday season together since Bethany's passing. So far, Sam wasn't handling it well.

"Hey, at least we've got pumpkin pie," he said, picking up the frozen treat he'd grabbed at the market. "Let's see if it's thawed." He tested it with a knife. The point went in partway, then met icy resistance. "Sorry," Sam said. "I guess I should've given it more time out of the freezer."

"Let's have some anyway," Maggie said. "It'll be like eating pumpkin ice cream!"

Using the force of his big hand, Sam managed to hack out two slices of pie, slide them onto saucers, and squirt canned Reddi-wip over the top. Exchanging a thumbs-up and a smile, they each broke off a piece and took a taste.

"Yuck," Maggie said, putting down her fork. Sam did the same. Even with topping, the half-frozen pie was nothing like ice cream. It was more like mushy ice. Maybe he should have cooked it in the oven instead of just trying to thaw it.

"Sorry, honey," Sam said. "If I hadn't needed to work this morning . . ."

"I know, Daddy," Maggie said. "Your job is to keep people safe, even on Thanksgiving. That's why I'm going to make dinner next year. We've got Mom's big red and white cookbook, the one that was Grandma's. I can read and learn how. Hey, the Christmas specials are starting on TV. Want to watch them with me? We can make popcorn."

"Sure." Sam's heart had been set on football, but if his little girl, who had just eaten the worst Thanksgiving dinner ever, wanted to watch Frosty and Rudolph and Charlie Brown, who was he to spoil her day?

Maggie put the popcorn bag in the microwave and punched the buttons. As the sound of popping and the buttery smell filled the kitchen, Sam found a bowl on a high shelf and had it ready to hold the popcorn when it was done.

With the bowl between them, they settled on the couch to watch the kiddie shows. Sam sighed as the folksy voice of Burl Ives rolled out "Frosty the Snowman." Things could be worse, he told himself. At least Maggie appeared to be holding up all right. She'd always been an upbeat kid, choosing to see the sunny side of things. Or, more likely, she was just being brave. But he knew she missed her mother every day, just as he did.

As she munched her popcorn and watched her show, Sam studied her stubborn young profile. Maggie had her mother's curly auburn hair, green eyes, and the same sprinkle of freckles across her nose. But the rest of her was all Delaney. She was going to be a pretty woman one day. And tall. How tall remained to be seen.

There was a reason people referred to their sheriff as "Big Sam." At six-foot-four and a husky 250 pounds, there was no more descriptive word for him than *big*. He'd played defensive line in college and had been a likely candidate for the NFL until he'd blown his knee—blown it spectacularly in a nationally televised game. Damned knee. It still gave him a slight limp and pained him in cold weather.

With his pro football hopes gone and his athletic scholarship ended, Sam had come home to Branding Iron, married Bethany, won the election for county sheriff, and gotten on with what he'd thought of as his real life—real, until last year when a drunk driver on an ice-slicked road had changed it forever.

The program had gone to a commercial. Maggie stirred beside him. "Daddy?" she said.

"Mm-hmm?" he muttered, giving her his attention.

"I've been thinking about something. Do you know what you need?"

"What, honey?" Maybe she was going to suggest that they replace their geriatric TV or the rusting Ford pickup he drove when he wasn't on duty.

"I can tell you're lonely, Daddy," she said. "You need a wife—or maybe, for now, just a girlfriend. What do you think about finding one?"

Sam's throat jerked tight. His daughter was full of surprises. But where the hell had *that* come from?